# Murder among the Stars

Adam Shankman

# Murder among the Stars

*A Lulu Kelly Mystery*

Laura L. Sullivan

Atheneum NEW YORK LONDON TORONTO SYDNEY NEW DELHI

An imprint of Simon & Schuster Children's Publishing Division
1230 Avenue of the Americas, New York, New York 10020
Text copyright © 2017 by Adam Shankman
Jacket photographs copyright © 2017 by Getty Images (Castle in Fog:
Kerrick James; Moon over Palm Trees: Grant Faint)
For information about special discounts for bulk purchases, please
contact Simon & Schuster Special Sales at 1-866-506-1949 or
business@simonandschuster.com.
The Simon & Schuster Speakers Bureau can bring authors to your live
event. For more information or to book an event, contact the Simon &
Schuster Speakers Bureau at 1-866-248-3049 or visit our website at
www.simonspeakers.com.
Book design by Debra Sfetsios-Conover and Irene Metaxatos
The text for this book was set in Baskerville MT.
Manufactured in the United States of America
First Edition
10 9 8 7 6 5 4 3 2 1
CIP data for this book is available from the Library of Congress.
ISBN 978-1-4814-4790-4 (hc)
ISBN 978-1-4814-4792-8 (eBook)

*Murder among the Stars*

# One

**H**ollywood starlet Lulu Kelly gazed through the brilliant California sunshine at the castle that rose like an enchanted dream from the mountainside. She was so awestruck by the grandeur that she almost didn't notice when Freddie Van—former billionaire, former hobo, current private eye, and Lulu's boyfriend—held the car door open for her.

"Holy cats!" the actress said as she looked up at the mansion that was to be her home for the long weekend. "Freddie, are you sure this belongs to Mr. William Randolph Hearst and not a sultan? It's rather . . . a lot."

"Being 'rather a lot' is what Mr. Hearst is best known for," Freddie said. "Why do you think everyone who's anyone is here?"

"I'm here to get the part of a lifetime," Lulu said as she

marveled at the castle. In her successful year in Hollywood she'd gotten used to luxury and high living. Though her own rented home was fairly modest, she was often invited to the luxury estates owned by such luminaries as Mary Pickford and George Cukor. But their establishments paled in comparison to the estate known modestly as the Ranch. This was a castle, plain and simple, built for an American prince.

Not satisfied with a single splendid house, Hearst had built four. La Casa Grande with its two towers and stunning blue tile work held the place of honor as the main residence. Surrounding it were guesthouses that were mansions in their own right. Casa del Monte had a stunning mountain view. Casa del Sol faced the setting sun. And Casa del Mar overlooked the crashing waters of the Pacific Ocean. Together it was called La Cuesta Encantada—the Enchanted Hill.

"And I'm here as private eye, junior edition." After helping Lulu clear her good name following an accidental shooting (that proved to be no accident), Freddie had fallen naturally into the investigative business. Right now he was assistant to Mr. Waters, the most sought-after PI in Hollywood.

"What a shame our first holiday together has to be a working holiday," Lulu said a little sadly.

Freddie groaned. "Only in Hollywood would they turn a party into a tryout. Do you even have any idea what you're supposed to do there for four days?"

"No. It's all very hush-hush. The invitation said 'WR and Marion Invite You to Reveal Your True Character' in big embossed gold letters. That's all. Veronica says that nearly every starlet in the biz will be competing for the role of a life-time, but no one knows any more than that."

Freddie looked sly. "Maybe I know a *little* more than that."

Lulu gasped and grabbed his hand. "Oh, my own personal investigator! Come on, spill!"

"Well, Waters may have mentioned to me that none other than Anita Loos will be in attendance."

Lulu's heart began to race. Anita Loos! The author of *Gentlemen Prefer Blondes*, the funniest book of the last decade, maybe even of the last century! Now she was a screenwriter of considerable renown, working with her husband, John Emerson, on only the choicest projects.

"Do you think she could possibly be writing something completely new for Cosmopolitan Pictures? A real Anita Loos original screenplay?" Her eyes were aglow at the possibility.

"I wouldn't be surprised. Would you like to work with her?"

"Like to? I'd kill for—" She caught herself short and swallowed hard, as Freddie laughed.

"It's just an expression," he said, excusing her.

Lulu shook her head. "But one in very bad taste for yours truly." Not long ago, she'd very nearly killed a rival starlet. In the peculiar way of Hollywood, it had launched both of their careers to new stellar levels.

"I have to meet with Waters and find out why I'm here," Freddie said. "I'll find you as soon as I can." He bent over her hand, kissing her knuckles with elaborate gallantry.

A slew of photographers was waiting for Lulu and the

nineteen other starlets invited for the weekend. A little while before, Lulu had submitted her tired face to the skilled hand of her friend and publicist Veronica, and now she was daisy-fresh and glowing, her platinum hair fetchingly curled around her ears, her sleepy eyes painted wide and alert. She smiled gamely for the cameras while she held her little terrier, Charlie, in her arms.

Lulu did what she was required to do, but after her official photo shoot she declined to pose and ham it up with the other girls. A brassy, buxom blonde sidled up to her. Lulu knew most of the other actresses—a mix of newly established A-listers and the relatively unknown group of this year's Baby Stars. But this girl was unfamiliar.

"Are you too dumb or too smart to be out there mugging with those publicity whores?" the girl asked, fanning herself with her slim crocodile pocketbook.

Lulu, momentarily too shocked by the girl's language to speak, let her mouth gape. "Oh, too dumb, I see. Well, *I'm* not bothering with those photographers because they don't count for a hill of beans. Joan Crawford and Jean Harlow are the only ones who will get any ink tomorrow. They'll hold the rest of the photos until they see who wins. And, sister, when I win, I plan to have a photo shoot with diamonds and doves, looking like a queen slumming as a pinup. I have no time for snappers of me with a greasy morning face and bad lighting. No thank you!"

"I'm Lulu," she began, holding out her hand.

The girl ignored it. "I know who *all* of you are. You're no competition. Why do you think I'm here? After that business with Ruby Godfrey they'll never cast you in a comedy or a romance. It will be gangsters' molls from here on out, toots. I'm Juliette Claire. Ugh, look at Joan Crawford, flapping those giant hands around. More like Joan Crawfish."

"Joan's a friend of mine," Lulu said.

"Then you ought to tell her to keep her hands behind her back if she doesn't want to look like a lobster. Too bad Bette Davis can't hide those bug eyes behind *her* back. Oh my, look at all the bad bleach jobs out there. Pure chlorine, you can tell. Half of them will be bald in six months." She looked Lulu over critically. "What do you use, then? It almost looks real."

"It's my own color."

Juliette snorted. "Sure, and so is mine. Forget it. Just trying to be friendly."

It was Lulu's turn to snort. Still, she tried to be polite to this unpleasant girl. "Which studio are you with?"

"I'm freelance, sister. I have two movies coming out next year, so watch out! Let's see, who else have they dragged out of the woodwork? That tall drink of water is Boots Mallory. She posed in her scanties, so WR will never consider her. Because he's such a pillar of virtue! Ha!" Juliette erupted in a hideous honk of a laugh that pierced the air and made Lulu physically recoil.

"WR?" Lulu asked, composing herself. "You're that intimate with Mr. Hearst?"

Juliette shrugged. "I will be, if that's what it takes. You got a problem with me, sister? Didn't think so. There's Eleanor

Holm, still wet from the swimming pool. I hear she's a champion *on her back*."

Juliette snickered, and Lulu bristled. She'd recently seen a photo shoot with the Olympic swimmer turned actress, and admired her confident physicality. "She won a gold medal for the backstroke."

Juliette shrugged. "Oh, is *that* what they call it these days? These girls all think they can get this part by impressing Marion. I know its WR who holds the purse strings—and owns Cosmopolitan Pictures. Once he finds out about some of these girls' reputations, they won't have a chance."

"These are some of the sweetest girls in the business," Lulu said hotly. "Most of them don't have a reputation for anything other than beauty and professionalism."

Juliette glared at her. "Well, hoity-toity. Don't you know a reputation is easier to get than the clap out here? And easier to give. Hey, will you look at that! Who the hell invited Toshia Mori?"

Juliette indicated a striking Japanese girl standing a little apart from the others.

"I hear there's a part for a brunette, but not someone *that* brunette," the actress said. "What's next, they audition our colored maids?"

Lulu felt her face redden. "And why shouldn't Toshia be up for a part as much as you? She was a Baby Star, after all, and she's filming with Frank Capra right now. How dare you imply—"

She was interrupted when several other girls joined them.

Lulu felt relieved. One more minute alone with Juliette, and she'd likely find herself involved in another murder investigation.

Juliette looked amused to be challenged. "I never *imply*," she hissed to Lulu. "I make myself perfectly clear." Then she smiled at the new girls and said loudly, "Make sure you give Lulu here plenty of room and don't jostle her. She's in a delicate condition." Her hand hovered briefly over her own stomach and she winked.

"What?" Lulu cried. "I'm not!"

But she could already hear some of the other girls whispering behind their hands. *Who's the father? Will Lux fire her?*

Lulu protested as strongly as she could, and the other girls said they believed that it was only Juliette's joke. But she could still see the doubt in some of their eyes. How could one quick lie have such power?

Lulu tried to act natural, but it was hard. *A better girl,* she told herself, *would be plotting revenge.* Or a worse girl. In any case, a more typical girl. She still wasn't used to the way girls out here could sabotage each other so viciously. She longed, more than anything, to be quietly alone with Freddie. But he was already on the job, and she didn't know when she'd have a chance to see him.

An imposing older woman in black came up to the young actresses. Her dress was of such good material, so finely tailored, that it took Lulu a moment to realize it was essentially a servant's livery. It was as simple and chic as a Chanel frock, and the shining chain holding the housekeeper's collection of keys might as well have been a platinum accessory. Her steely hair was severely coiffed, her lips a long, elegant line. She'd been a beauty in her day, Lulu thought.

"I am Mrs. Mortimer, the housekeeper," the woman introduced herself, giving a stiff nod of her head. "I am in charge of your comfort and will ensure that your stay here at the Ranch goes smoothly and without incident. Miss Marion does not care for incidents." She looked sharply at a couple of girls. Her gaze seemed to rest the longest on Juliette. Lulu suspected the housekeeper was competent enough at her job to have done her homework about all of the guests.

"Should you have any difficulties, please come to me before they get out of hand," Mrs. Mortimer went on. She gave a hint of a smile and briefly met Lulu's eye. "Early intervention can prevent a host of problems. Please follow me."

She gave another sharp bow of her head and walked purposefully away without a backward glance, trusting that the girls would follow. Lulu watched her with admiration. What a strong, competent-seeming woman. She supposed being a housekeeper at a place like the Ranch might almost be like being an executive at a big company, hardly like a servant at all.

Much to Lulu's annoyance, Juliette maneuvered to walk beside her. "Why the sour puss? Oh, my joke earlier? Well, what's a little reputation? They'll know it ain't true . . . in nine months or so."

Lulu gave her no encouragement, but Juliette seemed to like having an audience. "I was talking to Dolores, that giant over there." She nodded toward a tall, striking, dark-haired beauty of superbly buxom proportions. "She told me Marion herself was originally up for the role we're all here fighting over. Even old WR had to shoot her down. Whatever the part may be, if they have all of us here, it's obviously for a young beauty queen. Can you imagine an old hag like that trying to play twenty?"

"Hush!" Lulu hissed. Ahead of them, she could see Mrs. Mortimer stiffen, though she didn't turn. Lulu was sure she could hear.

"She's nearly forty, and WR still has her playing ingenues. It's ridiculous. She should shove off center stage and leave it to the next generation. You know, girls like me who don't have to provide *favors* to the lighting supervisor to make sure we're shot in flattering light."

Lulu gasped. "Marion is a beautiful woman and a great actress." This last might have been a slight exaggeration, but Lulu felt the situation called for adamance. "She could adapt herself to any part. That's why this job is called *acting*. A skilled actress doesn't have to rely on being eighteen. But for some, that's all they've got." She looked pointedly at Juliette, who sniffed derisively.

"Oh, I'm going to put on one hell of a show for Marion . . . and a different kind of show for WR, if that's what it takes. She won't know I think she's a ridiculous has-been, and he won't know I think he's a disgusting old lecher. And if Marion tries to get that part, I'll show her exactly how easily a prettier, younger woman can take her place." Juliette snapped her fingers and strutted off, following Mrs. Mortimer to her room. All the while Mrs. Mortimer stiffly ignored her. She had to have heard, though. Lulu wondered if any of it would make its way back to Marion Davies.

As the rest of the girls were directed to their rooms in the main house, Lulu and some of the others waited in the hall. Veronica pulled Lulu away for a private chat. She wanted to share her theories about what might be expected of Lulu this weekend.

"The scuttlebutt is that whoever can make Marion laugh the most gets the part," Veronica said. She tossed back her sensible brown bob. "I miss the innocent, simple old days when all an actress had to do to get a role was show a little leg. Or heaven forbid, be able to act. But this! Everyone is determined to be funny, but they know they have to toe the line with WR. If it were up to Marion, whoever got drunkest and danced longest on the tabletops without falling off would take the prize."

"Doesn't this all seem a little desperate to you?"

"Now you're getting it!" Veronica said. "I have no idea what this script will look like, but based on the buzz, it's going to be the biggest thing ever. And you can bet that Marion Davies was behind these ridiculous shenanigans. She's bored! A gin-soaked bird held prisoner in a gilded cage. The whole thing smacks of one big spectacle for her personal entertainment."

"Are we really all supposed to act like fools for her amusement?" Lulu asked.

"Who knows? But she was a Ziegfeld Follies girl, and then

did mostly comedies until Hearst pushed her into dramas. She's basically a champagne bubble ready to pop. She can't be as wild as when she was a sixteen-year-old chorine, but she still surrounds herself with all the funny and bright young things. Maybe she's looking to relive her stolen youth through you all. To see herself as young again. I'd say a bawdy joke and a squirting boutonniere might be the way to win her over."

"That's sad," Lulu mused. "If I were her I think I'd rather—"

Veronica interrupted her. "Take it from me, you have to put on a show. Don't worry. We'll figure something out once we have the lay of the land. Luckily I know you're a girl who can think on her feet."

The ladies were led back outside by courteous staff members to their respective guesthouses. As she was ushered along the shade-dappled tile pathway, Lulu did a double take when she thought she caught sight of a familiar—and unwelcome—face near the trucks that were unloading copious amounts of liquor. Black hair, flashing eyes, the sensuously curving mouth of a Caravaggio . . . She gasped. It couldn't be Sal! What on earth could he be doing at the Ranch? An icy chill ran down Lulu's spine even as the hazy San Simeon sun beat down upon her.

Sal had been an unexpected hit in the Hollywood social scene, schmoozing with some of the biggest names, and everyone seemed willing to ignore his shady profession. Gangsters were superstars, and Sal seemed to have a knack for buying his way into the right society. She'd heard there was a movie in the works based on his life story. Some even said Sal was going to star in it.

She craned her neck behind her, trying to get a better look. But the man, whoever he was, had vanished. *My mind must be playing tricks on me,* Lulu thought. *Sal would never manage to get an invitation to the Ranch.*

"Looks like you're with me," Boots said, tucking her golden-brown hair behind her ears. "Casa del Mar, right?" Lulu had never met her before, but she liked her right away for her easy, straightforward manner. She was all legs and angles, but she carried herself with a natural grace that gave her a sylph-like beauty.

"Me too," said Eleanor. The catty Juliette was right—Eleanor's dark hair did almost seem like it was fresh from the pool, slicked back away from her face, wet-looking, curling at the tips. But it was a good look for her. She seemed strong, ready for anything. Lulu saw her eyeing the unloaded liquor.

"Guess I didn't have to smuggle this in," Eleanor said, giving them a peek at a flask from her satchel.

"Better to be prepared," Boots said. "Hearst might have enough booze to fill his swimming pool—*both* his swimming pools—but I hear he restricts his guests to two drinks apiece, and I intend to have a good time while I'm here, even if I know I don't have much chance of landing the role."

"Ditto," Eleanor said. "We might as well live it up for a weekend, right, girls?"

Toshia joined them. "I don't know why I'm here," she confessed. "We all know they'll never give me the part, unless there's one for a maid or a concubine. And if the concubine is the star, it goes to Myrna Loy in eyeliner. All I'll ever get are the roles Anna May Wong turns down."

Boots gave her a hug. "Just enjoy the party, lady. We Baby Stars have to stick together. This one, though." She patted Lulu on the back. "She might have a chance. She's got the goods, dimples and all."

"I think Juliette is the one we have to watch out for," Eleanor said. "She's sneaky, mean, and ambitious. The trifecta of successful starlets."

"I agree," Toshia said. "Girls like her might get theirs in the end, but in the beginning they usually do pretty well."

Boots and Eleanor exchanged a quick look. "Well, maybe we can fix the odds a little bit," Boots said.

While the maids unpacked their suitcases, the girls were summoned to the main house for a cocktail party. Drinks—all two of them—would be served in the Assembly Room. But as Lulu was about to leave, Charlie made his needs known with a yip, so she slipped away with him for a quick stroll around the grounds before getting dressed.

She found something fantastic around every turn. In one fountain, dolphins sported around naiads. In another, a cunningly placed conch hid essential parts of a naked and brawny Poseidon.

"Guess I don't have to bother going to Europe now," she told Charlie as she gazed at a row of armless marble statues imported from Greece and Italy.

She whipped around, startled, when she heard a giggle

from the foliage, and a dark-haired, impish head poked out.

"Don't go even if you get the chance," the girl said. "It's deadly dull, and no one speaks properly, even the English."

"Hello," Lulu said. "Are you family?"

Charlie pushed his way into the shrubbery and looked pleased when he emerged again not only with an entire girl, but with a graying, portly dachshund on a leash. When Lulu could only see her peeping face she'd thought the girl must be a teenager. She had bright precocious eyes under arching brows, and a hint of lip rouge.

But when she emerged completely from the bushes she looked like a totally different girl. Her hair was gathered in long twin braids that fell over her shoulders, tied with pink bows. She wore a high-waisted short frock with frills and petticoats, ruffled white socks, and black patent-leather shoes. Her body was slim and straight, her chest perfectly flat. At first Lulu thought she must be a very small woman dressed for a costume party. But no, she was a little girl after all, and apparently much younger than she first appeared.

"I'm Patricia, Marion's niece."

"I'm Lulu." She held out her hand.

"I know that," Patricia said, giving it a businesslike shake. At their feet, the two dogs struck up their acquaintance with posterior sniffs. "Golly, everyone knows who you are now. Did you really, truly shoot someone? Gosh, how exciting!" She heaved a dramatic sigh. "I never get to do anything. Dinner in the nursery, bed by eight. It's a sad and sorry life for a girl like I."

"Well, at your age . . . ," Lulu began, then stopped herself. How old was Patricia? She talked like a young woman and dressed like a child. Lulu was perplexed. Perhaps children raised by millionaires matured differently than poor children. She'd have to ask Freddie later.

"Tell me what it felt like," Patricia begged. "Did the blood get on you?"

What a morbid little person she was. But her eyes seemed eager as Charlie's when he smelled a treat. Lulu could tell she was simply longing for experience—any experience. Lulu remembered that feeling. It had been replaced only a few weeks ago with a fervent hope that nothing dangerous or exciting would ever happen to her again.

Against her better judgment, Lulu told her about the terrible ordeal that had been cleared up only a few weeks before. She left out many of the more sordid details that the studio lawyers had managed to conceal from the press. "The scene called for me to shoot the gun, so I did. I had no idea it was loaded."

"And they never figured out how the bullets got in there? Strange. I pored over the stories in WR's newspapers. It always seemed to me as if the relevant particulars were somehow . . . missing." She gave Lulu a canny look that made the actress feel decidedly uncomfortable.

"Accidents happen," Lulu said, neglecting to mention that the victim, rival actress Ruby Godfrey, had loaded the gun herself in a desperate play for publicity.

"I bet Ruby had something to do with it herself," Patricia

said. Lulu kept her face resolutely expressionless. A few of the papers had speculated on that, but no one seemed to take it seriously. This girl was too perceptive for her own good.

"She has an interesting face, that Ruby," Patricia continued. "Always looks like she's up to something. Which is good for an actress, maybe, but not so good when you actually *are* up to something. You, on the other hand, look as innocent as a May flower." Patricia scrutinized Lulu's face, and Lulu got the distinct impression she was trying to imitate her expression. "You could get away with anything. That must come in handy."

"How old *are* you?" Lulu finally couldn't help but ask.

She thought it would be an innocent question. After all, children got asked that all the time by tedious adults who couldn't think of anything more interesting to ask. So she was surprised to hear Patricia give a sharp intake of breath, almost a sob, while a look of something strangely like fury flashed across her face.

Then, just as suddenly, it was gone, replaced by a bizarre look of affected innocence. "I'm ten," Patricia said, and now her voice was pitched up an octave, squeaky and girlish.

*Two*

**L**ulu wiggled and struggled into a formfitting strapless Elsa Schiaparelli cocktail dress of burnt orange silk velvet with a fiery pink satin-lined train, and entered the Assembly Room. She accepted a poison-green cocktail, though she didn't really have a taste for alcohol beyond an occasional glass of champagne. Still, it was a decorative thing to have in her hand, and less noxious than the long cigarette holders some actresses thought were fashionable.

Though the twenty actresses were the guests of honor, the party didn't lack for male company. Anita Loos's handsome husband and cowriter, John Emerson, was there, resplendent in a gray suit and shimmering lion-head tie tack. For some reason, the Lux Studios doctor Harry Martin was there too, neat scotch in hand as always. Lulu wondered how he'd finagled an invitation. There were newspaper men and Wall Street men, novelists and actors, and a few more exotic specimens, too—at least one unattached man for every woman. Freddie and his boss were nowhere to be seen. There was a palpable tension in the room as everyone waited for Hearst and Marion to arrive.

"They have spy holes everywhere," Veronica whispered into Lulu's ear. "I even heard they have the rooms rigged with microphones. I bet Hearst is watching us right now. Now, make with the shenanigans! There have already been three whoopee cushion incidents, a cloud of itching powder, and one gal who keeps trying to shake people's hands with an electric joy buzzer."

Lulu noticed Patricia sitting quietly by herself, her legs in lisle stockings kicking against the sofa as she watched the elegant crowd around her. "How old is Marion's niece?" she asked.

Veronica, who made it her business to know absolutely everything, thought a moment and said, "Ten."

"Are you sure?" Lulu asked.

"Yes. They had a photo spread on her last birthday party. It had ten peacocks, ten flamingos, ten baby tigers, ten unicorns, for all I know. Yes, definitely ten."

"She seems so much older," Lulu said.

"You've only been in this life for a year, and I bet you feel a million years older at seventeen than you did at sixteen. Without the crow's toes to show for it. Patricia has probably seen and done more in her ten years than most people do in a lifetime."

The girl seemed so bored and alone that Lulu sought her out and—with great effort and an alarming creak in the Schiaparelli's stitches—sat down beside her.

"Oh, thank goodness it's you," Patricia said, her voice jaded now, almost adult. "Can you believe someone actually patted me on the head? What do I look like, a dog? Why do people think children can be treated like dumb animals?"

"People *don't* think, most of the time," Lulu said, feeling sorry for this precocious girl.

"See, you can speak to me like an adult. Other people do baby talk and call me a good girl and ask what I want to be when I grow up. Is that what passes for conversation? Should I ask them where they plan to retire when they get wrinkly and washed up? Honestly, I detest these parties." She flopped back on the sofa.

"Isn't there something you'd rather be doing? Surely in a place like this there are more suitable things for a . . . younger person such as yourself."

"I want to dance!" Patricia said. "I want to drink absinthe and flirt and creep off into dark nooks with Douglas Fairbanks Jr. and . . ."

Lulu couldn't help but burst out laughing. "There's plenty of time for that when you're older."

Patricia gave her a withering look. "When I'm older. Do you know that phrase has been the bane of my existence for half my life? That's what Marion is always saying. Just a few more years, and . . ." She clamped her mouth shut.

"Tell you what," Lulu said. "I might not be Doug Jr., but

I can cut a mean rug." She inhaled deeply and stood without ripping a stitch, which was something of a miracle, then exhaled as much as possible and held out her arm. "May I have this dance?"

Patricia looked delighted. She turned on the Victrola and dropped the needle on Cole Porter's "Let's Misbehave."

At once Lulu was caught up in the joy of dancing. She forgot all about the competition for the lead, the uncomfortable dress. Juliette's nasty rumor even ceased to sting. Lulu had passed many of her happiest moments dancing with her mother in their cramped and squalid tenement. Even when they didn't have food, they still had music they sang and hummed, and the lively swinging steps of her mother's favorite dances.

Now, taking the lead and swirling Patricia into the middle of the floor, Lulu felt totally unconcerned about the tittering crowd. She was happy and carefree. Patricia seemed joyous, too, because she flung her head back, laughing and wild as a maenad, and danced with such abandon that for a moment the rest of the guests fell silent and simply watched.

It was at this moment that Hearst and Marion slipped into the room through a secret panel beside the fireplace.

"Now, that's what I like to see!" Hearst boomed. "Dance, everyone—dance!" He clapped his hands loudly, slightly out of time with the rhythm.

No one disobeyed an order from Hearst. Almost instantly couples formed and found an open spot to finish out the tune.

Marion bounced beside him in a flirty polka-dotted dress.

"Come on, Daddy," she cooed, dancing a quick step around him, looking like a tiny kitten frisking around a bloodhound. "I get you first."

Hearst made a rather ludicrous figure, bearish and lumbering beside the effervescent Marion. But he put on a game show, laughing at his own clumsiness. Lulu thought it must be easier to accept being a figure of fun when his signature on a check could buy anyone or anything. That would numb the sting.

No, she realized a moment later. He was *ordering* them to laugh at him, just as he had ordered them to dance. If they'd done it on their own, they might be banished, ruined. But he enjoyed having the power to tell people to laugh at him. *Look*, he seemed to say with his antics, *I can be ridiculous and still be above you.*

The music stopped, and Marion clapped, then flitted from guest to guest, saying charming nonsense to each until she was interrupted by Mrs. Mortimer, who whispered something in her ear that made her frown. They had a quick, hushed consultation before the housekeeper left and Marion resumed her flitting, though it seemed a little more forced now.

To Lulu's surprise, Hearst introduced himself to her after a while.

He was daunting close up. Even the president wasn't such a public legend as William Randolph Hearst. A president would be gone in four years, or eight. Hearst had been head of an empire for decades and seemed to have every intention of living to rule for many more. Though nearly seventy, he was hale. If he stooped a bit, he still towered over everyone in the room. If his fair hair was graying, it nonetheless flowed in a thick wave across his forehead.

His eyes were the strangest of all, an unnerving pale blue that seemed somehow less alive than the rest of him. Lulu couldn't tell if they were the eyes of a child that still turned to some secret inner world of his own, or the eyes of a monster.

If he was a monster, he was a perfectly cordial one. "Welcome to the Ranch," he said. "Are you the gal who was caught up in all that ruckus a while back? Marion was sure it was that one over there." He pointed to the tall and sultry Dolores. "She looks more like the shooting type. But I remember your face from the *Los Angeles Examiner*. I never forget anything that appears in any of my papers. I peeked out and said yup, that's the face."

"So you really *do* have spy holes?" Lulu couldn't help saying.

"Wouldn't you?" he asked, and tapped the side of his nose.

"I don't think I'd like to know what people are saying about me behind my back," Lulu admitted.

"Oh, the microphones are just a rumor I started to keep everyone on their best behavior. And the spy holes are mostly so Marion can make sure no one is wearing her dress when she makes her entrance. Now, tell me, young lady, do you like art?"

She caught Veronica's eye across the room. The publicist made a pushing gesture that Lulu interpreted to mean she better take advantage of her moment with Hearst to be funny.

"Art? Never met him," Lulu quipped, embarrassed at the inanity of the joke.

But Hearst gave a belly laugh. "Thank goodness, someone who didn't bone up! Do you know, every guest who comes here knows I have an art collection and decides to impress me, so they look up some tidbit about Caravaggio's knife fight or Titian's tint, and try to talk like a professor."

Hearst gave Patricia a fond kiss on the head and went to chat with other guests. Patricia left the Assembly Room in search of cookies, making Lulu sure she really was ten after all.

With Hearst and Marion now in attendance, the Pranks Olympics began. Certain that this was the way to make an impression, everyone pretended to be chatty and social, but they all had plans to make Marion laugh. Instantly, as if she were in on the gag, Marion plopped down on one of the several whoopee cushions hidden around the room. She squealed and jumped up. "Excuse me!" she said, looking far too ladylike to ever produce such a sound herself. Then she gave a mighty belch, and laughed.

Jean Harlow, her hair almost exactly the same platinum shade as Lulu's, offered Marion a tray of candied apples. Marion gamely bit into one and scrunched up her face into a grimace as sweat broke out on her forehead. "Spanish onion!" she gasped, fanning her mouth and raising her arm blindly for a drink.

"You've probably had enough," Hearst said gently as Marion downed a gin, honey, and lemon concoction called a Bee's Knees.

"Water ain't gonna cut it, Pops," she said, and called for another. "Whew-ee, Jean, you are one hot lady! And the pale horse takes the lead."

Joan Crawford supplied Marion's next drink—in a dribble cup. "And Joanie edges up," Marion said, wiping her chin.

"I'll give a hundred dollars to anyone if I crack three eggs over their head!" Juliette suddenly announced.

"I'd volunteer," Hearst said, "but it would just put me in the next tax bracket."

Juliette batted her dark lashes around the room, finally settling on the Lux Studio doctor, Harry Martin. "How about you, big boy?"

"A hundred dollars? Really?" he asked. His voice was slurred with drink, but his eyes perked up at that remarkable sum.

"If I crack three eggs over your head," Juliette confirmed.

"I'm game," he said. "If you're really good for it."

"And if not, make her pay you off some other way," said John Emerson with a lascivious leer that brought a disapproving look from Hearst. "I'm sure she can think of *something*."

"I always keep my word," Juliette said staunchly. "To the *exact* letter." But Lulu could tell she had a plan. Juliette looked sidelong at John, a look that seemed to promise something in the future, but then turned her attention squarely to the man known on the Lux sets as Docky. Marion, eager to see what would happen, told a servant to fetch three eggs.

"Drumroll, please," Juliette said as she held up the first egg. Everyone began tapping their fingers on the furniture.

Juliette basked for a moment in the spotlight. Lulu saw Louella Parsons—gossip columnist extraordinaire, known to her friends as Lolly and her enemies as something unprintable—sidle up to Docky and whisper something in his ear. He shook his head brusquely and turned away from her. He seemed to like being the center of attention too, particularly when his audience consisted of so many pretty girls.

With great fanfare she held up an egg . . . and smashed it down on top of Docky's head. He flinched, but kept on a game face even when the gooey yolk dripped into his eyes.

"Should I do another?" Juliette asked, holding up the next egg. When she was answered with cheers, she smashed that egg, too, onto Docky's balding pate.

Lulu didn't want to look. It was humiliating.

"That's what this whole business is about," Boots said from beside her. "Doing anything for money."

Juliette held up the last egg over Docky's slimy head. His face was red, but he looked eager, too. For the hundred dollars? Lulu wondered. Didn't a doctor make enough that he didn't have to embarrass himself for money?

"No," Juliette said after a long pause. "I think I'm in the mood for a flip." She summoned a maid and instructed her how to froth the last raw egg with brandy and spices for the unusual cocktail. Then she sat down next to Marion.

"What about my money?" Docky demanded, hot and hoarse.

Juliette looked at him with big, innocent eyes and said guilelessly, "But I didn't break three eggs." She shrugged her shoulders as if she were just too helpless to do anything about it.

"But you said . . . ," Docky began.

Marion laughed. "Oh, I get it now! She never said she *would* crack three eggs over your head—just that *if* she did, she'd pay you a hundred dollars. Oh, it's too funny. Docky, you look an absolute fright! I've never seen such a mess. And the dark horse takes the lead! What's your name, kid?"

"Juliette Claire," she replied, her eyes big and innocent, looking like she had no idea what everyone was laughing at.

Marion's face instantly darkened when she heard the name, and she turned away. Lulu guessed that Mrs. Mortimer had shared the cruel, catty things she'd overheard Juliette say.

Docky sputtered and fumed, his face going from red to purple in his rage. Lulu saw him clench his fists and take a step toward Juliette. Lolly put a hand on his shoulder.

"Why don't you go and clean up, Docky," she said. "Here, I'll help you."

"Exit, pursued by a bear," Lulu murmured, which might have earned her comedy points if anyone present had read *The Winter's Tale*.

"Has anyone told you that you look ravishing tonight?" a low voice whispered in her ear. Lulu shivered, and turned to find Freddie. She shook her head. "Good, because I'd have to beat him silly."

"Did you find out why you're here?"

He guided her farther away from the others. "Not a word to anyone, but . . . blackmail! Hearst got a letter purporting to know something terrible he did thirteen years ago and demanding money."

"How very mysterious!" Lulu said, her eyes lighting up at the thought of a mystery. They'd worked so well together uncovering Ruby Godfrey's plot. It would be fun if she could help him on something like this.

Before she could offer her help, they heard Hearst sputter from across the room. He was mopping his face with a linen handkerchief that seemed dwarfed by his hand. Someone had unleashed that old comedic standby, the squirting boutonniere, on their host.

"What the hell is going on?" he thundered. All of the actresses avoided eye contact, and the whole room fell silent. "You!" He jabbed his finger at the pretty little actress with baby-doll curls still clutching her trick flower. "Why is everyone acting like a lunatic? I demand an explanation!"

"B-because we all want the part!" she squeaked.

"What?" Hearst bellowed.

The little actress quailed, and Lulu felt sorry for her. She stepped up to take the harsh, frightening focus onto herself and said, "Because we were all told that making you and Marion laugh would get us the part." She held Hearst's steely gaze.

Hearst looked around the room. "You ladies think that squirting water in my face and breaking eggs on a fellow's head is the way to get the finest role Cosmopolitan Pictures has ever offered?" He frowned, looking to Lulu like a sulky, overgrown child, though his millions seemed to stand behind him like a child-king's personal army, making him incredibly intimidating. "You should know that practical jokes are the lowest form of comedy," he said witheringly. "You better start taking your craft more seriously if you want to get ahead in this business . . . and at the Ranch. After all, you only have one chance to make a first impression. So far, very few of you have impressed me favorably." Lulu was almost certain his small blue eyes flickered her way.

The actresses all looked abashed, and Marion pushed her way in front of Hearst, pulling a funny face to chase away his ire. She clinked her cocktail glass with a backgammon piece and called everyone to attention.

"Thank you so much for coming to our humble abode," she said, making a little curtsy. "I'm sorry to have kept you all in the dark about the nature of this party. Oh, who am I kidding? I *loved* keeping all of you in suspense!" She laughed merrily. "Now, I've heard the rumor that's going around. Whoever can make me laugh gets the coconut, right? Wrong! But oh, what a show you girls have put on so far! You know how I love a good chortle. Juliette, that egg joke was . . ."

Hearst flashed her a quick scowl, and Marion's face grew a shade more serious. "You saw that the party invitations said we'd reveal your true character this week. Well, that's exactly what we plan to do. WR and I have come up with an absolutely revolutionary new way of making a grand film. Instead of finding a story, writing a script, and casting an actress who fits the part—or more likely, one who the public is already mad for—we're flip-flopping the whole tedious affair. Look at how fascinating all of you girls are! Some of you I know well, and some of you absolutely intrigue me already." She winked maliciously at Juliette.

"You are all being judged this week," Hearst said. "By the end of the party, Marion and I will have chosen the actress who interests us the most, upon whom to base my friend Anita Loos's next screenplay. Ably assisted by her husband and a brilliant new writer we just discovered, Mr. Paul Raleigh, Anita will write something the likes of which the world has never seen. Art will imitate life as it never has before. One lucky girl will not only be the star of the biggest Cosmopolitan Pictures hit—she will be a muse. She will be a goddess, with the story molded to her in every way. She will ennoble great cinema with her most radiant virtues . . . and her terrible secrets!"

Around her, Lulu heard the actresses gasping. Lulu gasped too, but not, she thought, for the same reason. The other girls were awestruck that a movie might be custom-tailored to their unique personality. Lulu was for a moment horror-struck. Though she strove every moment of every day to be a good person, her past haunted her. She knew that her secrets were far too grisly to be revealed. They could end her. Permanently. She always suspected that deep down she was flawed. Why else would she have lied to protect a gangster and advance herself?

When she sat in the witness stand and swore that Salvatore Benedetto had not shot the man who killed his father, she had betrayed everything her mother taught her and everything she knew was right. She knew she probably would have been killed if she hadn't played along with Sal's demands. And look what it had gotten her! A soaring career, fame, love, enough money to pull her family out of abject poverty. But she was always left with a sick feeling of her own moral failure. However good, however kind, however brave she might be now, she had folded when it mattered most.

*No*, Lulu thought, *I don't have the kind of character worthy of a movie heroine.*

"In four days," Marion went on, her words more than a bit slurred, "we will hold a talent competition. And you thought you were all above such nonsense, didn't you!" She shot a look straight to Joan Crawford, whose square jaw set tightly just as one eyebrow arched skyward. "The winner will get the part. Simple, right? Wrong!"

She downed her cocktail. "The talent show will only be the—what was that fancy word you used, 'Nita? Culmination! Long before that, though, you will all be judged." She dropped her voice to an ominous modulation. "And sadly, some of you will be found wanting. Every night two of you will be bundled into Daimlers and whisked away home. An honor to be nominated and all that, right? The lucky ones who remain in four days' time will grace us with their artistry in the final competition, and a winner will be chosen by myself, WR, Anita, Emerson, and Paul." She turned to Hearst. "Darling, where is Paul?"

Hearst shrugged, but Lulu, within earshot, heard his private secretary murmur into his ear that Paul Raleigh had called, saying he was unavoidably delayed and hoped to arrive before dinner.

Lulu felt warm breath on her neck and turned, letting her cheek brush against Freddie's. "What do you say you commit an unpardonable faux pas and get kicked out, I quit my job, and we spend the rest of the weekend fooling around on the beach?"

"Tempting, but Veronica would never forgive me. Hell hath no fury like a publicist scorned."

They wandered toward a dark nook, and might have managed to avoid dinner entirely if Veronica hadn't spied them and tried to hustle Lulu back into the social circle. "You're not doing yourself any good being a wallflower," she said.

"We're just trying to get some time together," Lulu said. "I have several days to be thrilling and inspirational."

"You have to focus on the competition first."

"Just let me have a little while with Freddie, and I promise tomorrow I'll pull out all the stops."

"Oh, very well," Veronica grumbled. "Just turn on a couple of lights, will you? Hearst will think you're up to no good."

"Don't we wish!" Lulu said with a dramatic sigh.

Veronica turned the switch on an unlit nearby lamp—and screamed.

The bright bulb illuminated the silhouettes of half a dozen huge roaches clinging to the underside of the lampshade. Veronica jerked away, knocking the lamp down with a crash. One of the insects seemed to fly through the air, landing at Lulu's feet. She managed not to cry out—after all, roaches were a familiar sight in her slum childhood—but she backed hurriedly away.

Juliette, who had been deep in an animated conversation with John Emerson, gave a grunt of distaste and said, "You simpering namby-pambies make me sick!" With that, she stomped on the roach.

"That would have done it in for sure," Freddie said, picking it for inspection, "if it hadn't been made out of paper." He upended the lampshade, showing the cleverly cut-out figures of bugs designed to show up alarmingly when the lamp was lit. "Just another practical joke, left over from when they were still all the rage a quarter hour ago."

Marion laughed, along with everyone else, and gave Toshia a hug when she took credit for the prank. Only Hearst was manifestly displeased.

"I don't allow anyone to hurt animals in my house or on my land," he said ominously.

Juliette snickered, then saw that he was serious. "But . . . it isn't even real! And even if it was, who cares about a disgusting roach?"

Marion came up behind him and slipped under his arm. "Ladies, when we had a mouse in the house, this man caught it in his hat, made a nest for it, and fed it for three days." She looked up at Hearst. "Not everyone feels the same way you do about animals, Pops."

"True," he said, still angry. "But they have to respect my wishes in my house."

He looked to Lulu like a cross between a domineering company president and a petulant child.

"Oh, please don't be a grump when I'm having such a good time, WR," Marion pleaded.

Hearst looked down at his treasured mistress, then slowly to Juliette, his eyes narrowing. "Tell you what we'll do," Hearst told Juliette. "Take it outside and give it a decent burial. Then we'll be square."

Juliette looked at Hearst like he was nuts.

"But it's *paper*," she said again. Hearst stared icily down at her. "Okay, fine. But this is dingy, I tell ya!" She snatched the paper roach out of Freddie's hand and stomped out the door.

A servant came a little while later and summoned Hearst on some newspaper business.

"Now, where were we?" Lulu asked Freddie, edging closer.

But almost as soon as their hands touched, Mr. Waters called Freddie away. Lulu closed her eyes and sighed. Would she never get any time alone with Freddie? She didn't care what they did, as long as they could be together.

"There you are," Boots said, dragging Eleanor and Toshia behind her. "We have a plan to take Juliette down a notch or two. Are you in?"

"I don't know," Lulu said. "What do my odds look like?"

Boots pulled out a little notebook. "Ten to one right now, alas. Jean and Joan pulled ahead, and stand at three to one each. Juliette, darn her, is at five to one thanks to that egg stunt. She knows her audience, in Marion at least. Not so much in Hearst, though."

The look of mischief in Boots's eyes made Lulu think she'd better pass.

"Have you seen Honey or Dolores?" Boots asked. Those were the other two girls sharing Casa del Mar. "They might want to help."

Dolores was busy looking sultry in a corner while an up-and-coming young artist praised her figure. Adorable, black-eyed Honey, though, was nowhere to be found.

"Well, the three of us ought to be strong enough to manage," Boots said mysteriously.

"Heavens!" Lulu gasped. "What are you planning to do to Juliette?"

"Come with us if you want to know," Boots said deviously. "No? Well, you'll find out soon enough. Suffice it to say that a good scare might be enough to make Juliette quit this game for good."

The three young actresses slipped out of the room on their secret mission.

Left alone, Lulu looked around the Assembly Room for someone to talk to. Marion saw her at loose ends and pounced. She took her arm and said, "I didn't get a chance to thank you earlier for showing Patricia such a good time. The poor girl is absolutely dying for some fun, and nobody pays much attention to her. You're the first person to make such an effort."

"Your niece is an interesting girl," Lulu began.

"Oh Lord!" Marion said, smacking her forehead. "Interesting? That means crazy, doesn't it? That's one of those backhanded insults clever people do. A critic once walked out of my premiere, and when I asked what he thought, he smiled and said 'words fail me.' Boy oh boy, words didn't fail him in the next morning's review! Ouch!"

"I didn't mean . . . ," Lulu began.

"Don't worry your pretty little head about it. And it *is* a pretty little head. You remind me of someone. Who could it be? Oh yes, me!" Marion threw back her head and laughed. "Seriously, I'm so grateful to you for dancing with my niece. She said she met you earlier with your little dog, Charlie. Why not have him stay in Casa Grande so he can pal around with my dogs? You'll be here twenty hours out of the day, anyway. Have you met everyone yet?"

She walked Lulu up to Anita. "This is 'Nita, my bosom friend. At least, I think she is. Most of the stuff that comes out of her mouth is so clever I can't understand it, so she might be insulting me all the time, for all I know. Have you read *Gentlemen Prefer Blondes*?"

"No, I'm sorry, I haven't. I didn't have many books growing up."

Anita moaned. "*Growing up*, she says. These kids make me feel ancient. She was an infant when the book came out."

"Don't remind me," Marion said. "This week I want to be forever seventeen. Oh, you should have seen me at seventeen! WR would buy two seats in the front row just to stare at me at the Follies—one seat for him, one for his hat." She looked around the room. "Where did our fellows get off to? I wonder."

"Yours is doing that mysterious thing called business,"

Anita said. "Mine isn't being mysterious at all. This is his day off. Just figure out which starlet is missing, and that's what—or who—he's doing."

"How do you mean, day off?" Marion asked.

"Never mind," Anita said lightly. "I'm starving! Someone ring the dinner gong."

*Three*

**T**he missing guests began to filter back in. Boots, Toshia, and Eleanor reappeared looking like the cat that ate the canary. Honey slipped in a moment later, distinctly tumbled, and John Emerson came in by another door, looking smooth and crisp as ever.

"You changed your suit," Anita observed dryly.

Docky and Louella came in, whispering heatedly. Lulu wondered if they were having an affair. She didn't know anything about the gossip columnist's personal life. Louella thrived on other people's secrets but was a cipher herself.

Freddie entered without Lulu seeing him, and managed to startle her by whispering from behind, "I was on a secret mission."

She jumped. "What were you up to?"

"Hearst needed to talk to Waters some more, but again I wasn't privy to it. I guess mere assistants aren't to be trusted with state secrets. I had to wait in the hallway, which gave me ample time to sneak away and change the place cards in the dining room. They had us miles apart. Wait until you see the dining room. My father would turn pea green and explode with envy, which makes me think I should arrange for an invitation. That would be a sight I'd rather enjoy." Lulu would have laughed had she not felt a chill at the mention of Freddie's monster of a father. How very far the apple had fallen from that tree.

"Now we're right next to each other. I know it's terribly gauche to seat couples together, but what does a former hobo know about good manners?" He snuck a light kiss on her cheek, making a swooning sound like Groucho Marx.

Hearst returned last of all, slightly out of breath and with a sheen of sweat on his forehead. "Sorry, folks. Life of a publishing magnate." Now that he was there, dinner could begin.

Lulu stopped dead in her tracks when she entered the palatial dining room, known as the Refectory. "Where's Henry the Eighth?" she asked in a breathless whisper, gazing at the royal magnificence.

Veronica, coming up beside her, gestured to Hearst. "So watch your head."

The Refectory looked like it belonged in a medieval castle. The scale was cavernous, at least three stories high. Figures in bas-relief looked down from the ceiling. Lulu couldn't tell if they were saints or goddesses or Hearst's old girlfriends, but they made her feel disturbingly like she was standing wrong way around and might fall from floor to ceiling any moment.

There were banners flying, and feudal tapestries of hunting scenes hung on the walls, deer getting elegantly slaughtered in centuries-old thread. In the center of the room was a huge banquet table with fifty or more chairs. Footmen were already seating Hearst and Marion in the middle, directly across from each other.

"Yoo-hoo, Lulu!" Marion called, wiggling her hand at Lulu. "Some sap put you at the end of the table, so I switched your place card to be closer to the action. Perks of being the hostess."

Lulu cast a despairing glance at Freddie.

Hearst protested that the change would mean men and women didn't alternate like they should, so there was a last-minute shuffle as cards were exchanged, to everyone's annoyance, until Hearst was satisfied.

"Who is this?" Hearst asked, holding up Juliette's card. She hadn't yet returned from her humiliating burial duty, though, so Hearst ordered her card to be put at the less prestigious end of the table, the place reserved for lowly accountants or writers. "Serves her right for being late," he said pettishly.

As Lulu was taking her seat, a new man walked in and took a seat at the far end of the table. Lulu gasped, and froze with her derriere hovering above her chair.

"No," she whispered. Her breath came hard, and her heart beat wildly in her chest. That glimpse she'd seen as they arrived hadn't been her imagination. Sal Benedetto was really here!

She shot Freddie a frantic look. What was Sal doing at the Ranch? How had he attracted the attention of a man like Hearst? She couldn't guess the answer to the latter, but she began to tremble in fear that his main purpose in coming here was to continue his unwanted pursuit of her. He'd already bought off police and threatened her with prison in his attempt to procure her. Though she'd offered him no encouragement, he was obsessed and had told her directly that it was only a matter of time before she was his. He was a man accustomed to getting whatever he wanted.

Even if she hadn't been head over heels in love with Freddie, she would never yield to Sal's advances. The man terrified her. He was a callous gangster who had happily taken over his father's criminal empire and subsequently created a patina of culture around himself. But there was no amount of money or artificial suavity that could eclipse the fact that the first time she'd seen him, she had witnessed him shoot a rival in the head in cold blood. Her impression of him hadn't improved since.

Though her first impulse was to flee, Lulu soon found her steel. She sat and tried not to stare at him down the table. Sal wasn't just a dangerous man; he imperiled the entire life she'd worked so hard to build. He knew about the past that she hid so carefully. If Sal chose to casually pull one silken thread, the entire fabric of her life would unravel, and no one in this mercenary business would glance back or remember her. If he bothered her, she'd have to deal with it privately, hidden away from the hundreds of prying eyes that surrounded them at the Ranch.

Sal only glanced her way, a smile playing on his sensuously curving mouth. He gave her the barest nod, then turned his attention to the luscious starlet on his right. Lulu might have been no more than a passing acquaintance.

Her jaw dropped. Inexplicably, she became aware of a heat in her cheeks. How dare he!

Unaccountably annoyed, Lulu settled herself uneasily in her chair and looked around the room. She was sitting directly across from Freddie. It wasn't as close as she was hoping for, but at least they could talk. John Emerson was on her left, and an artist named Hugh d'Or was on her right.

Neither was shy in expressing their admiration of her. By the time the asparagus soup was cleared away for the next course, each had made her a proposal of sorts. John dropped his napkin and ham-handedly brushed her thigh retrieving it, then told her that, perhaps, if the stars aligned, even if she didn't get the starring role, he could write a noteworthy part for her. He said it as other men might ask the time of day, and she assumed it was one of his standard pickup lines. Anita caught Lulu's eye and gave a little shrug.

Hugh the cubist talked about himself, slyly offered to paint her, then talked about himself some more. "You would be nude, *naturellement*, for the human form is the expression of the divine, no? But you would be rendered in flesh-colored geometry, cones and spheres, indistinguishable from other females. You can be nude without fear, for no one will know it is you."

"So I could be anyone?" Lulu asked archly.

"*Oui.*"

"Then I don't see why I should let you paint me when an ice-cream cone could serve just as well as a model." She tried to talk to Freddie across the table, but she had to shout to make herself heard above the lively din, and most of the things she wanted to say to him were meant to be spoken in loving murmurs. The other things were about Sal. Neither was appropriate dinner table conversation.

It might be too far to conveniently talk, but perhaps they could communicate another way. She reached out her foot, feeling for his, catching his eye, and looking meaningfully down at the middle of the table.

He must have understood, because after a moment of discreet searching, Lulu found his foot. She stroked it with the side of her kitten-heeled shoe and found bare flesh. Her lips curling into a secret smile, she looked demurely at Freddie across the table and slipped her own shoe off. Clever boy! Though she wondered what he'd done with his sock and how he'd get it back on when dinner was over.

His foot was chilly, and she placed her own silk-stockinged foot over it to warm it up.

"Cold in here, isn't it?" she shouted across the table at Freddie. He smiled but gave her a funny look.

His foot was strangely inert. But then she realized that he must be extending his leg as far as it would go to reach her.

He probably couldn't move it to stroke her foot without being obvious. It was a compliment to Lulu that he could flirt with her at all, given the gorgeous women on either side of him. Jean Harlow was on his right, a dancer named Ginger Rogers on his left. The last-minute card switcheroo had put him in an enviable position.

So Lulu did the work for both of them, caressing his foot with hers as she pretended to be impressed by the artist's inflated ego and John Emerson's poorly concealed advances amid bits of acid wisdom.

"Hearst claims he's such an animal lover," Emerson said as the main course was served. "But look at his table. Foie gras. Veal. And do you know what this is?"

"Duck, I think," said Lulu, salivating at the rich aroma and the crispy fat. Her physical culture coach would have a fit if she saw Lulu eating something like that. Lulu planned to ask for seconds.

"*Pressed* duck. Just this morning our fine feathered friend was decorating the pond for the pleasure of WR's guests. Next thing he knows he's being slowly strangled to death." A look of malicious pleasure crossed Emerson's face as he mimed squeezing the life out of someone. "Not for him the quick death of the guillotine. This duck's blood had to be saved for nefarious purposes. Next he was plucked and half roasted—let's pray he was *quite* dead, not just faking and hoping for the best—and his tender bits removed. The rest of his mortal remains were clamped in a sterling-silver vise and squeezed until they yielded their juices. See that delicious-looking sauce? Blood and marrow, semi-raw. Spanish Inquisition duck, I call it. And yet they say Hearst won't kill a bug."

At the center of the long table, Hearst was shoveling crisp, fatty duck into his mouth.

Lulu shuddered. She'd suddenly lost her appetite.

Louella's shrill voice rang out. She was one of the only people—besides Hearst himself—who could command the attention of most of the table. She might be Hearst's minion, writing for his papers and commenting on his radio stations, but she was powerful in her own right.

"Mr. Hearst, I cannot understand why Marion hasn't talked you out of your disgraceful habit."

Hearst looked momentarily alarmed, until Louella went on. "You have built the biggest and most beautiful home on this part of the continent, have a staff that's larger than the population of many smaller European countries, the finest china dishes, the most delicate glass goblets . . . and yet you use these . . . these *paper* napkins! It's appalling! And ketchup and mustard bottles right on the table, too."

"This is a ranch, after all," Hearst said amiably. "We can't get too far above ourselves."

"Some of us can," Lulu heard Emerson mutter beside her, but she couldn't tell who he was referring to.

"Oh, dear me, I'm just teasing you, Mr. Hearst," Louella said, not pushing her criticism too far. Even a favorite could fall. "I think it is charmingly unpretentious. If you don't mind, I'll even write about it in my next column." To show her approval, she snatched up a bottle of ketchup and prepared to desecrate her meal.

But the second she opened the top, the ketchup exploded in a red volcano, covering her and everyone around her with a spray of tomato gore. She screamed, then tried to laugh because she knew she was supposed to, but failed miserably. She dabbed at her silk and chiffon gown, but it only made it look more like blood on her chest.

"Baking soda in the ketchup bottle," Marion howled. "A classic." No one claimed credit though. They didn't want Louella as an enemy.

The scarlet image, so familiar to Lulu, made her feel momentarily queasy. Ruby had looked like that, with the blood of her gunshot wound blossoming on her breast. Added to her duck-induced nausea, she really didn't think she could make it to dessert. And there went John Emerson's napkin again, so she was in for another feeling-up.

Regretfully, she gave Freddie's toes a last caress and slipped her foot into her shoe.

"Excuse me," she said, pushing her chair back and standing.

John, who had been in an awkward position with his attempt to subtly reach Lulu's leg, fell sideways to one knee on the floor as Lulu stood. He reached for the table to catch his balance, and caught Lulu's wrist instead. A delicate bracelet of pearls, given to her by Lux Studio head Niederman to mark the signing of her new contract, broke, and the gems clattered to the floor.

"How clumsy of me," John said, managing to sneak in another fondle. A girl can only take so much, even in Hollywood, so Lulu stepped down hard on his hand before she knelt and tried to pick up the pearls.

Undeterred, John stooped to help her, brushing her hip.

Lulu screamed!

"I was only being friendly," John whispered.

But Lulu wouldn't stop screaming. She staggered back, pointing under the table.

Freddie launched himself over the centerpiece and was at her side. He flung back the tablecloth.

Underneath the table, still and staring and cold, was the body of Juliette Claire, her bare foot splayed near Lulu's chair.

Just then the door burst open and an auburn-haired young man strode in.

"Sorry I'm late, everybody. What did I miss?"

## Four

**C**all the police!" Freddie shouted as he felt Juliette's wrist for a pulse. But even Lulu could see that there was no hope for the young actress. A silk scarf in shades of pale sea green was wrapped so tightly around Juliette's neck that there were livid bruises on her skin. Her eyes were wide and staring, her painted mouth agape.

"No, don't call the police just yet," Hearst commanded in a low voice. "Everybody out of the room, now. You stay, Waters, and you, too, Docky."

"Stop," Freddie said in a firm order, surprising a roomful of people who were decidedly unprepared for any more surprises. He released Juliette's wrist, and her hand fell to the floor with a limp meaty sound that made Lulu shiver. "Everyone has to stay right here."

Even amid the horror of discovering Juliette's corpse, Lulu was impressed with the young man she loved. Half a century younger and infinitely poorer than Hearst, he still faced the tycoon down with steady eyes and a confident stance, as if he owned the room.

"She was killed by someone in this house," Freddie went on. "Maybe even someone in this room. The first thing we have to do is account for everyone's whereabouts." He pulled a little notebook from his inside jacket pocket. "Please, no one leave until I've gotten your name."

He seemed to suddenly remember that he was only a junior assistant detective under Mr. Waters. No one knew that he had until recently been Freddie van der Waals, son of a man even richer than Hearst. Now he was just Freddie Van, assistant gumshoe.

He looked to Mr. Waters. "Isn't that what you taught me, boss?" he asked. Waters seemed flummoxed. Freddie knew that even though Waters was at heart a fine detective, he'd been in Hollywood a long time and was used to bending the rules—and maybe even the truth—to help his big-name clients. Hearst was by far the biggest. But Freddie himself had once lived in a world of luxury surrounded by yes-men, and he wouldn't ever let himself be one.

Mr. Waters recovered himself and looked sharply at his protégé. Beckoning Freddie, he crossed the room to Hearst's side and whispered confidentially into his ear, "Don't worry, Mr. Hearst. We understand the need for discretion to a man such as yourself, and we will conduct the inquiry with the utmost tact and consideration for your position."

Hearst nodded, looking relieved, until Freddie said, loudly enough for those closest to hear, "Still, we must not forget that a girl is dead. What is scandal compared with a human life? The police have to be called."

"Of course," Hearst said. "I only thought that since Mr. Waters and the good doctor were here, it was better that they begin the investigation, instead of waiting. The nearest police station is a good hour away through the mountains."

Freddie wasn't the only one with a notebook. Louella Parsons was already hunched over the corpse, scribbling furiously into an ostrich-skin journal. Lulu, watching her, felt a fresh quiver of revulsion. The woman—dressed in a black satin gown with black feathers on the shoulders—looked exactly like a vulture. She feasted on anything rotten.

Lulu's heart was still pounding loudly in her chest, but she found herself filled with a strange new calm. The sense of moral rightness that had so treacherously deserted her once now rose up stronger than it ever had been. Someone had murdered poor Juliette in cold blood. She might not have liked the girl, but as she looked at her cold, lifeless body she was overwhelmed with a desire to bring the murderer to justice. It didn't matter that Waters, Freddie, and soon the police would be on the case. She knew right then that she had to do whatever she could.

Marion, who looked annoyed rather than horror-struck, took Lulu's arm. "This kind of thing always seems to happen to me," she said, nattering pathetically.

"Funny, I thought this happened to Juliette," Lulu countered archly, gesturing to the corpse.

Marion didn't seem abashed. "First there was that scandal at my sister Reine's party. Some drunken dame shot up her husband in the road outside her house. The papers said that she was jealous of me, but I'd never met them. I wasn't even at the party! And of course you know about poor Tom Ince."

Everyone had heard about the Thomas Ince scandal, even Lulu, who had been no more than ten at the time. Though the official story said that the famed producer had suffered a massive heart attack while on board Hearst's yacht, other people swore to a different version. Hearst had supposedly caught Marion *in flagrante* in a hallway with Charlie Chaplin, and tried to shoot him. He missed, and shot Ince in the heart. To this day, gossips whispered their own ideas of the truth.

"The worst part is that my name will be in the headline," Marion said. Lulu's opinion of her hostess had been falling steadily, and her attitude now—that she was the one suffering when a girl lay dead underneath her dining table—was unconscionable. But then Marion added, "It's disgusting. *She's* the one who has suffered. *She's* the one whose life has been brutally snatched from her in the prime of her youth and beauty. But no, if it happens near me or WR, we're the news. We're the story." She looked down at Juliette's body. "The poor, pretty child. What a rotten world it is. I need another drink."

Marion moved to the table, picked up someone's half-drunk glass of wine, and neatly polished it off. Mrs. Mortimer came in and made a beeline toward Marion. Someone must have relayed the news. The two women conversed in a whisper, their heads bent close. Marion was weeping quietly, and the housekeeper pulled a handkerchief from her sleeve and dried Marion's cheeks with a surprisingly tender gesture. Then she helped Marion out of the room, half-supporting the much smaller woman.

Freddie and Mr. Waters were writing down names, letting each person exit to the Assembly Room to be interviewed as soon as possible. When she was released, Lulu decided to do a little investigating of her own. Since the incident with Ruby, she knew that the best course of action was the systematic elimination of plausible suspects, which Freddie and Mr. Waters would inevitably take far too long to do, since they had no entrée into the inner circle of the guests. Obviously people would be much more likely to blab to her than to them!

She squinted and looked about the room, imagining the dreadful things Juliette had said to each person there, and thought, *Good Lord, not a single person in this room, except Marion, demonstrated any sadness when they discovered that Juliette was dead! They all loathed her.* And with that in her head, Lulu began her probe. She took a deep breath, and gliding casually across the room, cornered Boots, Eleanor, and Toshia by a bookcase at the far end of the great hall.

"Girls like that get theirs in the end?" she said at once to Boots, glaring at her with her hands on her hips as she quoted the girl's words back to her.

"What are you talking about?" Boots asked, leaning her lanky body against the bookcase.

"Juliette, of course!" Lulu said hotly. "You three said you had a plan to take her out of the running. I never dreamed you meant permanently."

"You can't be serious," Eleanor said.

"You came to me just before dinner with some cockamamie scheme. You even said the three of you should be strong enough to handle whatever it was you were doing. Well, I guess three of you could move a body pretty easily!"

Toshia had tears in her eyes, which could either be a sign of guilt or innocence. Lulu was excruciatingly aware that she was dealing with actresses. Turning on the waterworks came with the territory. "How could you even think that of us?" Toshia asked. "We would never hurt anyone."

"Is that so?" Lulu needled.

"Not much, anyway," Boots muttered under her breath.

Eleanor nudged Boots in the ribs. "Oh, all right, so we did have a plan to do *something* to Juliette. Something just a teeny bit horrible. But she deserved it! She was telling everyone you were expecting, and when she got bored of slamming you, she started in on me, ratting out to a few carefully chosen people of influence my not-so-dignified past! Sure, I posed in my scanties, but I never took 'em off for anybody! Juliette had it coming, but good."

There was a part of Lulu that wanted to agree . . . almost. It wasn't a part of her that she liked, or planned to share with the world.

"Whatever you did," Lulu said, "it went terribly wrong. What did you do to her?"

"We didn't kill her," Eleanor said. "Come upstairs. We'll show you what we had planned. It was nothing, I swear! Nothing much . . . ," she added in a mutter.

The four young actresses slipped out of the Assembly Room and upstairs to the suite of guest bedrooms where the most fortunate guests were staying. "This is Juliette's room," Boots said. The door was slightly agape. Boots, Eleanor, and Toshia lingered in the hallway, looking ashamed. Lulu, however, moved cautiously toward the door, uncertain but mindful that she might be walking into the scene of a heinous crime.

"No! Stop!" the other girls cried, and Toshia grabbed for Lulu's arm. "Look out for the . . ." Lulu shook her off and shoved her way inside.

Her shoe squelched into a puddle and she slipped down to her backside into freezing water. "What the . . . ?"

"Are you all right?" squeaked Toshia.

"Peachy," muttered Lulu. As she gasped and sputtered, trying to stand and slipping, she kicked a metal bucket.

"See!" Boots said triumphantly. "It wouldn't have killed her, even if she *had* gone to her room."

It took Lulu a moment to catch her breath after the sudden shock of her cold bath. When her friends had hauled her to her feet, she said, "You had a bucket of water set up over her door? That was all you were going to do to her? Give her a drenching?"

"Cross my heart," Boots said. "We figured she'd go back to her room after digging in the dirt to bury that paper bug. We thought it would be a big comedown to get soaked before dinner. She'd have to show up all wet, or else be late for dinner. Hearst would be furious either way."

"But she never showed up to her room, did she?" Lulu said, squeezing out the skirt of her dress. "She was dry when I found her, and her hair and makeup were perfect. Who set off the booby trap, then?"

Boots shrugged. "All I know is that we three are in the clear."

"I almost hoped it *was* you three," Lulu confessed, to their shocked stares and gaping mouths. "Oh, I didn't really want you to be guilty—though at the moment I'd be happy to send the three of you to Sing-Sing for what you've done to my clothes. I knew in my heart that you wouldn't kill anyone on purpose—and were probably too sensible to kill someone by accident. But I'd hoped that maybe it was just an innocent prank gone wrong, somehow."

"I don't see how a girl can be accidentally strangled to death," Eleanor pointed out.

"Call it wishful thinking," Lulu said. "Because if you three didn't do it, that means there is a real honest-to-goodness murderer in this house. And I think I know who he is."

The girls gasped. But though they pressed her, she wouldn't give them a clue. She had to talk to Freddie.

Anxious as she was to get to him, she knew she had to start thinking like an investigator if she was to be of any help. Juliette obviously hadn't gone to her room after completing Hearst's preposterous, childish punishment. Still, there might well be a clue inside. If the murderer was who Lulu thought it was, he probably had some personal connection to Juliette. If she could find some proof and bring it to Freddie, the case would be all but solved, and her life would become exponentially less dangerous.

Mostly, Lulu wanted to solve Juliette's murder for the good and simple reason that life was precious and killing abhorrent. But a tiny part of her—again, the part she didn't particularly like, or wish to share—knew that the sooner this case was wrapped up, the sooner she could spend more time with Freddie.

"I'm going to look around," Lulu said.

"Are you sure you should?" Eleanor asked.

"The police will want to look first," Toshia said.

"I won't touch anything," Lulu said, and dripped and sloshed her way around the room.

Like all the rooms in the castle, Juliette's bedroom was more of a way to display art and artifacts than it was a living space. The overall theme was French, but the decor spanned hundreds of years. Tapestries crowded with paintings along the walls, gilded walnut tables perched cheek by jowl with heavy brocade chairs, and the bed was canopied in blue and gold. On the pillow sat a small opened box, empty, with striped crimson and silver paper strewn nearby.

It was certainly an impressive room, Lulu thought, but not a very comfortable one.

"She's a slob!" Boots said.

"*Was* a slob," Toshia said sadly.

Every drawer and door in the room was half open.

Juliette's clothes were strewn haphazardly over chairs, and makeup and cold cream littered the tables. Lulu bent over a hairbrush with tangles of blond hair. She could see dark brown at the root of each strand.

"No one should die with their roots showing," Lulu said, then flinched inwardly at the shallow thought. Had she really said that? Hollywood was changing her. "Poor Juliette. Look at all the clothes she brought. Enough for a month."

"Why didn't she take care of them, or put them away?" Boots asked. "If I had all these clothes, I'd make sure they were hung up neatly. And her underthings are thrown 'round like confetti."

Lulu gasped. This wasn't just random chaos. "Juliette wasn't a slob. This place was searched! Probably by whoever set off your surprise."

"Unless it was just an unfortunate chambermaid," Toshia said.

"Either way, whoever got drenched might know something," Boots said, looking excited to be part of an investigation.

"Or they might be the murderer. I have to tell all this to Freddie. Immediately!"

But when she ran up to Freddie in the Assembly Room, he greeted her with a smile and said, "Good news—they've caught the murderer!"

*Five*

**R**eally? Are you certain? I just found some very strange evidence in Juliette's room, and I was so sure that . . ." Lulu trailed off, strangely disappointed to have the mystery solved so quickly.

"I'm so sorry that you find this news disenchanting. One is usually happy when a murderer is caught," Freddie said, putting his arm around her in mock sympathy.

"Oh, stop teasing me!" she said, pushing his arm off in annoyance. "Someone absolutely ransacked her room. Her clothes were everywhere, and not like a messy-girl kind of everywhere. It was a definite ransacking kind of everywhere. And there was a missing present, but I don't know what it was, and . . . Freddie, where's Sal?"

Freddie's eyebrows twitched upward. "Smoking upstairs in

the billiard room, I think. Why do you want to know? I'd have thought you'd want to stay as far away from him as possible."

"Wait a minute. You mean Sal's not the murderer?"

"Darling, I don't like him much either, but for the life of me, I can't imagine why he would kill Juliette. Not that I wouldn't be happy to see him locked away. I don't very much care for the way you and he—"

"Well, why would anyone kill anyone? He's the only person here who I positively *know* has killed before. The first time I met him, he . . ." She stopped.

"When you first met him, what?" Freddie asked. There was always something strange between Sal and Lulu, and confident as he was, it made him just the slightest bit uneasy.

She bit her lip. As intimate as she was with Freddie, as much as she trusted him, she had never revealed the story of her first meeting with Sal, or what she'd done afterward. Freddie knew that Sal was obsessed with her, but she'd never corrected his natural assumption that Sal had become intrigued with her after seeing her on-screen.

"I just knew that he was dangerous. That's all. I'm sure he's killed people in the line of work, or at the very least, he's ordered his goons to do it for him. He has everyone out here convinced he's just a businessman, but I know that he's a criminal. He *must* have been the one who killed Juliette. Now, if we can just figure out why . . ."

"Much as I hate to disappoint anyone as charmingly enthusiastic about a murder as you are, and as happy as I would be to throw that crook in jail, it really doesn't look like it was him," Freddie said. "Just a few minutes ago Hearst's private security team found a trespasser on the grounds, and apparently, he had some stolen items on him."

"I'm telling you, something's off about Sal being here."

Just then Hearst came back into the Assembly Room. "My friends and guests," he said in his booming pompous voice. "I apologize for the unfortunate interruption."

"Unfortunate interruption!" Lulu couldn't help but repeat audibly. How could he be so blasé, as if a rainstorm had spoiled their picnic? "A girl's life was interrupted—permanently! How can you say . . . ?"

Veronica rushed to her side and shushed her. "Admirable sentiments," she hissed, "but no opinions, please, if someone wants the job of a lifetime."

Lulu rolled her eyes, and Hearst went on, watching her warily for further interruption.

"An intruder was spotted on the grounds near the Neptune Pool. The suspect was handily apprehended and knocked unconscious, thanks to my outstanding security staff. Now, given his insensible state, taking him into custody should be well within the prowess even of our rural police force. The murderer has been caught, and we are all safe! Cheers!"

He raised his glass, and everyone in the room followed suit. Not Lulu. She stepped forward slowly, eyebrows furrowed with frustration.

"But how do you *know* he was the one who killed her?" Lulu asked. "Who is he?"

"The culprit is a colored man in his twenties," Hearst said. "I never saw him before in my life, and neither has any of the staff. The man had scratches on his face and arms, clear evidence of a recent battle with one of the fair sex. When my men searched him, they found a diamond ring in his pocket."

The women in the gathering murmured in great alarm, checking their fingers, as if the prisoner might have escaped, slipped into the room, and snatched their jewels. *How awful and self-absorbed these people are,* Lulu thought.

"It appears the intruder's plan was to rob us while we gathered before dinner," Hearst went on. "He must have searched the rooms and found the ring, then left. Miss Claire must have surprised him, perhaps even confronted him, and met her sorry end at the hands of the desperate criminal. Please, let's have a moment of silence for the lovely, unfortunate Miss Juliette Claire, struck down in the prime of her youth."

The whole room bowed their heads and went silent, but Lulu could feel all eyes shifting around, knowing full well that this was a bona fide viper's nest full of enemies Juliette had made. Many that very day.

The capture of the trespasser was certainly damning, but something was gnawing at Lulu. If the man had broken in to steal jewels, why would he stop at one ring? The actresses' rooms were most certainly littered with valuable gems, owned or borrowed from the biggest jewelers in Hollywood to add glitter and a sense of entitlement, if not outright envy, to the party at the Ranch. And if he had indeed killed Juliette, why would he still be hanging around the estate? He should have been halfway down the mountainside, not lingering by the swimming pool.

She had a lot of questions. But right now one seemed to be the most important. Despite the thick, agitated silence of the partygoers, heads bowed in insincere reverence, Lulu felt compelled to ask, "The man you caught—was he wet?"

Hearst looked at Lulu as if she'd lost her mind. And Freddie, head popping up, had to pinch himself to keep from bursting out with laughter. She just couldn't help herself, and he loved her all the more for it, though her timing could use some work.

"I think the strain has been a bit much for her," Freddie said. "I'll escort her to her room, if you don't mind."

He took her by the upper arm and began to hustle her away. Lulu couldn't believe it. "Why, of all the condescending, insulting . . . Strain? I'll show you strain! How dare you? You think you're superior because you're a man, and I'm just some weak female! Well, I'll show you who's weak!"

When they were outside Freddie released her.

"You're lovely when you're angry. Your eyes are so pretty when your face turns red like that."

"You are a monster!"

"Entirely possible, but we'll save that conversation for another time. For now I simply thought that was the most convenient way of getting you out of that room—and outside, where they're keeping the suspect. You want to see him, don't you? You might sound crazy to the rest of them, but I've seen you in action and I have a fair guess you can out-sleuth me in a heartbeat. When you start talking about missing presents and wet murderers, I know you must be onto something."

"Oh, Freddie!" she said, and kissed him in the silvery moonlight.

The police were pulling into the driveway when Lulu and Freddie arrived. Mr. Waters was already there, talking with Hearst's security. At their feet lay a man trussed like a Christmas goose.

The young man appeared to be in his early twenties. He was handsome, even in his unconscious and unfortunate state. His hair was trimmed neat and very close to his head, as if he had just had a fresh haircut, and he sported a pencil-thin mustache. He was nattily dressed in a well-tailored checked suit marred only by a damp, muddy patch on one knee. An expensive and fashionable paisley bow tie was neatly knotted on his neck. In the harsh headlights of the police cars, Lulu could see a dark stream of blood running down his head.

"He's not just unconscious," she said. "He's badly hurt."

"But not wet, evidently," Freddie said, and knelt by the man's side.

Lulu bent to look closer. "See that shine on his shoes? And look at those fingernails. They're buffed. I'd swear to it. He doesn't look like a thief."

"Doesn't look like a murderer, either," Freddie said. "Why did you want to know if he was wet?"

Lulu told him about the prank that Boots, Toshia, and

Eleanor had planned to play on Juliette. "Someone was in that room and set off their ridiculous trap. Hearst said that this man was inside the house. I thought maybe he was the one in Juliette's room, that it was her ring he stole. But if it was him, he'd be drenched."

"Unless he went in after someone else set off the prank," Freddie pointed out.

Lulu shifted in her squelching shoes. "The rug was soaking, and there was a deep puddle inside the door. Check his shoes."

The soles were muddy, but the shoes were dry.

"So he didn't go in Juliette's room. That doesn't clear him. He still has the stolen ring."

"But there's nothing connecting him to Juliette. Look at all that dirt on his feet. If he'd gone inside he would have left tracks. And if he killed her outside, why would he take the risk of going back inside, where it's crawling with guests and staff, to hide her in the dining room? And how do you know the ring is stolen? If his suit, shoes, and grooming are any indication, this man is hardly hurting for money!"

"Good questions," Freddie said. "Mr. Waters, any chance we can speak with the suspect?"

Waters shook his head. "Boy's out cold. The officers will take him down to the chokey and see if a bucket of water can't revive him. Then they'll get the truth out of him."

"I don't think he did it," Lulu said resolutely.

Waters smiled indulgently and took a long tug off of a flask nestled inside his coat pocket. "Well, ain't you a softhearted little missy. What else would a colored boy be doing hanging around a mansion?"

Racism did not sit well with Freddie. He had made too many friends and shared too many hard times with men of all backgrounds during his time as a vagrant to pass judgments on a man simply because of his skin tone. But he valued his job and knew that men like Waters had to be handled carefully.

"All due respect, sir, we have no clear evidence here that ties this man to the victim. No murder weapon, no motive—"

"That we know of," Waters sneered. "But we'll get it out of him. This man had no business here except for evil."

"He could have been looking for a job, or coming to see someone, or his car could have broken down along the road," Lulu said indignantly. She shared Freddie's distaste for bigotry.

"You have too much faith in human nature," Waters said dismissively. "When you've seen the things I've seen, you'll realize that most of the world is bad, and the rest of it is downright rotten."

"I promise you, Mr. Waters, I have seen things," Lulu said with a frown. "Perhaps too many. But I don't think this man killed Juliette."

She watched as the handsome young suspect was carried away and tossed, still unconscious, into the backseat of the police car. She would have given anything to be able to talk with him.

As the car pulled away, Lulu tugged Freddie back toward the house. "I want to see the body. Well," she amended, "I don't actually *want* to see it. *Her*, I mean. Juliette is still a person."

"You want to look for more clues?" Freddie asked.

"Tell me to butt out if you think I should."

"Never," Freddie said, arching up his left eyebrow mischievously. "If you have a hunch, I trust you. I don't know why, but I do."

Lulu smiled and looked into his beautiful eyes, and felt more love for him in that moment than she had ever before. "I don't know what I think. I just want to have another look."

When they got to the Refectory, they found a dignified-looking butler standing watch over Juliette's corpse at a respectful distance. Lulu wondered if this was the most unusual thing he'd had to do in service for Hearst.

"I have been instructed to inform you not to touch the mortal remains," he said, his lined face expressionless.

"We won't," Freddie assured him. "I'm Mr. Waters's assistant."

The butler nodded but stopped Lulu from entering. *He must think I'm just a vile tourist eager for another glimpse of something macabre in the castle.* "And I broke my pearl bracelet, and I desperately want to find the missing pearls!" Lulu explained, acting the part of the scatterbrained actress to the hilt. "It was of untold value! Rudolph Valentino gave it to Theda Bara while they had a torrid affair, and a very nice gentleman who Miss Bara then gave it to as payment for some chandelier repairs in her house after she lost all of her money gave it to me as a gift when . . ."

The tortured butler winced and said, "Of course, madam. Good luck," as he ushered Lulu into the room.

She dropped to her knees and forced herself to look at Juliette while she pretended to grope the ground for her pearls. Then she stopped pretending and just sat back on her heels, looking at Juliette.

She had been close to an actual dead person only once before, when she'd witnessed Sal shoot a man in the head. She'd done her best to avert her eyes. Besides, there had been so much else to look at in that moment—Sal's gun pointing at her face, the police arriving seconds later.

Juliette was different. Though Lulu could see the bruising on the girl's throat, it was mostly hidden by the flowing ends of the scarf. She looked so lovely, so alive! Only her vacant stare showed that all that really mattered of her had left this world. *You can't really be dead*, Lulu thought. *You're so young—my age!* In disbelief, she reached out to touch Juliette's curled fingers, recoiling at their chill. Then she steeled herself and took the girl's hand, holding it, warming it with her own living flesh.

"I'll find out who killed you, I promise," Lulu whispered. "And what's more, I'll find out why." To her, that seemed almost more important than *who*.

"You were right. No water on her," Freddie said. "So she never made it back to her room. I don't see any signs of a struggle. No scrapes or bruising on her hands."

"She must have fought back. Juliette was no shrinking violet." From the acidity of her verbal attacks, Lulu couldn't imagine Juliette succumbing quietly to anything.

"Maybe not, if she was attacked from behind. She might

have been unconscious in a matter of seconds. See, her nails aren't broken, and her clothes aren't mussed."

"They said the man they caught had scratches and marks on him, so there should be signs on her hands and wrists . . . ," Lulu said. "And if he killed her because she saw him, wouldn't he have attacked her from the front?"

"Not if she was running away."

"She would have screamed. Someone would have heard."

"Not necessarily," Freddie said. "This is a huge place. We were all inside. The staff was busy preparing for dinner, and the groundskeepers were home for the night."

Lulu scanned the ground. There were no telltale footprints or mud. "They said he killed her outside and dragged her here, but he would have left dirt."

"Maybe he walked in the dirt afterward."

"It just doesn't all fit," Lulu said in frustration.

"We won't know what happened until the suspect wakes up and the police question him. Things might not look like they fit now, but that's because we don't have all the information. Though if he didn't do it, who else could it have been? All the guests were together in the Assembly Room."

"Not all of them," Lulu said. "Not you, or Waters, or Emerson, Lolly, Docky . . ." She scrunched her face up, trying to remember. "Who else was missing when you came back?"

"I haven't a clue—quite literally," he said. "I was only looking at you."

"Oh, Freddie! Stop flirting. This is serious."

"I'm dead serious. Well, not as dead as *her* serious, but,

well, you know what I mean. I think you're right, though. Something's all wrong. Listen, let's get out of here. We can't help Juliette just kneeling here."

Freddie led her out of the dining room. The butler expressed his opinion of them with one small, dignified sniff.

They discovered from the staff that the rest of the guests had been herded to the in-house theater. Hearst had the latest releases driven up to the Ranch every weekend to entertain his guests. If the movie proved a dud, he'd replace it with one of Marion's films.

"I couldn't watch a movie now," Lulu said. Neither of them knew the layout of the house well yet, but they made their way back up another of the small winding staircases that led to the second floor and tried doors until they found a room that looked quiet and comfortable. It might have been a library, because books lined the walls, or it might have been an office, because there were several desks with typewriters on them. Each machine looked brand-new.

"My head feels like it's going to explode," Lulu muttered, massaging her temples as she flopped onto a sofa. "I can't think about corpses and murderers any more today. It's absolutely exhausting."

"Very well . . . Hmm. I wonder how I can distract you." Freddie had a number of excellent ideas and proceeded to distract her as best he could until her mind could focus only on the feel of his skin, the taste of his mouth.

All too soon, the door burst open. "There you are!" Waters

said. "Been looking all over this pile for you. Hearst needs us both. Something's happened."

"What is it? Did the man confess?" Lulu gasped.

"Not yet, but he will, mark my words. This is something else. Now, get moving. Hearst is waiting."

Freddie left her with a regretful backward glance.

For a while Lulu sat in silent contemplation. When the door opened, she looked up expectantly, eager for a little more of Freddie's skillful distraction. But it was another man— auburn haired, about twenty, with clear, pale brown eyes and a sensitive face.

At first she didn't recognize him. Then she gasped and jumped to her feet. She didn't know his name, but he was the man who had arrived late to dinner just as Juliette's body was discovered. She hadn't seen him until that moment. Where had he been before that? He could be the killer!

*Six*

**W**ho are you?" Lulu demanded, her voice sharp and apprehensive. Then she realized what she was doing. The slight, owlish young man had committed no offense except being late for dinner. While the controlling, rule-obsessive Hearst might think that was a crime, it wasn't enough for her to look at him like he was capable of murder. "Sorry," she said, softening. "I'm just a little on edge. It's been a rather challenging day." She eased herself back down onto the sofa.

"That's perfectly all right," the young man said. "We're all on edge right now."

His voice was soft and slow. It wafted toward Lulu like the bouquet of whiskey in the deep South, though the man had no discernible accent. He seemed to Lulu like some curious woodland creature, shyly inching his way into a glen. He hesitated by the door as if he might turn and run if she made any sudden movement.

"After something like that, I'd really rather pack up and go home," he said. "But for better or worse, I know which side my bread is buttered on. Hearst wants me here, so here I stay." He edged forward, holding out his hand. "I'm Paul Raleigh." His fingers were long and elegant, his skin soft as Lulu's own.

"The writer! I just saw your first film."

"My only film," he said, inclining his head modestly so that his just-too-long auburn hair fell into his eyes.

"But what a film!" *The Thousand Cuts* had been a smash, heralded as one of the greatest psychological masterpieces Hollywood had ever produced. "Eva, the wife. She was the most completely realized female character I've ever seen in a film. How is it that you could possibly understand the female nature so intimately?"

Paul blushed. "I don't know all that much about women, really. At least, not from practical experience."

That was refreshing in Hollywood. Most men prided themselves on being self-minted Casanovas and Don Juans.

"But I pay attention," Paul went on. "To women, for sure, but not because they are so different from men, but because they are superior versions of the same species. Men and women are both motivated by the exact same things. Survival. Fear. The need to be safe. The need to be loved. But their modus operandi are vastly different. They are the physically weaker sex, but spiritually they tower above men. Whereas men live to conquer and rule, they are ultimately inferior because they don't possess the ultimate power: to give life. So God himself tipped the scales in favor of the fairer sex, and all we men can do is beat our chests in defiance and lamely attempt to exert superiority over that which has given us our existence. To simultaneously worship and detest our makers. It's in our blood. Eva understood that, and perished standing up for her place in this godforsaken world. . . ." Paul stopped, and suddenly grew self-conscious. "Oh dear. I'm rattling on. I apologize. I just feel very deeply for my characters. They're really my only children."

Lulu, hypnotized by Paul's overwhelming passion and dizzying worldview, came out of her haze. She paused, then patted the sofa cushion beside her. She longed to talk more with this sensitive, brilliant man, and felt like she was a better woman simply by proximity. Paul sat at a respectful distance. She was a beautiful young starlet, so virtually any other man, whether actor, writer, or lighting assistant, would have sat as close as possible. But Paul was deferential, a natural gentleman. She silently prayed that he wouldn't hold her earlier, childish behavior against her.

"Well, then! What do you say we sit back and compare notes on our technique," she said, and settled in for a chat with a kindred spirit.

"I want answers now!" Hearst thundered, slamming his fist down on the desk of his private office. A letter, damp with sweat, was crumpled in his fingers.

"Sir. If I may? You're destroying the evidence . . . sir,"

Freddie said, and gently unclasped the tycoon's fingers. He smoothed the paper onto the desk and read it through.

This, apparently, was the second threatening letter Hearst had received. The first message had been cryptic: I KNOW YOUR SECRET—AND MARION'S. It had been written on ordinary stock paper in black-inked block letters, so perfectly uniform that Freddie surmised it was meant to disguise the writer's natural hand.

As a publisher of some of the most widely read newspapers in the country, Hearst received a vast wealth of hate mail. Freddie wasn't sure why this particular letter was exceptionally distressing. Perhaps because it mentioned his mistress. But what could the secret be? The world—both the young, rich, fashionable world of Hollywood and the gossip-loving public—had by now accepted the fact of Hearst and Marion's affair. They had been together so long that Marion was considered by most to be a second wife, concurrent with his actual wife, Millicent, who ruled the East Coast while Marion dominated the west. That indiscretion was so public that Freddie didn't think there could be any room left for secrets. Waters had told Freddie that the first letter had been found in the regular mail, but in an envelope without a stamp or postmark. Someone had evidently delivered it directly, slipping it in with Hearst's mail and bypassing the post office. Whoever it was had gotten uncomfortably close, though none of the servants reported being handed a letter. It had just appeared.

This second letter had arrived in a much more troubling way. When Hearst had retired to his private office to make a few calls, ensuring that his empire was running smoothly, he'd discovered it placed carefully in his desk drawer on top of his personal gun.

"He's here! In this house!" Hearst shouted. Freddie noticed that he was far more alarmed now than when faced with a dead body and the knowledge that there was a murderer loose at the Ranch. Or could it be the same man? He raised the possibility, but Hearst shot it down.

"This is my private room," he said. "I let the maid in once a week to clean it, but I'm the only one who ever goes in here."

"So there's only one key?" Freddie asked. Hearst nodded. "And you always lock it?"

Hearst admitted that he sometimes forgot.

"So it could have been left by anyone in the house." Freddie glanced over at his employer. Waters was beginning to slur, but was now doing his level best to appear steady and sober in front of Hearst. Poorly. He nodded at everything his protégé said, but didn't seem capable of adding any insight or assurances to the problem before them. Freddie knew he'd have to lead the investigation despite his limited experience . . . for tonight at least.

He peered intently at the letter. He hadn't thought people really crafted cliché blackmail letters like this outside of dime-store novels. Maybe this was no more than a prank, designed by one of the starlets before Hearst's joke moratorium. Each word had been cut out of a newspaper and carefully glued to form the threat. The lines of the cuts were a little uneven, slightly curled, definitely cut by an unskilled hand. Some words, huge headlines, stood out boldly, while others, snipped from tiny advertisements, hunkered in their shadow. It read:

i KNOW WHAT yoU did
13 yeARs aGo.
pAY $30,468, oR
thE WoRLd WiLL KNOW Too.
aWait instRuCTiоNs.

"If I may ask, sir," Freddie said in his most respectful voice. "Can you recall anything of special significance happening thirteen years ago?"

Hearst mumbled something about his life being too busy to recollect every day's occurrences, and stared out the giant iron-framed window in front him into the darkness.

"And why that amount of money?" Freddie wanted to know. "Does that number mean anything to you?"

"The thirty thousand? I have no ide—" Hearst began, then stopped as if an electric charge had just shot through his body. "But no, it couldn't be that. The number's not right. That extra four hundred and sixty-eight dollars. It can't be." He turned slowly and sat down in the massive cordovan leather chair behind the desk.

Whatever Hearst was thinking of, Freddie was pretty sure from the look on his face that it decidedly *could* be.

"Sir, whatever it is, I promise you nothing leaves this room. We can't do our jobs unless we have some idea what this is about, and I can guarantee total discretion. It would help us narrow down suspects."

Hearst looked dubious. "I will only say this. Thirteen years ago I paid someone—it was actually more of a donation—thirty thousand dollars to deal with a particular issue. It was handled quietly, and everyone involved was satisfied with the outcome. No one knows outside of those immediately concerned."

"And those people?" Freddie carefully prompted.

Hearst's eyes moved to the blackmail letter. "I assure you, they have every reason in the world to keep it a secret, and nobody else knows."

When everyone finally retired in the small hours of the morning, Freddie, his head full of a million questions about both the murder and the blackmail, went back to the library where he'd left Lulu, hoping against hope. Surely she'd gone to bed by now, resting up for what would be an arduous day of strictly scheduled and enforced fun, obscure tests of character, and preparation for the talent show on the following Friday.

But when he lingered outside the door, he heard murmured voices and Lulu's low, musical laugh. With vague apprehension, he opened the door silently. Lulu was sitting thigh to thigh with a handsome young man, looking adoringly into his eyes.

Once she spied Freddie, she jumped to her feet, which seemed to him a rather guilty piece of behavior. "Oh, Freddie darling, we were just, er, um . . ."

The man stood too and approached Freddie with his hand out and a soft, fanciful smile on his face. "Paul Raleigh," he said. "Miss Kelly was helping me run the dialogue of a scenario I'm working on. A sister who is seeing her brother off to war. I'm so grateful to her."

"Yes. She's quite a girl," Freddie said carefully with an uneasy smile. Seeing Lulu so physically close with another man, and so obviously flustered at her discovery, made him . . . *Well, there's no other word for it*, he thought. *I'm jealous.* He knew that she was an actress, and as long as he was with her, this was likely to always be an annoying reality. It was her job to act the part of the beautiful young woman in love, or the sexy temptress, and that was annoying enough when she was on the clock.

Still, a well-bred gentleman would never let anyone know he felt jealous, least of all the girl he loved. He would prove his trust by confidently leaving them alone . . . though perhaps not cheerfully.

"Good night, my dear," he said, nodding to Lulu and cursing himself for that childish, possessive use of the endearment, showing off to Paul that he had the right to call Lulu "dear." "I'll see you in the morning. Lovely to meet you, Mr. Raleigh."

He turned to go, clumsily saluting them with two fingers as

he tried to affect a casual, happy-go-lucky attitude that made him wince when his back was to them, but Lulu dashed after him with a backward wave to Paul. "I had no idea it was so late. Good night, Mr. Raleigh! It was lovely to meet you. Until tomorrow!" Then, whispering to Freddie, she said, "We were talking about how similar our jobs are, how deeply we have to get inside the heads of the most troubled characters. You should hear how brilliantly he expresses himself! He puts into words things I've half felt for the past year but could never articulate. Hearst is right—he's a genius."

Freddie didn't like Lulu's eyes to glow like that for anyone but him. Was this to be his life now, always sharing her with other people? People who understood her Hollywood life and artistic passions better than he ever could? He kissed her on the cheek stiffly as they walked, another possessive gesture, and then, vigorously, told himself to knock it off.

After all, he trusted Lulu.

He just didn't trust Paul Raleigh.

*Seven*

**V**eronica shook Lulu awake at six a.m., a mere three hours after she'd collapsed into bed. "Up and at 'em, sunshine!" she said in a voice far too chipper for the early hour. She held up a beautiful white silk floor-length day dress with big orange polka dots.

Lulu regarded the dress, teeter-tottering between being euphoric from her talk with Paul, then lost in doubts about the suspected murderer. Pensively, Lulu set about the business of making herself look like a fresh-faced and well-rested star, her mind focusing on everything but.

When she was almost ready, there was a rap at the door, and a sharp yip. "I come bearing pooches!" Patricia announced as she let herself in.

Charlie jumped onto Lulu's lap and licked her frantically,

undoing half the work she'd done on her makeup. She rubbed his ears and kissed his nose.

"Now, I'm dying to know, what present did you get?" Patricia curled up on Lulu's bed and looked around the room eagerly.

"Present?" Lulu glanced at Veronica, who shrugged.

"On special occasions, Marion and Uncle Will give all the guests presents each night," Patricia explained. "The girls all get the same thing, and all the boys get something else. Emerald shoe clips or platinum cigarette cases. Mrs. Mortimer, the housekeeper, told me you'll get something every night you're here, and the gifts keep getting better as the days go on. So the girls who don't get eliminated will probably end up with a whole sack of loot and a diamond tiara or something truly splendiferous. Oh, I hope it's you!"

"Glad to know I have someone in my corner," Lulu said, laughing.

"Glad to know it's someone with Big Daddy's ear," Veronica said in a muted aside.

"But it seems I'm on the outs with someone," Lulu went on as she reapplied the makeup Charlie had so excitedly removed. "I didn't get any present."

"That's strange," Patricia said. "Let's check with the other girls." And with much more self-possession than most girls her age, she marched into a couple of the other bedrooms to investigate. A few minutes later, with knitted brow and folded arms, she returned with her report: No one else had gotten anything, either.

"Peculiar," Patricia said. "They should have been put out while everyone was in the Assembly Room before dinner, so you'd all find them when you went to bed. I saw them all wrapped in one of the pantries, so pretty in silver and red."

Lulu drew a sharp breath and turned away from the mirror resolutely. "There was one in Juliette's room—unwrapped. So she got her present." Lulu frowned. "But we know she hadn't gone to her room, because she wasn't wet."

Patricia and Veronica just looked at her quizzically as Lulu's investigative mind began to race again. "What could it possibly mean? I wonder . . ." And then her voice trailed off.

Veronica winced. "Uh-oh. I've seen that crazy look before. This is going to take some time, and will definitely not end well," she said, flopping onto the bed and grabbing an old copy of *Photoplay* to flip through.

Lulu dashed out of the room and knocked on Boots's bedroom door. Boots hadn't gotten as far as Lulu in her beauty rituals, and her hair was still in curl papers. "That unwrapped present we saw in Juliette's room—was it there, still wrapped, when you set the trap for her?"

Boots yawned and said, "Yes, still wrapped so prettily, and I was dying to open it and see what it was."

"But you didn't, right?"

"'Course not! Though I did wonder how that sly coyote had sniffed out prey so quickly."

"I think it was from Hearst," Lulu said.

Boots's eyes opened wide in shock. "*He* was her . . . ?"

"No! Not that! I mean he gave a present to all the actresses.

Only he didn't. Or he did and they were taken away." She rubbed her forehead. "I don't really even know if it means anything, but something's not right about it."

"Lulu, you need to stop focusing on Juliette," Veronica said, coming up behind her and slipping an arm around her shoulders. "They caught the man who did it. Let it go."

"Yeah, kiddo, I know it's terrible, but you can't let it drive you bananas," Boots said.

Patricia came to her defense. "Lulu's the only one here who has even an inkling what crime is all about. *And* her boyfriend is a private investigator. If she's worried, I'm worried."

"No," Lulu said, "they're right. I feel like I'm going crazy. I can't stop thinking about it. Poor Juliette."

"You want to do something," Veronica said gently. "That's just your way. You can't help it. But there's nothing left to do here."

"I know," Lulu said, and tried to make herself stop thinking about the crime.

The first item on the day's agenda was a tour of La Casa Grande. Neither Hearst nor Marion made an appearance, but left it to the butler to guide them through the innumerable rooms and point out the many pillaged treasures of Europe. Patricia decided to tag along.

"Won't you be bored?" Lulu asked. She must have been playing in the rooms and corridors all her life, privy to every hidden nook and secret passageway.

"Not with you around!" Patricia said brightly. "Trouble

always seems to find you, and I'm positively desperate for some trouble in my life. Did you really find the body yourself? Gosh, you have all the luck."

The butler led the twenty actresses through the house. The torturous task of playing Sherpa to this gaggle of nattering self-obsessed women seemed to shake even his unflappable dignity.

Lulu, though, was enjoying herself immensely. The decor was confusing, lavish verging on garish, and little of it was what she would have chosen for herself. Still, it was beautiful, and gave her a glimpse of places she had never been, ages she had never seen. Most of the furniture was from Europe, some of it older than the United States itself. Parts of Spain and France seemed to have been ripped whole from their native lands and transplanted in California.

Just as Lulu was about to ask the butler a question about a painting of a particularly cuddly looking Madonna and child, Patricia pulled her down a corridor.

"What are you doing?" Lulu whispered, yearning for the art.

"I know everyone wants you to let it drop, but I can see the gears still churning in your brain. *Please*, let me help you investigate. I never get to do *anything* exciting, and if I can help you catch a murderer, it will just be the bee's knees!"

"Everyone is sure they already caught the murderer," Lulu said, discouraging the girl though she felt the prickings of renewed excitement.

"Well, what if they have? I heard one of the maids

gossiping in the kitchen, and she said he hasn't said a lucid word yet, and she knows because one of the local policemen is sweet on her and told her so, so they don't know anything about how or why he did it! You could surely whip together enough evidence to convict him before he's even conscious."

"I don't know . . ."

"Please? Pretty please?"

"It isn't exactly a suitable pastime for a young lady like yourself," Lulu said, feeling unpleasantly like a prissy old governess as she spoke.

"I'm not some baby!" Patricia almost shouted. She bit her lip, and then more calmly, whispered, "I won't be seeing any bodies or blood, so what's the harm?"

"So, where are we going?" Lulu asked, giving in to the persuasive junior sleuth.

"To find out what the present was," Patricia said with a conspiratorial grin. "Come on—you know you're dying to find out. Even if it had nothing to do with the murder, which would be unlikely because it simply *reeks* of a clue."

As she led Lulu through the house, they could hear the muted sound of the group of actresses through the walls. "Oh, before we do that, I want to show you something else," Patricia said. "Hurry, before they get to the next room."

She pulled Lulu into a little alcove. "Stand up on that step. Now feel along the wall. Got it? Move that aside and you can see everything."

Lulu found the hinged cover and opened it, revealing a small breach in the wall. She put her eye to the peephole and saw a richly decorated room. Something glittered on the table. Lulu squinted. It was a slender diamond-encrusted watch, carelessly left behind by someone.

"Now look across the room," Patricia directed. "See that nook with the wooden saint? Look into the ironwork at the back and tell me what you see."

She stared for a long time without seeing anything in particular. Then she thought she saw a shadow pass behind the opening, and then . . .

"Is that an eye?" she asked, pulling back from her own peephole.

"Yes!" Patricia squealed. "That's Uncle Will, or Marion, spying on the actresses to see how they behave. They're judging all of you every moment you're here."

Lulu was mortified. "Then I should be out there. What will he think if I'm not with the group?"

"Don't worry. I'll tell him I asked you specially to do something with me. He knows we've bonded, and I can see that he's grateful, so we'll be A-OK. Ask him a question about his Byzantine tilework later, and you'll be golden. Quick, look again! Here come the others."

Lulu pressed her eye to the opening and watched as the embittered butler elucidated the room's splendors to the dozen or so actresses who remained. They milled around the room, examining the finery or yawning outright.

When the butler left the room, the actresses slowly trailed in his wake, but one lingered a bit behind the others. Lulu knew her only slightly, a girl named Gloria who worked for another studio. She watched Gloria scan the room furtively, then skillfully palm the diamond watch and slip it down the front of her dress.

Astonished, Lulu stepped back and told Patricia what she'd seen. How could Gloria do something so despicable after Hearst had invited her into his home? "Shouldn't I tell someone?" Lulu asked.

"Oh, believe me, *someone* already knows," Patricia answered, and winked at Lulu.

Next Patricia led Lulu down some stairs to the cool basement area of the house. "The wine cellar and storage," Patricia explained. "This is where I saw all the presents the other day."

Sure enough, there they were, wrapped in red and silver paper.

"Hmm. Some of the bows are mussed, and the paper is torn in places," Patricia noted pensively.

"Almost like they were delivered . . . and then taken back again," Lulu offered. "But why?"

Patricia took one of the identical boxes off the shelf and tore open the paper.

"Oh, pretty," she said as she pulled out the gift.

But Lulu gasped and fell backward, catching herself on the wall. Trailing through Patricia's fingers was the same scarf whose swirling hues of sea-green silk had strangled the life out of Juliette Claire.

*Eight*

**A**s he sat musing alone in his room, Freddie came to the disheartening realization that no case a private eye takes on is ever going to be completely clean, with one party totally innocent. Having been raised in a nest of corruption, he wasn't inclined to think anyone was free and clear of sin anyway. Hearst was clearly withholding crucial information that would help apprehend the blackmailer and reveal his identity, and Freddie wanted to know why.

And then there was the nagging feeling that Lulu might be right about the murderer of Juliette not being the man the police had in custody. Though he should have been wet from the prank, he could have killed her, gotten wet, and changed. But something was bothering Freddie about the motive. Mostly, that there wasn't one. In a house full of precious jewelry, he couldn't imagine that this well-dressed young man would have killed a young woman whom he could have so easily overpowered. Especially in what appeared to be a very calculated manner. No, something was wrong, but for now he would have to focus on the blackmail, and keeping his boss sober enough to not get fired.

But first he needed to shower up and dress. He chose a particularly handsome navy chalk striped suit that Lulu had purchased for him for a party at Louis B. Mayer's estate, but he had just paid her back, not interested in being perceived, mostly by himself, as a gigolo. As he splashed on some vetiver aftershave, he scolded himself again for succumbing to jealousy last night. Lulu and he were puzzle pieces that fit. When he thought about her, surely waiting for him now in the Assembly Room, he relaxed. Everything in the world felt calm and perfect, and serene.

Lulu's mind was spinning and her breath short. Her thoughts racing, she muttered the facts as she knew them. Patricia, now thinking herself a pint-sized Dr. Watson of sorts, tried to sift through Lulu's rapid-fire speculation. "Juliette was strangled with a scarf that was given to all the actresses. Was it her own scarf, from the box in her room? Did anyone else open their present? Were they all identical scarves? Why were all of the gifts repossessed and stored?"

Lulu pushed the boxes around, counting. "There are nineteen here, unopened." She spun around to Patricia. "How many boxes were there last night?" she asked. "Did just the actresses get one? Or all the female guests? Were there extras?"

Patricia's mouth spread into a slow smile. "Does this mean I'm on the case?"

"Of course! Well, wait . . . No! Er . . . maybe. Fine! Unless it gets dangerous."

"Deal! I don't know, but I know who does."

She and Lulu hunted down the housekeeper, Mrs. Mortimer, who knew more about the ins and outs of the Ranch than anyone else, even Hearst himself.

"Why, there was a scarf for every actress," she said, not looking up from the accounts she was working on. The pencil looked tiny in Mrs. Mortimer's large, competent hands. She dressed well for a housekeeper, and her makeup was impeccable, but her hands and muscled forearms showed that she'd worked hard in her life. "Twenty, exactly. The other guests got something else. Opera glasses for the ladies, silver clothes brushes for the gents."

A maid knocked and stood in the doorway, waiting for permission to enter. "Here are your shoes, Mrs. Mortimer," the girl said with a bobbed curtsy. "I got every bit of mud off, and spit-polished the toes for you."

The housekeeper took them without a word or a glance, while her other hand kept scribbling figures in a ledger.

"And you collected them after the . . . the incident?" Lulu asked.

The housekeeper erased a miscalculation and said, "When Mr. Hearst saw that his gift had been used in the crime, he had them recalled immediately."

"And you got them all except Juliette's?" Patricia asked.

The housekeeper eyed the girl briefly but was apparently used to her meddling in adult affairs. Mrs. Mortimer bobbed her head. "Hers was already open when the maid got there."

So Juliette had definitely been strangled with her own scarf, Lulu thought. But her dry clothes and shoes showed that she hadn't gone into her room. Who had gotten the scarf? Surely that was the person who used it to kill Juliette.

At the end of her calculations now, the housekeeper took off her rather stylish tortoiseshell reading glasses and looked at them directly for the first time. Lulu noticed with some surprise that she was wearing false eyelashes.

"Why so many questions? Ah, wait, I know you. You're Lulu Kelly. That explains it. Actresses usually stick to their first starring role, and Ruby Godfrey's shooting certainly made you a star. Of course you want to meddle in every morbid scene you stumble across now."

Lulu, feeling both chagrined and defensive, wasn't sure how to respond. Mrs. Mortimer didn't seem to be making accusations. In fact, she spoke as if she had a deep and resigned understanding of humanity. She cast no blame, only commented.

"Something's off about the whole thing," Lulu said cautiously. "I don't think they arrested the right man. Or woman."

Mrs. Mortimer looked at her sharply. "Do you have evidence to support your wild assertion?"

None that Lulu cared to share. "Just a feeling. Do you

know anything about what happened?" She turned on a bit of flattery. "I'm sure you know more about what goes on in the Ranch than anyone. From what they say, this place couldn't function without you."

Mrs. Mortimer looked pleased, and settled more comfortably into her chair . . . though she did ask, "Who is 'they'?"

"Oh . . . Marion, of course." Lulu waved her hand airily. She usually didn't lie, but this obviously pleased the housekeeper, and after all, Marion *might* have said it. It was almost certainly true, whether she'd said it or not.

"I didn't hear anything myself," Mrs. Mortimer confessed. Her entire attitude seemed changed. She unbent, became confiding and somehow softer. *Amazing what a little judicious flattery can do*, Lulu thought.

"But Ginnie told me about the ruckus she heard, right after it happened last night," Mrs. Mortimer went on. "I didn't pay it much attention, to my regret. I never dreamed it would amount to anything like this. Mr. Hearst's guests are usually much better behaved."

Lulu's eyes widened. "Someone actually heard what happened?"

The housekeeper nodded. "Ginnie's my niece, one of the maids. Last night when she was taking out the rubbish from dinner, she heard a man and woman arguing. The woman said something like 'No, you can't do that to me,' and he said 'Watch me.' But she didn't hear anyone scream or anything, so she came in. I feel just terrible I didn't tell anyone about it, but at the time it didn't appear that there was anything much to report, and gossip is strictly discouraged here at the Ranch."

"Can I talk to Ginnie?"

"She had to stay home in bed today with a sick headache."

"Did she tell the police?" Lulu asked.

"Heavens, no! Junior maids don't talk to the police!" the housekeeper said, aghast. "They tell senior maids, who tell me, who tells Mr. Hearst, who *then* tells the police." She huffed at the very idea of anyone so gauchely violating the servants' chain of command. "Who would listen to a fifteen-year-old maid, anyway?"

"I would," Lulu said firmly. "I'd like to talk to her. Can you call her in?"

"If it's entirely necessary."

"It is."

"Of course, ma'am." Her congenial softness evaporated, and she became the rigid housekeeper again. She stood, and Lulu took an inadvertent step back. Mrs. Mortimer was so much taller than she remembered. She loomed over Lulu, majestic and dignified. Like a great ship pulling little boats in her wake, she ushered them out of her private office and locked the door behind her.

As soon as they were out of the room, a maid approached Lulu and Patricia. It was the one who had come with the housekeeper's shoes a moment before.

"Oh my! You are Miss Kelly, aren't you? I'm Kitty. Oh, I cried my eyes out when you died in *Six Sisters*. The rest of the movie was trash, but you were just heavenly. I read all about you in the papers, when you shot that nasty Ruby Godfrey."

"I didn't—" Lulu began, but Patricia shushed her. The maid was obviously on a roll.

"I heard what the housekeeper told you Ginnie said. About the fight she overheard. Well, sure as I stand here, I heard it too, and it didn't go anything like that. I heard the good part. It was a gentleman and a lady arguing. The man said 'I'll never let you go.' And the lady said 'Leave me alone; you're killing me.' He must have had her by the throat right then. I was going to run and get help, but it was surely none of my business, and if I didn't finish my chores, Mrs. Mortimer would definitely give me the old heave-ho. It was a terrible row!"

Lulu thanked her and made good her escape.

"You look like you want to punch someone," Patricia said. Lulu's hands were clenched into tight fists.

"I do, starting with the police. I don't think they even investigated the murder with any seriousness. They didn't talk to the servants. There are witnesses, for heaven's sake! They might not have seen anything, but they certainly heard something. And the police didn't question anyone about it at all. They just arrested someone who looked suspicious. I'm sure it didn't help matters that he was black." Lulu was fuming now. "They just assume he did it, without a shred of evidence."

"It does look awfully suspicious, him lurking on the grounds uninvited at the very moment someone is killed," Patricia said.

"True. But let's not forget, it also looked a lot like I tried to kill Ruby Godfrey a few weeks ago. Everyone believed that, but there wasn't a shred of truth in it. Lord knows I would have gone to prison if it were up to the police. Freddie and I had to investigate on our own to clear my name. I won't let an innocent man take the blame." She took a deep, steadying breath. "And if the killer is free, I won't let him get away with it."

Lulu and Freddie met in the Assembly Room before dinner when everyone gathered for their two-drink limit. With great difficulty, Lulu managed not to tell Freddie what she'd learned about the scarf and the argument. There were just too many missing pieces, and she wanted to be sure before she made a fool of herself.

"Just focus on the competition, my angel," he said, sneaking a kiss on the soft curve of her cheek. "I can see those little detective wheels whirling in that beautiful head of yours. I wish I could show you a copy of the blackmail letter. It's straight out of a gangster movie."

"I'm sure many criminals get their best ideas from the movies," Lulu said.

"I've heard criminals are running the whole town," Freddie said as a joke. He sobered quickly when Lulu's eyes slid to Sal, chatting with the curvy, sultry Dolores across the room. "To be clear, I was thinking about the studio heads and producers," he said, sipping at what remained of his highball.

"No, you're right. Sal Benedetto is getting his mitts into this town. I don't know how, but it worries me."

"Well, his background isn't exactly a secret. Everyone knows what's what with him, but everyone in the world seems to be fanatically obsessed with the crime syndicate. If the Hollywood big fish want to welcome him into the fold, that's their lookout."

"I suppose," Lulu said, still watching Sal out of the corner of her eye. "Why do you think he's talking to Dolores?"

"Call me crazy, but he's a man, and she's falling out of her dress," Freddie guessed. "But more to the point, why do you care who he talks to? Should I be concerned?" he asked in as cheeky a manner as he could muster.

Lulu dragged her eyes away from the couple. "Oh, don't be silly. I'm only thinking of Dolores. He's trouble, and she should know."

"She looks like more than a little trouble herself," Freddie said. "I think she can handle him." He snuck one more kiss and, seeing a freshly sobered up Waters beckoning to him from across the room, left to strategize their next moves with regard to the blackmail.

Annoyed, Lulu settled down with a thick book she didn't read and watched Sal over its cover. *Why is he talking to her?* she asked herself again and again—which she was vaguely aware translated to *Why isn't he talking to me?* She was relieved to be free of Sal's attentions, of course. But only a few weeks ago he'd bribed policemen and rather dramatically vowed to move heaven and earth to claim Lulu as his own, like some piece of art on an auction block. Now he was all but ignoring her.

She couldn't tell which was worse: being disregarded or being irked about it. Neither idea sat well with her.

He caught her staring before she could look away, and his mouth twitched in a fleeting smile as he returned to lavishing attention on Dolores.

To Lulu's relief, Paul Raleigh found her and sat down on the sofa next to her. He perched a little closer than last time, she noticed, but that was probably so he could be better heard in the noisy room. And she thought she detected the faintest odor of gin about him, which likely accounted for his newfound confidence.

"Do you remember your dreams, Lulu?" he asked quietly.

"Oh, yes," she said, trying to make herself sound as interesting as possible. "I feel like there's a movie reel playing in my head every night. Such wonderful things! Why, do you?"

He shook his head. "Far too rarely. There's always a magical moment just when I wake up, when I feel like I can hold them in my hands. But they turn to dust and blow away. I'm left with ghosts of ideas. So I'm forced to resort to waking dreams."

"You mean like daydreams?"

"No . . . actually, nothing like daydreams!" he said, his eyes full of passion and intensity. "My waking dreams are real. They're . . . hard to explain." He took her hand eagerly. "Please forgive my excitement, but it's so rare I meet anyone who I think could possibly understand me. I could show you what I mean. Come with me. I know a place where I can show you exactly what I'm talking about."

He stood, drawing her up with him. His eyes blazed with unreadable complexity and emotion, and Lulu was caught up. She'd felt glimpses of this kind of passion in her acting class, and occasionally when she would lose herself in the scene and fantasy became real for just that brief time. But Paul was all profound conviction. The personification of creative inspiration, she thought, and she longed to know more about him and the deep well of his artistry.

"Of course," Lulu said breathlessly, and moved to follow him.

But before they had gotten very far, the doors burst open and a dozen uniformed men stormed in.

"Nobody move! You're in violation of the National Prohibition Act. You're all under arrest!"

Women screamed and men shouted. Lulu turned to Paul to see what to do, but he gave one horror-struck look at the authorities and snuck out the back of the room at top speed, abandoning Lulu.

She didn't have a drink in her hand or alcohol on her breath, but that might not matter. She was in the midst of utter pandemonium in a place where prohibited alcohol was being served, and that could be enough to lead to her arrest. She looked frantically for Veronica, who she spotted across the room trying to hide behind a massive hanging tapestry. It might not be the end of Lulu's career—a few actresses before her had been taken into custody for violating prohibition, and bootleg alcohol was served at every Hollywood party. But Lux Studios already had to deal with drama from Lulu. True, it hadn't been her fault, and as Lolly so often said, there is no such thing as bad publicity, but still, they might decide she was more trouble than she was worth.

She turned this way and that, seeing other actresses grabbed by the agents of the Bureau of Prohibition. Dolores slapped one of them across the face. Eleanor climbed up on a table and kicked at the one who came after her. Honey cowered in a corner, while Boots let loose a string of creative curses. Toshia, though, slipped out of a side door and disappeared. That looked like the best idea. Lulu started for the exit but was immediately blocked by a hulking agent who looked oddly familiar.

"Hands behind your back," he said gruffly.

Suddenly Sal Benedetto was between her and the agent. He flashed her a smile and punched the agent in his solid jaw, sending the man reeling. Then he grabbed Lulu's arm and dragged her out of the room. Once in the hallway, he hustled her up the stairs, into a closet, and closed the door.

They were pressed together in the darkness. She could hear herself panting and could feel Sal's warm almondy breath, calm and steady, against her forehead. He smelled of smoke and amber and starch and brilliantine. He felt uneasily safe and inviting. She shuddered.

"I shouldn't . . . ," she began.

"Hush," Sal said. "They'll clear out in a few minutes. We have to hide until then."

Lulu tried to inch away from him, but there was no place she could maneuver where she wasn't touching him. Why would a castle ever have a closet this tiny? she wondered with irritation. Every time she tried to get away from him the movement only made her seem to wiggle against him. She heard him laugh softly in the darkness.

"I'd pay good money for this, minus the cops," he murmured into her ear.

"I thought you said to be quiet," she hissed at him. "I don't hear them anymore. I think I can go out now." She reached for the handle, but he took her shoulders.

"Not just yet, dollface. Play it safe and stay a while."

"Those agents out there are a thousand times safer than you!"

"Aw, I'm wounded, baby. What have I ever done but help you out?"

Lulu stammered, momentarily speechless. Sal had killed a man before her eyes, threatened her life unless she lied to protect him, made his goons impersonate police to scare her into giving herself to him. . . .

All at once she realized why that Bureau of Prohibition agent looked so familiar. *He was the man who had impersonated the Los Angeles police detective!* The one who had frightened her. Who had struck her and sent her running into the gangster's arms. He was one of Sal Benedetto's stooges.

"You dirty rat!" she shouted, and stomped her heeled shoe onto his foot.

Sal only laughed as she stormed out of the closet. "I'm a patient man, Lulu," he said as she ran off. "That's why I always win in the end."

"It's a setup," she fumed when she ran into Veronica, who had escaped the room. "Those aren't real agents. They're Sal's men. I should have known no one would dare raid William Randolph Hearst's castle. We've been had. But why?"

The chaos had died down. The guests had either fled or had been arrested by the mock agents.

Veronica caught her breath, looking immeasurably relieved. "Thank goodness. I could never be introduced to David's mother as a felonious fiancée. Whew! Do you think that was supposed to be a test of character? Apparently I have the character of a rabbit. I hid at the first sign of a badge and then got the heck out of there."

"Would Hearst really do that? Stage a raid to see how the actresses reacted?"

"Was he there? Or Marion? Probably laughing at us from behind their peepholes." She chuckled. "What a madhouse."

"I'll say this for certain: Paul Raleigh wasn't in on it. He looked absolutely terrified when those men stormed in, like the whole squad had come specifically for him. Just wait until I tell the others," Lulu said, her fist clenched. She didn't know which had shaken her more—the fear of being in handcuffs again, or her brief imprisonment with Sal. She could still smell the spice of his cologne. It was reminiscent of her favorite scent, neroli, the essence of bitter orange blossoms. She felt a little dizzy.

"Over my dead body will you tell the other actresses!" Veronica said. "You might think they're all the cat's pajamas, but they're the competition, and you just got a leg up. If this is the game Hearst is going to play, all right, so long as you win it. I wonder what other kinds of setups he has in store for you."

Lulu thought she may have seen another one. She told Veronica about seeing the actress swipe the unattended watch.

"Well, *her* character is established. Gosh, makes you paranoid. Just stay calm, and remember that whatever you see around here probably isn't real. You can put on a real show, be brave in the face of anything because you know it's all been staged. Oh! Do you think Juliette's murder was fake?"

"I touched her, Veronica. Even the best actress in the world couldn't fake being dead *that* well."

"And Juliette, rest her soul, wasn't that good an actress. Come on, let's see how this plays out. And where is that good-for-nothing boyfriend of yours when we need him?"

"Veronica! He's working!" But Lulu couldn't help feeling a sense of disappointment in his absence.

The entire ruckus was soon cleared up. The actresses and guests were led to believe that Hearst had come to an arrangement with the agents that let everyone go free. None of them seemed suspicious that the raid hadn't been real. Before dinner, they gathered for cocktails. The girls regaled

Hearst and Marion with stories of what they had done when the agents burst in. Eleanor, Boots, and Dolores seemed to have won their approval by resisting the brutish officers. "I need some jazz!" Marion squealed, and turned on the Victrola. "None of that New York style. I need something dark and dirty, like some New Orleans jazz!"

She put on a Jelly Roll Morton song called "The Black Bottom Stomp" and started dancing, urging the others to follow suit. Most of the guests did. Lulu swept the crowd to see how her friends were doing. Boots and Eleanor were dancing up a storm, and Toshia was lounging on a couch with a rather dull but moneyed-looking man in tweed. But Lulu, scanning the group, noticed that Honey was at the edge of the room, looking utterly distraught. Suddenly, Honey darted out the door, and Lulu was almost certain she saw a shiny trail of tears down her cheeks. She hadn't spent much time talking to the petite, dark-haired actress, but she seemed to be a sweet girl. What could have upset her so much?

Freddie caught her eye, beckoning her to join him in a dance. Lulu bit her lip. She felt like she'd hardly spent any time with Freddie and longed to be in his arms. Only that, she thought, would take away the memory of Sal's touch in the darkness. She might not tell him about it—she didn't want the two men to fight, or for Freddie to wonder why she stayed so close to Sal as long as she did—but she wanted the comfort of her boyfriend's presence.

Still, she gestured to Freddie with an apologetic look to wait a moment, and went after Honey.

She found the girl upstairs alone in the library, weeping inconsolably and staring out of one of the great windows overlooking the estate. "He didn't do it! He didn't do it!" she moaned. "I can't take it anymore. It's all my fault!" With that she crumpled to the floor.

Lulu cleared her throat, and Honey's tear-streaked face jerked up as she realized she had an audience.

"Who didn't do what?" Lulu asked gently as she knelt beside the stricken girl.

Honey looked up at her with wet, black-smudged eyes. "Zing Babineau. The man they arrested. He's my boyfriend."

*Nine*

**H**oney grabbed Lulu's hands, clenching them so tightly she felt the small bones grind together. "You can't tell anyone! Promise me!"

"I promise! Of course I promise. Honey, you have to breathe or you'll make yourself sick! Just take a second, and then tell me what you mean."

Honey took deep, gasping breaths, but her level of agitation didn't seem to diminish. "He's not a thief, and he's not a murderer," she said. "He's a jazz musician!" She looked at Lulu with an imploring liquid gaze, as if she thought that would serve as explanation enough.

Lulu paused. She admittedly thought that Zing was innocent but found herself playing devil's advocate and said in a measured voice, "Honey, his profession isn't an alibi. Things do not look good for Zing. He was trespassing. He was in possession of an expensive piece of jewelry, and there have been rooms broken into and ransacked. All arrows point to him as the prime suspect."

Under Honey's searching stare, Lulu wondered if she was being evaluated for trustworthiness. But the girl looked so grief-stricken and overwhelmed Lulu thought she would confide her secret to anyone who offered even the slightest bit of sympathy.

Honey sniffed and sat up straight. She looked ahead, as if she were staring into a vast emptiness that overwhelmed her in every way, and then, warm tears filling her eyes again, she whispered, "He came to ask me to marry him."

"Oh!" Lulu exhaled involuntarily. She considered herself completely open-minded, and was more than a little shocked, and frankly, dismayed, at her own reaction. In her heart she knew there was nothing inherently wrong with a white woman marrying a black man. Lulu was hardly in a position to judge anyone, given her precarious history; nor had bigotry been tolerated by her mother. Yet Lulu had been fully aware of the prejudices that surrounded her. No matter what, Italians married Italians, Irish married Irish, and blacks married blacks. Until this moment, the idea of a young white woman marrying a black man had been unimaginable to Lulu. As soon as she heard Honey's admission, the part of her that had been schooled by society all her life told her that it was impossible. But why should it be?

"Then he really is your boyfriend?"

Honey nodded. "His name is really Alvin Babcock, but he changed it to something flashy that everyone would remember. We met in New Orleans before I came to Hollywood. I was just fifteen, and he was nineteen, but we fell completely in love. My family was terribly against it. My aunt, who I was living with, sent me out here to live with her sister, and Zing went on tour. I never thought I'd see him again."

But then, she told Lulu dreamily, Zing came to Hollywood. He got a plum gig at the Cocoanut Grove nightclub, playing his unique style of New Orleans jazz, and became a quick sensation. Only when he'd made enough money to buy himself a Stutz Bearcat and put a deposit down on a nice house in Echo Park, a suburb on the outskirts of Los Angeles, did he approach Honey, who was by this time an up-and-coming actress.

With her petite but decidedly curvy figure and her exotic dark eyes and hair, Honey was starting to make a name for herself playing a certain kind of character. In fact, Lulu thought, she often got the very roles that a girl like Toshia might also be trying out for—amorous concubines and proud Eastern harem girls, foreign vamps and dark seductive spies. Honey got more parts than Toshia simply because she was white. With a little makeup, though, she could pass for anything from a Tahitian islander to an Eastern princess.

"He said he hadn't forgotten me for a minute," Honey told Lulu, pride shining through her tears. "Everything he did, every success, he did in the hopes of winning me. I . . . I knew I shouldn't, but I started seeing him. We kept it secret, though, even from my aunt. If anyone knew . . ."

Lulu nodded understandingly. There were many things that could derail a young actress's career, but some of them, like drug addiction, alcoholism, or even past indiscretions, could be more easily hidden from the public. With a large portion of the country being either actively or passively racist, one published photo of Honey kissing Zing would ruin her forever.

She'd tried to break it off, but Zing followed her to the Ranch. He'd bribed someone to slip a note in her luggage as the train was leaving, asking her to meet him in the gardens that night. He'd parked his car in a hidden spot along the road and walked the last mile.

"I went outside to meet him," Honey confessed. "What else could I do? If I didn't show up, he might have knocked at the door and asked for me. I told him we were through, that he better just leave me alone. Then he pulled out this gorgeous diamond and platinum ring and got down on one knee, right there in the marigolds."

Lulu looked up excitedly. That explained the dirty wet spot on his knee. Honey's story was making sense, much to Lulu's relief.

"What did you do?" Lulu asked.

"I started shaking and crying!" Honey said. "If I married him I'd be an outcast, and everything I've worked so hard for would be gone. But I didn't want to live without him. He stood up and held me so tenderly, and I . . . I exploded! I screamed at him to leave, slapped him, scratched him . . .

and he said he'd never let me go. I told him my heart was breaking, that he was killing me, and he just looked at me with fire in those kind, sweet eyes, so stubborn. So strong. He wasn't going to take no for an answer."

Lulu felt a surge of elation. So that was the conversation Kitty had overheard. Not the murderer and his victim at all. That meant the other maid Ginnie had probably heard an entirely different argument—most likely involving the *actual* murderer.

"I have to tell Freddie and Mr. Waters . . . and the police," Lulu said.

Honey grabbed her hand again. "But you can't!" she gasped. "You promised!"

Lulu closed her eyes for a moment, cursing herself for her rash promise. But did a promise really count when a man's freedom was on the line? When the truth meant a murderer was still on the loose? And yet her sense of loyalty told her not to break a promise to a trusting girl.

"Honey, if you love him, how can you let him go to jail?" Lulu asked in a firm but gentle voice. "Everyone thinks he killed Juliette, and they're ready to throw the book at him. How can you live with yourself if he's imprisoned, or gets the firing squad, because you won't tell the truth?"

"I couldn't live with myself, of course!" Honey said miserably. "I'm destroyed either way. If he's charged, I'll just die. And if he's let go because everyone knows the truth, I'm done for!"

"Maybe it's not as bad as you think," Lulu told her.

"After all, no one ever said you have to tell the *whole* truth. What if you just said Zing has a mad crush on you, and even though you offered no encouragement, he came to propose. That would keep him in the clear but wouldn't tarnish your name. I could tell Mr. Hearst what really happened, just so he wouldn't lay trespassing charges on Zing, but no one else would know."

Honey shook her head, her lower lip trembling. "It won't work."

"Sure it will!" Lulu said, doing her best to throw cheerful enthusiasm into her voice. "Why, I guarantee it won't even make the papers. Certainly none owned by our host! Hearst hates any publicity he didn't orchestrate himself. Trust me, Honey, this will work. Your reputation will be safe, and Zing will go free."

"You don't understand, Lulu," Honey wept. "There's more at stake here than you know."

"What I know is that there's a murderer on the loose because they have the wrong man locked up," Lulu pressed, her temper fraying. "What if another girl dies because you won't tell the truth?"

Honey looked aghast at the thought, then covered her face with her hands, saying, "No, no, no! I can't! This can't be happening!"

"Honey, you've got to tell me what you're hiding or I can't help you," Lulu insisted.

"An actress might get away with having a colored man in love with her," Honey sobbed softly. "But we both know she couldn't get away with being colored herself."

Lulu exhaled slowly, understanding now what Honey was saying.

She told Lulu the whole story.

Honey was the illegitimate child of a white man and a light-skinned black woman from the Louisiana bayou. Her mother had died giving birth to her, and Honey had been raised until she was ten in her mother's community in Cajun country by a clan of loving aunts and grandparents. She saw her father only a few times, but he made sure she was taken care of financially. When her father died, he specified in his will that Honey should live with his family in New Orleans. She was taken away from the home she loved to live with one of her father's sisters.

It was then that the little girl learned to "pass."

Her new family was unfailingly kind to her, Honey made sure to point out. They just didn't want her to be black.

Her skin was creamy tan and her features delicate. Her hair was wild and curly, but her white aunts went out of state to consult specialists, and the end result was straight and silky. They gave Honey elocution lessons and began talking loudly in the beauty salons and other local gossip hubs about a Spanish contessa their late brother had been involved with. Once all the groundwork was laid, they presented charming little Honey, and the world believed she had aristocratic Spanish blood.

It worked well for a while. But Honey's black relatives refused to entirely give her up, and insisted on visiting. When this was forbidden, Honey started to sneak out, visiting her mother's family, absorbing the culture of her childhood, and eventually, as a teen, going to all-black jazz clubs. It was there she met Zing.

When her father's people found out, they were furious. They sent her to a distant family member in California where she had no connections, to try to wean her off her past. She was beautiful and exotic-looking—and accustomed to pretending to be someone she was not—and so Honey soon landed movie roles.

But she never forgot where she came from. And Zing never forgot her.

All the same, she'd been so bullied and threatened and shamed over the past years about the absolute necessity of keeping her race a secret that she was convinced utterly she couldn't live if the truth came out.

"You can't tell anyone," Honey insisted again. "You promised me."

But still it tormented Lulu: How much did a promise count when weighed against murder?

Though she knew it was wrong, Lulu found she couldn't betray Honey's confidence. "I won't tell the police," she said. "At least, not yet. Zing hasn't said anything, as far as I know. But he'll most likely start telling the truth soon."

"No, he won't," Honey said with absolute confidence in her man. "He'll do anything to protect me."

"Maybe at first," Lulu admitted, "but not when they start talking about the noose. No. The only way to save him without condemning yourself is if we find out who the real murderer is. When we have him, they'll let Zing go without asking too many questions."

"Then find the murderer! Please!" Honey begged.

"I will," Lulu answered with grim determination. "But for that I need help. I have to tell your secret to one person, Honey."

"No!"

"Don't worry. He's good at keeping secrets."

And with that, she left Honey weeping gently and went to find Freddie.

"We have to tell the police," Freddie said in an infuriatingly rational voice.

"It isn't our secret to tell," Lulu said quietly and firmly. "If we have to, eventually, then okay. But for now I think we can find the real murderer and clear Zing's name on our own."

"Darling, we'll find the truth much faster if there are more people working on it. Doesn't it make you nervous to know there's a murderer still at large, and most likely it's one of the guests?"

"Yes . . . and no," Lulu said. "When I was in that crime thriller *The Life and Death of Willa Langley,* the director brought in a psycho-thingamajig to tell us about killers and their minds. He said that most murders are personal. I mean, a killer murders a specific person for a particular reason. Either because he hates them, or loves them, or maybe both, or wants to cover up something else entirely. He said that the real maniacs—I mean the ones who kill because they actually *like* to kill—are extremely rare."

Freddie agreed. "And what's more, now that the real murderer thinks he's safe—"

Lulu interrupted him. "He or *she* is safe."

Freddie raised his eyebrows. "Really? You think it might be a woman?"

"Probably not, but don't underestimate us. There are twenty—er, nineteen—smart and highly competitive women trapped in a house with a once-in-a-lifetime prize dangling in front of our noses. One of us might very well be willing to kill for it."

"I don't know whether to be awed or afraid," Freddie said with a nervous chuckle. "Okay, granted that women are just as capable of anything, including murder, as men . . ."

"Thank you."

". . . whoever it is might be easier to catch as long as Zing is in custody. They think they're home free, so they might get careless."

"We can catch him—or her! I'm sure of it!" Lulu said excitedly.

"I'll give it a little while. Not too long, though. Then we go to the police."

"Deal," she said, shaking his hand. He didn't let it go, but pulled her closer.

"We have to go to the Assembly Room for cocktails," she murmured when she emerged from his kiss a moment later.

"Definitely," Freddie agreed. "Soon."

When she finally entered the Assembly Room (discreetly separate from Freddie), she waved away the offered drink. She felt tipsy enough on love without needing alcohol. In fact, she felt so good she scarcely even noticed that Sal and Dolores were canoodling all night. And if she noticed, she certainly didn't care. Much.

Lulu and Freddie made little headway that evening. Hearst had activities scheduled for his guests through midnight, and they could never escape. Engaged in games of darts, pool, and other assorted diversions, each tried to subtly ask questions about other guests' whereabouts the previous evening, but couldn't come up with anything particularly incriminating.

After dinner but before dessert, Hearst stood and said, "I have a very important announcement." Lulu looked up with eager eyes, hoping it was going to be about the murder. Had Hearst or the police found new evidence?

But it only obliquely concerned Juliette. Hearst was imperiously announcing which actresses were being sent home that night.

"Many of you have shown sterling character. Others have amused and entertained us, or shown your sweet dispositions. But a few of you have sadly disappointed us. Gloria Baker, please stand."

Lulu heard gasps, titters, a few murmured words of sympathy. But what she noticed most was that all the girls sitting near Gloria seemed to subtly lean away from her. They wanted to distance themselves from her immediately.

Gloria rose with a stricken face. She pulled herself together enough to ask defensively, "What did I do wrong?"

Hearst narrowed his small blue eyes at Gloria, and she quailed under the sternness of his gaze. "An actress may steal hearts, but not jewelry," he said. "You may keep the watch you pilfered as a consolation prize."

"I never!" Gloria began as the room erupted into shocked murmuring, but Hearst quieted everyone with a look.

"Though you may be disappointed to learn the diamonds are fake. Please leave now, Miss Baker. The butler will escort you to the door, where you'll find your bags already packed and waiting. I do hope you also enjoy the stolen decorative soaps that were found in your suitcase."

She was instantly ushered out without any further chance to defend herself.

"What a shame," Boots said to Lulu across Paul Raleigh as Gloria left. "And before dessert, too." She winked at Lulu.

The strawberry mousse was served, and conversation was just starting to build back up to its normal cacophony when Lolly piped up. "I thought there were supposed to be *two* girls eliminated each night. Who's the other one? I'm dying to know—and I bet she is too."

The room fell silent, and people looked at Lolly with shocked faces.

Lolly looked baffled. "What's wrong? What did I say?"

*Ten*

**T**he next morning, Lulu and Freddie went to the housekeeper's quarters to talk to their only real witness. Mrs. Mortimer was elsewhere. Ginnie, sleepy-eyed, was sitting in one corner of the spacious kitchen, sewing the torn shoulder seam of a woman's black dress. Her dark curls were delightfully tumbled, and she dimpled and perked up the instant she spied Freddie.

"I heard you had a rough night," Lulu said sympathetically as she slid into a chair next to Ginnie. "Here, let me do that for you." She settled the large dress on her lap and took up the neat, precise stitches where Ginnie left off. It was a simple dress, but made of soft black wool, and the tailoring was impeccable. Lulu's practiced washerwoman eye noted the fine details as she sewed, and she absently wondered whose dress it was. Not one of the actresses. They were all much too slender for this dress, and despite the exquisite cut, it was far too simple for any of them.

"You know how to sew?" the girl asked. "But you're a *movie star!*"

"Well, I'm not sure about that, but I'm trying!" Lulu smiled. "And I wasn't born one, you know." She often thought, with no small amount of amazement, that only one year ago she was helping her mother launder underthings for a living.

"Gosh," Ginnie said. "Then there's still hope for me. I want to be an actress more than anything. Are you an actor, too?" she asked Freddie as he lounged against the icebox.

"Not quite," he said with a wink.

"You're sure handsome enough to be one," Ginnie said, lifting her eyes up to him dreamily.

Lulu rolled hers, unseen by Ginnie, as Freddie charmingly grinned and played the handsome but modest boy next door, wiggling his eyebrows at Lulu when Ginnie looked away blushing.

"We wanted to ask you about what you heard the other night in the garden," Freddie said. Lulu bent her head to her sewing and let him take the reins, knowing full well that Ginnie would be much more likely to spill the beans to the cute, flirtatious boy. *Girls are so predictable,* she thought with a sigh.

"Well," Ginnie said, settling herself back to tell her tale, "I was taking the refuse out at around seven thirty or so, and I heard a terrible noise. A beast of some sort, I thought to myself, or something, well, something big. . . ."

"And you never saw it?"

"It was moving around in the bushes. Scared the bejesus out of me. It could have been anything! Once the lion got out and no one dared go outside for a week afterward, you know."

"Lion . . . ," Freddie murmured slowly.

"I dumped the trash as quick as I could and started to go back in. That's when I heard the argument."

It was a man and a woman behind some closely planted cypresses, Ginnie told them. The man growled, "How dare you? You'll pay for this. You're through!" Then the woman said piteously, "No! You can't do this to me! Stop!" The man said, "Just watch me, you . . ."

"You what?" Freddie asked, shooting a look at Lulu, who just looked at him dryly and continued to stitch.

"I can't say it out loud. It's too filthy."

"Can you whisper it?" he asked. Ginnie seemed delighted, and stayed nestled against Freddie's cheek for far longer than it could have taken to say one dirty word. *She could practically recite a sonnet,* Lulu thought, suppressing a sigh. But if he could tolerate the string of men who pursued her, she could endure the inept advances of an ambitious housemaid.

"'Take that,' the man said," Ginnie continued boldly, as if she were auditioning. "Then he must have attacked her, because I heard her shriek, just once, and then I didn't hear anything else."

"Did you tell anyone?" Freddie asked.

"I looked for Mrs. Mortimer, but she wasn't to be found. Which is strange. She usually goes over the accounts in the evening when the guests are all busy in the Assembly Room or at dinner. So I didn't mention it to her until much later."

"Why didn't you tell someone else right away?" Lulu asked.

Ginnie shot her a resentful look. "I wouldn't want anyone mucking around in *my* business," she said. "And I surely didn't know anyone was being murdered."

"Fair enough," Freddie said, suppressing a smile.

"Do you remember anything else? What did their voices sound like? Did either of them have an accent?" Lulu interrupted, finally putting down her mending.

Ginnie thought for a while. "They both sounded like you," she said at last. "Like everyone in the movies."

Lulu rolled her eyes again. Since sound had come to Hollywood, authentic regional accents had disappeared. Everyone studied with the same core group of voice coaches, who all had the same idea about what America wanted to hear. It was an accent that no one had ever spoken naturally before: an acquired mix of New England and Britain that stopped just short of being too posh for public consumption. By now it wasn't just the actors who spoke in that affected voice. Nearly everyone—from directors to writers to secretaries and waitresses hoping for a big break—used some variation of it.

"Will you excuse us for a minute, please?" Lulu said, pulling Freddie away far enough so that Ginnie wouldn't hear.

"Of course, ma'am," the girl demurred.

"Ma'am. Terrific. I sound like an old maid. In any case, that hardly narrows things down," Lulu said, aware that she was equally guilty of taking on the strange fictitious accent. "It could be absolutely anyone here."

"It actually helps a little," Freddie said. "We can be reasonably sure it isn't one of the staff members. Or Hearst himself." Hearst's voice had no pretension in it whatsoever.

"Or Paul," Lulu added, not noticing Freddie's faint look of annoyance. "Or that French painter, I suppose."

"That's good," Freddie considered. "It narrows the suspect pool. I'm guessing there are maybe ten other male guests who talk like that."

"Let's see," Lulu said. "That nice Cary Grant who all the girls like is English, but he's using his American accent most of the time, which is very distinct. There's Franchot Tone, whom I wouldn't put it past; Fredric March, who's an absolute dear; William Powell . . . I don't remember whether any of them were missing from the Assembly Room when Juliette was strangled. I honestly can't imagine any of them could have actually done it. They could all play very convincing murderers in movies, but actually killing? Not a chance. Most actors are *way* too fussy for that sort of thing."

"Anyone can do something irrational in a moment of passion," Freddie said.

"Do you really think so?" Lulu asked, reflecting on her own situation. "Do you really believe that someone could be good and moral all of their lives, and then do one terrible thing?"

"I think most people don't really know what they're capable of," Freddie said. "Who else?"

"Well, Sal doesn't have that accent, so he's in the clear." Lulu sounded a little disappointed. Pinning the murder on Sal would have solved a host of problems. Some part of her also felt relieved, though. Sal might shoot rival thugs, but she didn't want to think he was the kind of man who would murder a woman in cold blood. "What about Docky Martin? He's blotto half the time and he was pretty peeved at Juliette after that egg stunt, . . ."

"I'd forgotten about that! And he *left* with Lolly, right?" He wiggled his eyebrows again.

"I don't think I want to know what you're implying, and stop doing that with your eyebrows. It's very unsettling," Lulu said.

"What? You mean like this?" He did it again.

"I'm ignoring you now, and yes, he was out of the room when Juliette was murdered. And wait, there's your boss, Mr. Waters. Was he out of your sight while you were gone?"

Freddie frowned as he tried to recall. "He said he had to go back to his room for something. Probably a swig of a potion stronger than what Hearst was serving. So, excellent! Now we have two ill-humored alcoholics on the list. Anyone else?"

"Wait!" Lulu said. "Anita Loos's husband talks like that. What's his name again? Emerson. John Emerson! He seems the least trustworthy of all. When he looked at me, I felt like I immediately needed a shower. Something's definitely off there. Anyway, we have a decent list of suspects, so we'll have to . . ."

"Did you say John Emerson?" Ginnie asked suddenly.

Lulu and Freddie looked at each other and reddened. Apparently they weren't as quiet as they had thought. Lulu felt a surge of excitement. Did the name ring a bell to Ginnie? Did it tie him to the overheard argument?

"I forgot. I have to return his suit jacket to him! I don't suppose you happen to know what room he's staying in?"

"I'm not sure," Lulu said lightly, trying to cover her irritation. "Isn't there a master list?"

"His name's not on it. But did you say he's Miss Loos's husband? Well, that explains it. The room is under her name. I mean, everyone knows her, but who's ever heard of John Emerson?" Ginnie got a bundle from a shelf. "I hope he's not mad. Lord knows I did my best, but I couldn't get her lipstick stain off the collar. I had to spot clean it, of course. If I washed the whole suit, it would have shrunk." She looked at the stain admiringly. "Gosh, that Miss Loos sure has some elegant taste. It's a beautiful shade of lipstick. Very fancy."

She held it out so Lulu could see the smear of fuchsia high on the lapel. It was faded from Ginnie's attempt to clean it, but from what remained Lulu could tell that the original color had been garishly bright. *That's not Anita's lipstick,* Lulu thought as she took the shirt, studying it more closely. The writer had worn a delicate shell-pink shade. *That's the color Juliette was wearing last night.*

They saved the rest of their conversation until they were away from Ginnie in light of her apparently extraordinary auditory skills. They'd already given her enough to gossip about.

"I vaguely remember now," Lulu said. "Emerson was talking with Juliette in a corner of the Assembly Room before all the practical jokes started. Whatever they were talking about, it seemed like it was for their ears only."

"Scandalous," Freddie said acerbically.

"They're obviously not happy," Lulu said. "Anita said something about him having a day off."

"From what?"

"I actually think she meant from their marriage. She implied openly he was with another woman. When he came back in, I thought it might be Honey, because she looked disheveled and came in at the same time he did. But I think I know what she was up to. Emerson must have been with Juliette."

"But why would he kill her?" Freddie asked. "Didn't they just meet for the first time here at the Ranch?"

"Maybe not. How would we know?"

"We ask him," Freddie suggested.

"Or we ask Anita," Lulu said. "Not that I look forward to asking a wife if her husband might be a murderer. I can't really imagine that going well."

"What if Anita is the murderer?" Freddie asked. "Maybe her husband has cheated one too many times, and this time she snapped."

"Are you kidding? Anita is so tiny. She'd have to borrow a couple of inches just to make five feet. I don't think it's physically possible. But I like the way you think." She winked at him. "I told you, women are capable of anything."

"Darn right," he agreed, perhaps hoping for a kiss. It worked.

The two of them marched into the Assembly Room, but before they could track down Anita, the actresses were all rounded up for the big activity of the day: a scavenger hunt.

Veronica cornered Lulu before it began. "Remember, nothing you see is real," she whispered. "It's all a setup to test you. Go get 'em, tiger!"

# *Eleven*

**T**o her delight, Lulu was grouped on the hunt with Boots and Eleanor, though she wished Toshia were with them instead of with Jean Harlow and Ginger Rogers. Toshia cast a wistful glance over her shoulder as she left her friends, but it wasn't long before the ebullient Jean had her arm around Toshia's waist as Ginger cranked up the Victrola and tried to teach them a somewhat overcomplicated new dance step she had learned for an upcoming film.

"No fair!" Joan Crawford called out. "We only have two in our team. Where is that Dolores, anyway?"

No one could find Dolores. Household staff members were sent to search, but none of the other guests had seen her that day. Lulu knew that if Dolores had foolishly become involved with Sal, no good would come of it. That was simply thinking about Dolores's best interests, wasn't it? Or was there an irrational overtone of jealousy to her thinking? Lulu shuddered with annoyance and turned her attention back to her teammates.

"We'll give you a head start," Marion said, and handed Joan her team's envelope. Five minutes later the other girls got theirs.

Boots tore open the envelope and pulled out the first clue, embossed in gold on heavy cream-colored card stock. Charlie, bouncing at their feet, yipped excitedly. She read the clue aloud to the other girls.

> *Crawl ahead and ditch your fella*
> *In this modern Caracalla.*
> *Among the goddesses, heroes, and gods*
> *Gather your wits to beat the odds.*

"I have absolutely no clue where it might be," Eleanor said right away and so loudly that Charlie's head tilted.

"Do you think it might . . . ," Lulu began, but Eleanor hushed her and hurried her team out of the Assembly Room.

"I know *exactly* what the clue means," Eleanor said, hustling them along. "I did a photo shoot at the ruins of the Caracalla baths once. I just don't want those other doxies following us. Let them wander around the grounds while we get three clues ahead. Now, step on it."

She briskly led them along a route they'd taken for the tour. Charlie's toenails clattered on the floor. Lulu considered filling them in on everything she'd learned, but she knew she couldn't betray Honey's secret. She could, however, tell them about what Ginnie overheard and about Juliette's lipstick on Emerson's suit jacket.

"I've heard Emerson and Anita have some sort of under-standing. Not that she's happy about it, but apparently he didn't give her much of a choice, and for some reason she looks past it all," Boots whispered as they made their way down the narrow stairs. "He and Juliette were chatting away like old pals that first night. I bet they've known each other for a while."

"Well, that seals it, and how!" Eleanor said. "I wanted to bludgeon Juliette after I'd known her for ten minutes. If Emerson was having an *understanding* with her, I'd say he had plenty of motive."

"And no jury on earth would convict him." Boots snickered.

"Come on, girls," Lulu said. "Juliette wasn't nice, but she was a person. A living person, who, by the way, isn't living anymore."

"I know," Boots said contritely. "I'd like to waste whoever did that to Juliette." She balled her fists, and despite her slen-der wood-nymph form, she looked almost as if she could do it. "Not just for Juliette's sake, but for every girl's sake."

"What do we do now?" Eleanor asked.

"We talk to Anita Loos," Lulu said as they walked. "And we watch Emerson like a hawk. Maybe we search his room."

"And you're so sure that the man they arrested didn't do it?" Eleanor asked.

"Abso-tutely one hundred percent sure," Lulu assured

them. "It isn't just a hunch. I *know*. I just can't tell you how. You have to trust me."

Boots slugged her lightly on the shoulder. "Didn't anyone teach you that when you hear 'trust me,' you should run the other way, fast as you can?"

Lulu grinned at her. "So run."

"Nothing doing," Boots said. "I bet you any money that if you solve a murder Hearst and Marion will just hand you the part. You'll definitely be the most interesting person here this weekend!"

"Except for maybe the murderer," Eleanor chimed in.

Lulu hadn't thought of her obstinate curiosity and covert sleuthing as interesting fodder for a character before.

"But first," Eleanor said, "let's win this contest. Here we are! Girls, I give you—the Roman Pool."

Lulu had seen it briefly during the tour, but then she'd been in a gaggle of distracting girls, pressed to the back of the crowd. She hadn't been able to appreciate the indoor pool's full majesty. Now it struck her like an overwhelming dream of reflecting water and light. The cavernous T-shaped structure was somehow dark and bright at the same time. The massive pool was the dark blue of a calm sea and was connected in the center by a floating bridge bookended by two massive stone staircases. But what was most astonishing was that from pool bottom to ceiling, the entire expanse glinted with millions of reflecting tiles in deep blue and aqua, gold and orange. It was all the more disconcerting because the still water mirrored the glittering, elaborately surfaced walls, ceiling, and statuary, making a double world seem to float below the real one. For a moment Lulu didn't know which way was up.

"It sure is something," Boots whispered. "Can you imagine having this kind of dough?"

"Kind of makes me wish I could swim," Lulu murmured, overwhelmed. There hadn't been many opportunities to learn in a New York tenement, and though her publicist had it on her list, they hadn't gotten to it yet.

Even Charlie seemed speechless. Gingerly he walked to the edge of the pool and sniffed the water.

"Well, I've spent most of my life in pools, but I've never seen anything like this," Eleanor said. "In any case, before we find *ourselves* underwater, you girls look for the next clue. I need to duck into the changing area for a moment. I had one too many iced teas this morning!"

There was a worker sweeping the bridge that arched over the pool. All at once he gave a cry and tumbled headlong into the pool. The three girls started yelling, their cries echoing uncontrollably around the massive tiled enclosure. He thrashed wildly, screaming for help each time he came up for air, clearly unable to swim.

Charlie barked frantically. Without thinking, Lulu surged to the pool's edge, but the man was too far away to reach. "Eleanor! Eleanor! Help!" Lulu cried out for the Olympic gold medalist.

"Stay calm! Help is coming!" Lulu looked around desperately for something to throw the man whose frenzied gasps were becoming fewer as each submersion became terrifyingly longer, but there weren't any life rings.

Eleanor burst into the room and kicked her shoes off. She lurched forward to dive into the pool when, to Lulu's confusion, she stopped and gazed at the drowning, gasping man with a strange look.

"What are you doing, Eleanor? You've got to save him!" Lulu cried. Charlie began barking at the champion swimmer.

Eleanor merely propped herself against the golden tiles and lazily examined her nails. She glanced briefly at the drowning man. "Nah," she said. "I don't want to get all wet. I just set my hair."

Lulu gasped. "Eleanor, how could you?"

But there wasn't time for any more condemnation. Help would never arrive in time. The worker's head was slipping beneath the clear water.

There was nothing she could throw to him, nothing that would reach or float. Could she tie anything on to the long cleaning pole? No. There was nothing else in the almost bare room, except . . .

And then, with no trace of hesitation, she unbuttoned her blouse.

"Lulu, what are you doing?" Eleanor asked. "You don't have to bother. He's just . . ."

She'd already tied one sleeve of her blouse on to the scrubber and hoisted it over the water. The man reached out and just barely grasped the sleeve. The overweight, seriously weakened man almost pulled Lulu in, but she set her heels against the slippery tile and pulled with all her might. At that moment a very distraught Boots raced back into the pool area with several members of Hearst's staff, and they took over, pulling the exhausted man to safety.

Lulu collapsed against the knees of a marble Roman athlete with a strategically placed fig leaf. A servant politely handed her the sopping-wet blouse—which had been a rather nice seashell-pink silk not three minutes ago—and hustled the victim away. The three girls were alone.

Lulu looked up at Eleanor, her blue eyes steely. "Why didn't you help him?" she demanded.

"Because he wasn't really drowning," she answered flatly. Lulu gaped at her, and Eleanor gave a little shrug. "Real drowning is quiet and fast. Fake drowning is loud and splashy. Remember, I've shot reels upon reels of film where I pretend to save someone from drowning, and he looked just like someone pretending to drown."

"You can't be serious! I almost had a heart attack!" Boots said.

Of course, Lulu thought, feeling profoundly foolish. This was just another one of Hearst's tests. She knew full well that he'd be planning something, and yet she'd fallen for it hook, line, and sinker.

"What if you were wrong?" Boots challenged.

"I wasn't. The man was a terrible actor. No one actually drowning can sustain that many minutes of screaming and shouting. I could see his legs treading water in between bouts of hysteria, for crying out loud! He was fine. Now, *why* he would make all of that fuss and ruckus, I have no idea."

"More to the point," Lulu said dryly, "why didn't you tell me he was faking before I stripped naked?"

Eleanor giggled. "You looked like you really wanted to *expose* your true character! Who was I to stop you?" And with that the three of them burst into fits of laughter.

Lulu found she couldn't be mad. Her only real concern was that Hearst had been looking through one of his spy holes and caught her impromptu, manic striptease.

"I have a confession," Lulu said, making up her mind to reveal the truth to her new friends. She told them about the peephole, the setup of the diamond watch, and the theatrically fake raid. "I'm sorry I didn't tell you sooner."

She thought they'd be mad at her, but they seemed understanding. "So Hearst and Marion have just set up *all* these things to test us?" Boots asked. "They've got some nerve! What if I'd jumped in to save old what's-his-name and got knocked on the head and drowned? What if someone pulled a gun out of their handbag and put some lead in one of those imaginary agents? Hearst is asking for trouble."

"Should we tell the rest of the girls?" Lulu wondered. She knew Veronica would be dead against it. She'd be miffed Lulu had even told her friends.

"Nah," Eleanor said, helping to wring out Lulu's water-logged blouse. "It was pretty square of you to tell us— *eventually*—and give up your advantage." Then, handing the wet rag back to her, she added, "Hey, don't look so glum. I'm just ribbing you."

"We'll tell Toshia next time we see her and swear her to secrecy, and that's it," declared Boots.

"Deal," Lulu said, suddenly noticing a small freestanding marble pillar with a silver tray on top by the door at the other end of the pool. The three actresses hurried over to it and discovered a perfectly stacked pile of envelopes made of the familiar thick cream-colored stock. Lulu peeled open the top envelope and read.

> *Dear MGM girls: He's not your type;*
> *This handsome killer's of another stripe.*

*Twelve*

**W**ell, that's pretty obvious," Lulu said. "I know Hearst's private menagerie has lions, so why not tigers, too?" The animal enclosures hadn't been included on their tour, but overnight she'd heard growls and roars that sounded disturbingly like a Tarzan movie, without the appeal of having Tarzan to protect her.

"I don't like this one bit," Boots groused. "I don't trust wild animals. What if one takes a fancy to my Shalimar perfume and decides they'd like it for their own, even if it means tearing my throat out to get it?"

"What a lovely imagination you have!" moaned Eleanor.

As the girls bantered back and forth, Lulu remembered what Ginnie had said about hearing a beast in the shrubbery at night. But if Hearst was guiding them toward the area to find a clue there, the cages would obviously be securely locked. Besides, she recalled seeing a framed photo of Marion feeding a tiger from a bottle of milk. That must be the same animal. And since no one ever mentioned any attacks at the Ranch, everything in the Hearst menagerie was evidently tame.

"Come on," she said, linking arms with her friends. "Let's get this finished." She mulled over the clue again as they walked, struck by the words "handsome killer." There was still a real killer on the loose, and here she was playing Hearst's games. Of course, she did truly want to win the part. It was a chance of a lifetime. But the luster of personal gain faded in the face of Juliette's death. Lulu was anxious to continue investigating, but she couldn't just abandon the contest and start questioning people. She had to wait for the right opportunity. Anyway, Freddie was certainly on the case. At least she hoped so.

They left the main building and headed north, following the sounds, and before long the smells, of animal life. Hearst was proudest of his huge fenced enclosures that housed exotic deer and antelope, zebras, ostriches, and giraffes in fields that approximated their natural habitat and let guests feel they were in a wild area, not a zoo. But the most dangerous animals were kept in more traditional zoo cages.

The big cats were beautiful, and Lulu paused to marvel at an elegantly splotched jaguar pacing up and down along the length of his cage. At first she thought that was a good sign, because she'd worried a caged hunter would just sit in one place all day and get fat and lazy. She wasn't so sure when, five minutes later, he still paced in the exact same pattern, turning with ritualistic precision and doing it all over again. His golden eyes were vacant. She had to look away.

"Well, lookee here. Apparently *someone* doesn't think it's so safe." Eleanor indicated a glass-encased hutch tucked up against the cement wall containing a small armory of rifles and tranquilizer darts. "There's enough here to knock out an army of charging rhinoceroses.

"Mr. Tiger has got to be here somewhere." Eleanor looked around. "Here, kitty kitty! Do you think we're the first ones to get this far?"

"The tiles around the pool were dry when we got there," Lulu said. "So they hadn't played the prank on another team yet, unless the staff mopped it up in an awful hurry. Joan Crawford's duo headed outside, but they probably didn't figure out the first clue right away, despite their head start. Yes, I think we're in the lead."

"Won't that tiger be happy to see us!" Boots said, skipping ahead. "I bet he never met three more tender, tasty morsels than . . ."

And then she squealed, a high-pitched sound that seemed to pierce the vast blue sky above them.

Lulu froze for an instant, then ran to catch up. She stared at what Boots was fixated on . . . and then exhaled a deep sigh of relief.

"Have you ever seen anything more adorable in your whole life?" Boots gushed. "They're absolutely divine!"

Rolling about on the floor of the tiger cage in front of

them were two good-natured tiger cubs, happily playing with a women's beaded shoe, batting it around like overgrown kittens with a sparkling stuffed mouse. Charlie yipped and jumped up and down like a circus dog.

"Well, aren't they just heaven!" exclaimed Boots.

"Yeah, precious . . . until one of them eats your face!" mumbled a less-than-enchanted Eleanor.

"They certainly are having fun, aren't they?" Lulu smiled, then shook her head. "That's an expensive shoe. Now, how on earth would that have gotten in there? What do you think, Charlie?" She noticed the little dog was no longer bouncing by her side. "Girls, have you seen Charlie?"

"Oh dear!" exclaimed Boots. "I think he's making new friends! Look!"

Lulu followed Boots's eyes and saw that Charlie had gone around the side, squeezed through the bars, and was making his way toward the cubs, who were still cavorting about the cage.

"Charlie! Get out of there!" Lulu cried out.

Charlie, ignoring Lulu in the face of this new temptation, tried to get in on the game with the young cats. The cubs, after stopping for a tense few seconds while they all took stock of each other, went back to their entertainment. Charlie tilted his head, then went trotting off behind some potted shrubs inside the cage.

"Girls . . . what's that? Please tell me this is just part of another prank!" said Boots in a hoarse whisper, prompting the other two to turn and gasp. The cubs had disappeared through a flap at the other end of the cage, and Charlie was running about now, playing on his own with a very big, very bloody bone. When he saw the abandoned shoe, he ditched the oversized remains in favor of the cubs' coveted plaything.

The girls cautiously moved to the end of the bars to peer behind the plants. Eleanor screamed. There were big gnawed bones, gobbets of meat. One piece looked like a haunch of some lean and furless animal. *That must be it,* Lulu tried to tell herself. The lion had a lamb for dinner. The tiger had something bigger—a pig, maybe—that's all. The flap in the back of the cage swung open, and a giant mother tiger emerged from the other unseen chamber. She crouched against the far wall, massive and primal and beautiful, her orange eyes fixed on Lulu, her tail swishing. She dragged something big, which she dropped to the floor with a thud. It was a woman's mangled torso. The tiger flexed paws as big as dinner plates, and the corpse rolled slightly, dark hair falling as if she were tossing it seductively.

It was Dolores.

Lulu drew her breath for a scream . . . then stopped, deflating with a sound strangely like a laugh.

"No," she said again. "He won't fool us this time."

"We have to get help," Eleanor said in a very small voice. Boots said nothing, only stood like a pillar of salt.

"Don't you see?" Lulu said. "It's not real. It's just another one of Hearst's tests. A sick, terrible test." Her face burned with anger now. How dare he torment them like this? A drowning man and now a mauled woman? Not just any woman, but an effigy of a fellow actress. What a hideous, childish prank. It was a crass and terrible thing to do at any time, but especially after Juliette's real murder.

The likeness to Dolores was startling. Hearst must have used some of the industry's best prop designers. Was it a wax figure? The skin of the gruesome prop looked flawless, though paler than Dolores's own sun-kissed complexion. The blood looked real, too. Maybe they had used real animal blood to make the tiger more enthusiastic. Why, look at that poor tiger, slow and chubby and probably toothless and clawless. Like Boots said, she was likely a harmless old pussycat.

"I'm not going to be a part of this anymore," Lulu declared. She was furious. "And I'm not going to let Hearst get away with this. I'm going to tell all the other girls exactly what he's up to. Oh gosh, I hope Dolores doesn't see it."

"She's probably in on it," Eleanor said, recovering slowly from the shock. "That's why she was missing. She must have been working with whoever set this up to get her look just right. Oh, it's just too real! How did they do that? It's astonishing!"

Lulu leaned closer to the bars, trying to see the plaster, the wires, the wig that would show it was all fake. "Charlie, come back here!" Lulu commanded.

Charlie was so engaged with his shoe that he didn't seem to notice the tiger at first.

The tiger noticed him, though, and evidently found the live dog much more interesting than the waxworks prop. She heaved her bulk up and padded toward Charlie.

"Charlie, come here now. Please!" Lulu cried.

Charlie wheeled and his eyes went wide. He pulled back his lips in an almost silent snarl as the huge tiger paced closer, backing him into a corner. The wall was solid there, and Charlie couldn't escape except by darting past the tiger. Lulu could see his little body trembling. The tiger might be toothless, but she was still a tiger. One swipe of those massive paws would crush little Charlie.

Lulu took off her shoe and threw it through the bars at the tiger. She flinched when it hit her flank, but her focus didn't shift from Charlie. The tiger crouched slightly, the tip of her tail twitching as she began to stalk. Lulu ran around to the back of the cage to find the zookeeper's access door. It was held closed with a simple latch, and she pulled it open and stepped inside, brandishing her other shoe. "Bad tiger!" she said, and to her relief the tiger cringed in surprise and stepped back a pace.

"What are you doing? Get out of there!" Boots shouted.

"It's okay. She's not going to hurt me," Lulu said with complete confidence. Remembering the photo of Marion, Lulu knew that this was a pet tiger and, she told herself, another Hearst exhibition. Another big fake to "test their character." Well, Lulu had had enough. "Charlie, heel!" she said sharply, and Charlie slunk to her side. She looked down at him affectionately. What a loyal little dog. Anyone else, man or beast, would have run away as soon as the tiger was distracted.

"And as for you," she said, turning back to the tiger. But she wasn't where she was supposed be. While Lulu was looking at Charlie, the tiger had padded silently between her and the door. "Move!" she insisted, as if she were talking to a large, lazy Great Dane. She raised her shoe threateningly.

She tried not to look at the mangled mess of the Dolores prop. Even close up, it looked far too real. *Hearst*, she thought, *has gone too far.*

She shook her shoe and glared at the tiger. The beast took a step toward her, and another, but still Lulu didn't get frightened. It was so much bigger than she'd ever imagined a tiger could be. But she was a pet, toothless and clawless and gentle. She was probably just bored and as annoyed as any of them at having to carry on Hearst's tasteless charades.

And then she snarled. Lulu's pulse began to race when she saw the giant teeth, three inches long. Instinctively, Lulu threw her shoe, but the tiger batted it away easily. Lulu saw the deadly daggers of its claws.

"Oh no," she breathed.

Then she screamed . . . which seemed to be the right thing to do, because the high-pitched sound made the tiger wince and step back, shaking her head. Charlie, who had been relatively calm as long as Lulu was, sprang into action, yapping at the tiger's heels and dancing out of the way as she whirled and struck.

Lulu backed against the bars, looking desperately at the door. The tiger was still between her and safety.

The scuffle brought Charlie and the tiger back by the prop corpse, rolling it so that Lulu could see its glassy, staring eyes.

*Her* glassy, staring eyes.

With a shock Lulu realized that it was real. This wasn't

another Hearst setup. That was really Dolores, dead. This was really a man-eating tiger.

The tiger caught Charlie a blow that sent him flying, and Lulu screamed again, but that only brought the tiger's attention back to her. The tiger bared her terrible, bloody teeth and crouched, ready to pounce.

Lulu, nearly deaf from the thunderous pounding of her own heartbeat in her ears, could barely make out the sudden sound of glass shattering in the distance, and then a shot rang out. It was the third Lulu had ever heard in her life, and the only one she was happy to hear.

There was Sal Benedetto standing outside the cage, looking fiercer than any tiger, dripping wet in a bathing suit, his tan, muscled body in full warrior stance. He had a rifle in his hand. He shot the tiger again, and Lulu saw a dart lodge in the striped shoulder. After a long, terrible moment, the big beast crumpled at Lulu's feet. Lulu found herself incapable of moving.

Then somehow Sal was in the cage, and he scooped her up in his arms and carried her out.

"Don't worry, baby," he whispered as she hid her face against his hard, bare chest. "I've got you."

Dimly, as she curled against Sal's body, still soaking from the pool, she thought, *This jungle does have a Tarzan after all. . . .*

# Thirteen

**L**ong moments seemed to pass, during which Lulu kept her face pressed to Sal's warm, bare chest. Part of her brain said, *I need to do something.* But her body didn't seem inclined to obey. *Be the damsel in distress!* every muscle and bone seemed to say. *Rest here against this powerful man, this protector of yours. Let other people take care of all the big, bad, dangerous things in the world. You've done enough.*

Eventually her pounding heart slowed and she became gradually aware of her surroundings. There were women crying, Ranch staff members moving purposefully. She heard a man, his voice as echoing as if he were speaking on an empty soundstage, say wonderingly, "No, that's simply not possible. I always lock the doors. I always check twice."

*I can't be helpless,* Lulu thought. *I have to do something.* She had no idea what that something was, but she would find it and she would do it. She heard the weeping, the hysterics all around her. Maybe she could help simply by comforting others instead of being comforted herself.

She squirmed in Sal's arms and he released her, letting her step softly to the floor. She looked up at him gratefully in a way that made his hard face turn tender. Then she was hugging Boots, patting Eleanor on the back, telling Jean Harlow and a few others who, like Sal, had just come from sunbathing at the Neptune Pool, to look away.

"How did such a terrible accident happen?" Toshia wailed. "Why would she go into a tiger's cage?"

Lulu flushed with chagrin. She'd walked in there with hardly a second thought to save Charlie. But where was he?

"Charlie? Here, boy!" Lulu began frantically calling after her precious dog, but the brave little terrier was nowhere to be seen. "Charlie!" she shrieked.

She wove through the distressed onlookers until she spotted him, unmoving, crumpled in the bushes beside the cage. "Oh, Charlie!" she gasped as she fell to her knees at the little dog's side. She stroked his fur gently, and to her amazement felt his chest rise and fall beneath her hand. "Oh, you're alive! You dreadful, horrible angel!" She buried her face in his soft coat. It was amazing that he could have survived a swipe from the tiger's paw. He must have been small enough to have been caught by the velvet pads of the huge paw, missing the deadly claws.

She scooped him into her arms, and his plaintive whine

showed he wasn't entirely unscathed. Cracked ribs, she thought, and hoped it wasn't anything worse. He licked her chin, and Lulu began to cry silently, her tears falling onto his fur.

She heard someone speak her name, and looked up to find Freddie standing over her, a peculiar expression on his face.

"Freddie! You're here!" She moved toward him, still clutching the injured mutt.

"They told me someone got mauled by the tiger," Freddie said. "Thank heavens you're all right! What happened?"

It suddenly occurred to her that he might have seen her in Sal's arms. But the gangster had saved her life. And after that, she would have clung to anyone. Freddie couldn't be upset at that when there was so much else to be upset about.

She stood, still cradling Charlie, and told him as briefly as she could, wiping the last of the tears from her smudged cheek. But when she looked up into his eyes, she found them flashing with anger. "How could you be so stupid?" Freddie demanded, voice trembling as he gave her a little shake. "Running right into a tiger's cage? What in the name of all that's holy were you thinking?"

"I thought that the cat would be tame! And I had to save Charlie," she said, bristling.

"And *risk your own life*? How can you be so foolishly impulsive, Lulu? You always run right into danger without thinking!"

"How dare you speak to me like that after everything I've been through! I am not a child you can just chastise and punish! I'm a grown woman, and I was just almost killed try-ing to save the life of the one thing on this earth that truly cares about me, and . . . !"

By the look on Freddie's face, Lulu knew she had gone too far, and immediately regretted it.

"Freddie, I didn't mean . . . ," she began weakly, but he didn't let her get any further.

"I see how things are. Well. I am so very glad you have Charlie, then," he said coldly. "If that's the kind of careless life you want to live, full of stupid risks, maybe you should be with Sal. It's obvious he can protect you better than I can."

Lulu gaped at him for a moment, but Freddie was stone, and there was nothing she could say. She turned on her heel and walked away, her chest feeling oddly hollow, her eyes burning. *He's just upset. Don't think about that horrible thing he just said*, she cautioned herself. Not now. They would work every-thing out.

Another group of scavenger hunters arrived, and the screams started anew. Lulu wiped her face. She would talk to Freddie later, and he would understand, and they would kiss and have a glorious laugh about it. But right now Dolores came first.

Holding Charlie carefully, Lulu made herself look into the cage.

Her eyes squeezed shut with a will of their own, but she forced them open again. Why had Dolores gone into the cage? Lulu tried to remember when she'd last seen the tall, volup-tuous actress. Dolores had been at dinner, definitely. Had she seen her in the morning? No, Lulu had gotten out so early to meet with Freddie that the other girls had barely been stirring.

A shadow passed over her, and she felt Sal move beside her, his bare arm brushing the ruined silk of her blouse. "I wonder when it happened," she said.

She didn't really expect Sal to have an answer, but he said, "It was definitely not last night. She was with me until dawn."

A chill shot through Lulu, her breath growing strangely shallow.

"Poor kid," Sal went on. "She didn't deserve to end like that. She was so full of life."

Lulu tried to push aside the strange feeling that washed over her when she knew that Sal and Dolores had spent the night together. She felt her cheeks tingle with heat, but why? Flustered, she made herself focus on the matter at hand. Freddie had no reason to be jealous, so why should she?

"Did she seem okay to you? Was she sad or upset about anything?"

Sal's lip twitched in an almost smile. "She seemed like she was enjoying life to the utmost."

Lulu cringed. "And she left in the morning? And went back to our guesthouse?"

"She left around four or five," Sal confirmed. "I went to sleep for a couple of hours afterward."

Lulu made herself keep staring at the carnage. It helped her focus on what was important, and wash out the images of Dolores and Sal that wanted to flood her mind.

She couldn't help but ask, "Have you known her long?"

Lulu tried to keep her voice neutral and pretend the question was only about the investigation.

"A few weeks," Sal admitted. *So he met her not too long after the situation with Ruby*, Lulu thought. Right after he went to such great and immoral lengths to make Lulu his own.

"You . . . you seem pretty close to her."

"She's a hell of a girl, and a really swell actress. She's got the chops. *Had* the chops." He pressed his thumb and fore-finger briefly to the corners of his eyes. "I was doing every-thing I could to help boost her career."

Lulu knew exactly what Sal could do to help an actress's career. She wasn't sure how he did it, with threats or money or both, but when he sent Lulu to Hollywood in exchange for her favorable testimony, every door had been opened to her. Now that Sal had established himself as a Hollywood presence, she imagined his influence would be even more far-reaching.

"I've got such a good hookup with Hearst now, supplying him with liquor . . . and a few other necessities of life. I just about had this part in the bag for the kid. We shook on the bones of the deal last night but still had to flesh it out."

Lulu drew in her breath sharply. "You mean you'd talked Hearst into giving her the starring role in the movie Anita Loos is writing? The role we're all competing for?"

She was stung by the unfairness of it. Here were a bunch of talented girls working their hardest to get the role of a life-time, and the part was going to be handed off based on com-merce and sex. *The men are wheeling and dealing*, Lulu thought, *and we girls are hardly more than commodities traded on the open market.* Lulu knew she shouldn't be surprised. This was Hollywood, after all. But it was still galling.

Never in a million years would she admit it was galling that Sal was doing it for another girl instead of for her.

Sal seemed to think she might feel that way, though, because he said sincerely, "You're all set in this place, Lu. I might have given you a boost, but you've made your own way since then. Besides, I didn't think you'd like the idea of me doing any favors for you."

"Of course not," she snapped. "It's just . . ." Then she remembered that the girl she was definitely not at all jealous of was dead, and she bit her lip.

"I know. Life ain't fair. It wasn't fair to this poor kid."

*The part isn't important,* Lulu had to remind herself. She shouldn't let herself be dwelling on unrelated things like Dolores being handed the part when the statuesque young actress was dead. She tried to focus on that.

"Why didn't the keepers find her before I did?" Lulu wanted to know.

"Let's ask them," Sal said, his voice a menacing growl. He cornered a man in picturesque khaki jodhpurs and a pith helmet.

"She's such a nice tiger! So playful and gentle," the man was saying to other Ranch employees. "Still, I wouldn't ever be in the cage with her."

"Why didn't you find her before now?" Sal asked, looking like he wanted to grab the man by the shirt and lift him off the ground. "If someone had been here earlier, this might not have happened!"

"The big cats like to eat in the afternoon," the keeper said, obviously distraught, though Lulu couldn't tell if it was because of Dolores's death or Sal's sinister menace. Probably both, plus a natural fear of losing his job when Hearst found out. Where was Hearst, anyway? Word must have spread to him by now.

"So you didn't check them this morning?" Lulu asked.

"No. We fed the elephant, and the chimp, and all the grazers. But the carnivores are active at night, and lazy in the morning, so we leave them alone until later."

"The cage wasn't locked when I went in," Lulu pointed out. "Can anyone just walk into the cage?"

"There's a bolt and a padlock," the keeper said. "But the padlock wasn't on, for some reason." Lulu raised her eyebrows. "I always lock it, and I always double-check," he swore to her.

"I've heard that the lion got out before," Lulu accused. "So not quite *all* the time."

The keeper threw up his hands in exasperation. "I get days off, you know, and I don't sleep here. I always lock up. But I can't speak for my assistants. They're just guys who get paid to chop vegetables and shovel dung. If a cage is unlocked, it's their fault. I've told Hearst over and over—"

Lulu cut him off. "So it was locked last night. Where do you keep the keys?"

He pulled a key ring from his pocket and held one of the cluster out to them. It was a large brassy key with a stylized lion's head. "This is the key to every one of the carnivores' locks. I always have it with me."

"Does anyone else have a copy?"

He shrugged. "I don't think so. They shouldn't, anyway. I never really thought about it, though. What kind of an idiot would go into a tiger cage?" He looked at the gory scene behind the bars and shook his head sadly.

"Everybody back inside." Hearst's voice boomed through the menagerie as he strode in. It was so loud it set the chimpanzee, in some unseen cage, hooting and chittering. "There's no need for us all to gape at this horrible accident. I'm sure if it were you in there, you wouldn't want gawkers surrounding you. Have a little sensitivity."

"WR is right," said Lolly as she slithered around his bulk, craning her neck to get a look at the carnage. "Only necessary people should remain." She made a shooing gesture and herded Lulu and Sal away from the cage. Once the path in front of it was clear, she squatted down, took a Brownie camera from her ostrich-skin handbag, and started snapping pictures.

"The papers will never print those!" Lulu said.

"Private collectors," Sal whispered in her ear. "She'll make a killing, so to speak, off all this ugliness."

"Really?" Lulu asked, astonished. "Who would buy awful photos like those?"

"Kid, you'd be surprised at all the kinds of evil there are in the world. Fans who get their kicks looking at torture and disfigurement. Looking at—and doing—all kinds of things that you and I would never dream of."

Lulu shuddered at the mere idea that Lolly would participate in such hideous enterprise. Her eyes strayed reluctantly back to Dolores.

How had she ever thought it was a prop? Her skin, once so tropically tan, was pale as vellum, and the glint of drying moisture in her staring eye . . . Ugh, how could anybody get a thrill out of looking at a scene like that?

Then she noticed something she hadn't seen at first. When there's so much blood, and body parts strewn hither and yon, small details get lost by the wayside.

"Sal," she began hesitantly, "did you . . . ?" She stopped and bit her lip. This was far beyond her realm of experience. Sure, other girls had gossiped about their exploits, so strangely free of shame that Lulu assumed they were making half of it up. But Lulu had never done anything beyond passionate kissing and perhaps a little innocent petting. She knew a great deal about what came next from accumulated hearsay, but no one had ever taught her, or answered her questions—and she'd never been brave enough to ask.

She blurted it out as fast as she could, her face burning. "Sal, did you tie Dolores up last night?"

He looked at her with astonishment.

"I mean . . . for fun?" She looked down, deeply ashamed. An actress she knew had told her that some people enjoyed that during intimate moments. "It's just that she looks like she has marks on her wrists. Bruises, and a red shiny weal.

I had bruises like that after I was handcuffed." When she'd been arrested under suspicion of attempted murder, she'd been interrogated for hours. Although she'd been completely innocent, she had technically pulled the trigger. Investigating officers might have learned the truth sooner if Sal hadn't bribed them to charge Lulu right away. He'd wanted to make her afraid so she'd have no choice but to turn to him for help.

"No," he said gently. "I didn't do that."

"Well, look at her wrists," Lulu told him, stepping closer to the cage herself. "Doesn't it look like . . . ?"

At that moment a dozen burly men stomped into view. They were all in their shirtsleeves, and wore shoulder holsters openly. Lulu recognized some of them—a footman who had stood in livery behind Hearst during dinner, a gardener she'd marked as being particularly able-bodied but not otherwise noteworthy.

"Hearst's personal security force," Sal said. "Incognito most of the time. I guess now they're on official call-out."

"At least he seems to be taking this seriously. Do you think it's possible that . . . ?"

But four members of the security team imposed themselves between Lulu and the cage, blocking the scene. "You have to leave now," one said sternly. Elsewhere, other guards were hustling away the guests who had been reluctant to leave the exciting scene even after Hearst's command.

"But I have to check something! I discovered the body!" Lulu tried to explain, craning her neck to see around them. It was no use. The security force made a solid phalanx between her and the crime scene.

"There's nothing more to see here, miss. Go along back to the house."

She looked hopefully at Sal, but he didn't seem to like the odds. "Come on, babe. I need a drink, anyway." He put his arm around her and walked her back toward the house. Across the way she saw Freddie. Something was strange about him, she thought. He looked so imperious. His stance was uncharacteristically upright, far from the more casual and inviting slouch she so loved. His arms were crossed over his chest as he watched her. *He's on duty*, she mused. *That's it. Admittedly he might still be miffed, but surely that will pass, and he knows how I love him!* She broke abruptly away from Sal and ran to Freddie.

"Freddie, you have to take a closer look at Dolores. I don't think she went in there on her own. At first I thought she might just have been drunk, or foolish, or maybe suicidal, even. But now I think maybe she was forced to go into that cage. I'm almost sure I saw marks on her wrists. Freddie, I think Dolores was murdered too!"

For a long moment Freddie didn't speak. She gazed trustingly up into his face, but he looked eerily different than she had ever seen him. His face was pleasant, but formal and remote. There was a wintry distance in his eyes. The change, though subtle, was thorough, and chilling. He was that person again, she realized with disbelief. The billionaire he claimed to have despised and so thoroughly abandoned. He'd gone back to the personality he must have had when he was still living in New York on his father's ill-gotten fortune. He looked like a sophisticated autocrat who was so rich that nothing could possibly trouble him. Not death. Not love. He was above it all.

"Freddie," she asked carefully. "What's wrong?"

He regarded her with that insufferable, unflappable expression of the rich and said, "You get carried away with yourself, seeing murder everywhere, my dear." His voice was cold. "It's time to let the professionals handle this."

Even the words "my dear" sounded heartless falling from his downturned lips. There was no warmth in them. Was this all because of Sal? How could he possibly think that Sal meant anything to her?

"But, Freddie!"

"It's true, a pretty girl will be humored for far longer than the rest of the world," he said. "But even someone as beautiful as you gets tiresome after a while if she persists in ludicrous theories. You need to concentrate on your work, and I on mine. Mr. Hearst needs me to focus on the blackmail letter, which is what I fully intend on doing. If you want to meddle in things that don't concern you, you'll do it without me. I don't have the time or inclination to engage in wild-goose chases."

"But, Freddie, you have to help me," she pleaded, thinking all the while *Where has he gone? Oh, please be my sweet Freddie again.*

He shook his head. "You want help? It appears as if Sal is more than able to take my place. And you seem happy enough to let him."

She gasped in disbelief, torn between reactions. She

wanted to scream and slap him. She wanted to very calmly explain that he was being an ass, that she was naturally grateful to Sal for saving her life, and possibly she didn't hate him quite as much as she should, but her heart belonged completely and unequivocally to Freddie. Didn't it?

But if he could turn on her like this in a petty fit of jealousy, was he really the Freddie she knew and loved? Her life was so full of actors, of people skilled at pretending to be what they were not. Had he only been acting like a good and decent and loving and moral man, when in fact he was still the heartless young billionaire?

*No,* she told herself firmly. *I* know *Freddie. He's being stupid now, but I know his inmost heart. We'll get through this. We'll laugh about it later.*

She composed her face into a tentative smile and tried to explain everything to him in a calm and rational way. But he had already turned away, and her pride wouldn't let her call him back or chase him down. She stood, bereft, and watched him go.

# *Fourteen*

**K**nock *it off, van der Waals. This means nothing. Just keep your head down and walk. One foot, then the other. But if I see that lousy thug touch her one more . . . No, focus on the crime. What is it Mugsy used to say? Keep your head in the game, not on the dame? This is just a moment. One extremely aggravating moment. I'll be fine. She loves me. Doesn't she? But what if she's just playing me? I told you! Knock it off! Nothing happened. Nothing except that lowlife criminal pulled my girl out of the jaws of death and I wasn't there to do a thing about it. But that's the past. Just keep walking. You have a job to do.*

Freddie grimaced numbly as he strode away from the woman he loved, forcing himself with every fiber of his being to not offer her anything resembling a backward glance. When there was any question of a moral right or wrong, he always knew the answer. What's more, he was always able to do the right thing, no matter how difficult it was. Where honor was concerned, there was never any disconnect between what he *should* do and what he did.

That wasn't the case now. He knew in his heart that he was being petty, unreasonable, and small. He knew he should turn right around, take Lulu in his arms, and apologize for being such an ass. Why did he want to beat Sal to a pulp, then throw Lulu over his shoulder and carry her away? This was all pure ego and irrational foolishness. This insane jealousy had to stop. This was not a self he recognized, or could take any pride in.

But somehow he couldn't help himself. Even while he yearned to go back to her and make things right, he found he couldn't. It was some sickening remnant of the rich man he'd once been, the man who was so far above everything. Like a child throwing a tantrum, he knew he was doing the wrong thing, hurting Lulu and himself with his petty childishness, but he felt that if he ever saw Lulu in Sal's arms again, plain and simple, he would kill him. That was too much emotion for Freddie, so he needed to just keep walking. For now he needed to focus on his job.

*Waters and Hearst need me*, he repeated to himself over and over again.

Only, that brought him around to Lulu again. He'd come looking for her to talk through his new suspicions about the blackmail. It was a disturbing notion, but he couldn't quite shake it, and he'd wanted to get Lulu's opinion before he broached the idea with his boss. He didn't relish the thought of telling Hearst that the most logical prime suspect was, in fact, Marion Davies herself.

Marion had access to all of Hearst's secrets and was the only person with unhindered entrée to Hearst's private office at all hours, and to everywhere else in the castle. She could order the staff to be out of the way. No one else could move around without suspicion the way she could. She might easily have slipped the blackmail notes right under Hearst's nose.

But though she clearly had the opportunity, what about the motive? And the strange dollar amount? That's what Freddie couldn't fathom. Hearst gave her everything she wanted. Her latest shopping spree had probably totaled more than the blackmail amount. But there might be secrets he wasn't privy to. He knew all too well that every family had them, and despite their unconventional relationship, Marion and Hearst were very much family in every way that mattered. Maybe Marion was jealous of Hearst's wife back in New York—or of some other woman. It wasn't rational for her to blackmail Hearst, especially, given his extraordinary wealth, for this comparatively measly amount. But then again, Freddie was beginning to understand exactly how irrational jealousy could make a person.

Abruptly, he wheeled around, finally putting aside thoughts of Lulu and Sal. Waters had summoned him, but that could wait. Right now he needed to find Marion and see if he could unearth any truth to his suspicions. If so, he'd just have to bite the bullet and tell Hearst. And likely get fired immediately afterward. But integrity was integrity, and for Assistant Investigator Freddie Van, at this moment particularly, integrity was of paramount importance.

The servants were peculiarly evasive and no help in locating Marion. Neither the housemaids nor kitchen staff seemed to be able to offer even a clue as to where she might be or had last been seen. None of this made any sense to Freddie, having grown up in a similar environment where everyone in the house knew his every move. It was just how households worked, he thought. How could they have no idea unless . . . ? And then, acting on a hunch, he found her, and understood the staff's behavior.

Freddie knew that plenty of Hollywood types had drinking problems, and he'd seen Marion deeply in her cups often enough in their short acquaintance to gather that she was an alcoholic. He couldn't count the number of relatives of his own and his private school friends who'd been whisked away for some "quiet time" at one exclusive sanitarium or another. Addiction was just another whispered-about, poorly kept secret that seemed to accompany a life soaked in excess.

Like all addicts, Marion had constructed her own system of hiding her addiction, though in truth it was only a secret in her own mind. Hearst did his best to keep her sober, but the servants had been paid in bribes, gifts, and favors to facilitate her drinking on the sly. None of them would tell Freddie where Marion was concealed, but eventually he found her in the wine cellar, hiding her alcoholism in the most obvious place.

She had a little notebook in her hand and pretended to be going over the wine list for that evening's dinner. But it wasn't wine in her grasp. Wine didn't do the job efficiently enough. She sipped aggressively from a sweating highball glass of what looked like pure whiskey, and there was a half-empty bottle at her feet.

She looked momentarily startled to be discovered in her hiding place, but she recovered quickly and said with a provocative smirk, "Well, hello, sailor!"

*Ah,* thought Freddie, *the blatant flirtations of a seasoned lush.* He'd been accosted by plenty of party girls (and occasionally their mothers) back in New York and he knew how to handle them with kindness and tact. The trick was to deny them while preserving their dignity. You had to keep them happy by pretending they were irresistible . . . but still keep them at bay. It was even more important to walk that fine line here. Displeasing Marion could be disastrous to anyone's career. So could pleasing her too much—if Hearst found out.

"Looking for me?" she asked.

He gave her his most charming smile. "All my life," he said. "Though I know I'm too late." He sat down on a cask.

"Don't be so sure about that. May I offer you a nip?" she slurred, inclining her body toward him.

"Don't mind if I do," Freddie said, offering her a half smile. Knowing full well that an alcoholic likes nothing more than to get others to join them, he pulled a cut-crystal glass from the nearest shelf and poured a finger of the dark amber liquor as Marion repositioned herself, her dress sleeve slipping down her pale shoulder.

"But aren't you taken?" Marion asked artlessly.

"Aren't you?" Freddie countered.

"Ha! I'll drink to that!" she said, hoisting her glass into the air and spilling half of it. Freddie gallantly snatched up the bottle and refilled it.

"Mr. Hearst wanted me to tell you what happened," Freddie said, steering the conversation to something slightly more benign than illicit tipsy seduction. Briefly, he told her about Dolores.

All through the story, Marion sat frozen. The only movement Freddie could see was the gentle sloshing of her whiskey as her hand trembled. She didn't even seem to be breathing, so that when Freddie finished his tale, she gave a sort of gasp and suddenly sat up straighter.

"Another one," she breathed, as if to herself. Freddie saw her lips twitch, and at first he thought it must, improbably, be a flickering ghost of a smile. But no, who could smile at such news? It was a pained grimace, he decided, gone the next second.

"Which one was Dolores?" Marion asked. "The pale Polish girl?"

*Poor Marion must be even more upset than she looks*, Freddie thought, because he distinctly remembered her calling Dolores by name during the practical joke hijinks the first night. He caught her looking at him sidelong out of eyes that showed no trace of tears. In her deeply tipsy state he would have expected more feminine emotion. Wait. Could she be pretending to not remember who Dolores was? But why?

"No. Dolores was the tall, black-haired one," Freddie said, and watched her narrowly.

There was no look of dawning comprehension in her eyes, though she said, "Oh yes, I remember now. Nothing at all like me. Still, some like that type, I suppose." She picked up the whiskey bottle and looked at her own faint reflection in the smoky glass before sloshing in a little more. She smiled to herself. "I've still got it," she said softly. "Those others can't hold a candle."

Freddie wasn't sure if the alcohol was keeping Marion from fully realizing what had happened, or if there was something else going on.

"When was the last time you saw her?" he asked.

Marion shrugged. "I don't pay attention to most of the girls that come around here. They come, they go. Mostly they go." She giggled. "Dolores went." She clapped her hand over her mouth. "Oh, did I just say that? Bad me! Oh well, what's a girl to do?"

Marion gave a careless shrug, sending the other sleeve down to her elbow. Freddie began to feel increasingly uncomfortable about the amount of skin she was showing. If someone were to walk in . . .

"Dolores wasn't the worst of the lot, even if she did almost get . . ." She interrupted herself with a deep swig. "Much better than some, anyway. Not like that slut Juliette. You know . . ."

Marion dipped her heavily jeweled index finger into her glass, slowly swirling the thick dark liquid. "*She* had it coming but good."

Freddie hid his surprise. "What do you mean?" he asked.

"That—creature—had the nerve to tell me I'm yesterday's news. Can you believe it? That bleached-blond little travesty of an actress positively got into my face and told me I'm washed up! And Frances told me she'd been saying all kinds of horrible things about me behind my back."

"Frances?" Freddie asked.

"Mrs. Mortimer, our housekeeper. Now, *there's* loyalty. She's been with me since the beginning and always has my back. Without her bringing information to me, I might actually believe all of those sweetly smiling little tramps like and respect me."

"Some of them certainly do," Freddie said, thinking of Lulu. "But no one seemed to like Juliette much."

"One person liked her. She and John Emerson had a *thing*, you know." She leaned in close, exhaling boozily. "The part should be mine, you know. Anita is *my* friend. She should be writing the part for me. Not that horrible Juliette or that tramp Dolores, or . . ." She caught herself sharply and gave a little laugh. "Oh, what am I saying? You'll forgive me if my head's all muddled, won't you, dear boy? Poor, sweet Dolores. Such tragic times!"

Was she really so self-centered and conceited that she was thinking about a role she thought she deserved when two young women were dead? He supposed that kind of attitude wasn't too uncommon here in Hollywood, though most would have to be as deeply into their cups as Marion before they were so blatant. It made him grateful he had a girl like Lulu. He had to smooth things out with her, and soon.

But for now he tried to keep Marion's attention. She liked to talk about herself, so he encouraged her to do that. Maybe eventually he could steer the conversation to a point where he could get a clue about the blackmail.

"You hoped to get the part Anita is writing, then?" he asked, full of sympathy.

She nodded, and the movement almost made her fall off her chair. "But when I went to Pops and told him I wanted the part, he said I was too . . . too . . ."

"Sophisticated?" Freddie ventured with calculation.

Marion threw back her head and laughed grimly. "How clever you are. So sweet and *soooo* very handsome. That Lulu Kelly is a lucky girl. Too lucky, maybe. No, you silly! He suggested I might be just a tad too old to play a teenage ingenue. Even though Anita hasn't written the part, we all know the lead character will be young. I didn't push it after that. The world wants youth. Juliette had the absolute gall to corner me and tell me to stop trying to get Emerson and Anita and Paul Raleigh to tailor the part for me!" She tossed her messy waves. "God, how I hate these smart young things who think anyone over thirty doesn't count anymore." She leered drunkenly. "I'm glad some people, at least, can see the allure of a mature woman."

Freddie just forced a knowing laugh and ignored her

insinuation. "With Juliette . . . or even Dolores now out of the picture, do you think the part might go to you?"

Marion made a rude noise. "With all these sweet young things swinging their hips and pouting their lips at the men who make all the decisions in Hollywood? Not bloody likely I'm getting any parts, unless someone decides to strangle every last one of 'em." She laughed uproariously at the idea. "If only that were possible," she said. "Oh, darling boy, you make me say the most foolish things! What must you think of me?" She raised her glass and took a long, purposeful drink.

"I hope you don't mind, but I do have to get back to work. Miss Davies, I do not understate when I say that this has been fascinating." And with that, amid her drunken protests and giggles, Freddie left her to her bottle, consumed with a new idea.

It seemed ludicrous at first consideration. But the access that made it conceivable that Marion was the blackmailer also made it possible she could be the killer. She could go anywhere on the Ranch unobserved. She could have gotten the scarf. In fact, she selected them! Where had she been just before Juliette was discovered? She and Hearst had arrived late to the Assembly Room before dinner. Had they been together?

No, this was an insane idea. Marion Davies was a great movie star. Even more telling, she was a small, slender woman, not in her first youth. Juliette was bigger, younger, and no doubt stronger than Marion, and Dolores, who everyone compared to an Amazon warrior woman, was tall, sporty, and strong. It was almost impossible to imagine little Marion manhandling the two murdered starlets.

And yet, as Freddie climbed up from the wine cellar, it stuck in his mind. Her drunken admission of her hatred for Juliette was telling, though apparently almost every actress hated Juliette, and with good reason. But that offhand comment about strangling her competition revealed a hard streak in Marion that piqued his interest. She had shown Freddie a darkness and desperation that made him wonder how far down the rabbit hole she could go. In this state, what was she capable of?

But why talk so openly with him about her jealousies? Why confess? *In vino veritas*, most likely. When he'd first started working for Mr. Waters, the investigator had told him not to be surprised when people confessed. Especially Hollywood types. Show people are in love with their own stories, he said in a sober moment. They'll confess just because they crave an audience. How can they prove how interesting and important they are if they don't tell their darkest secrets?

And then, Mr. Waters had taught him, even those who don't confess will give you hints. *I didn't kill him*, a suspect might say, *but he stole my wife, my dog, and my job, so I'm glad he's dead.* Not a confession, but enough motive to warrant digging deeper.

When he met with Hearst and Waters later, he was still uncertain as to what he might say and how to introduce the subject. He had no idea how he could tactfully suggest that Marion Davies, Hearst's mistress and great love, might be involved with either the blackmail or the murders. Perhaps he could find some way to make Waters suggest it. Or best yet, put Hearst in a position where he couldn't help but think of it himself.

"Mr. Hearst, I know that we're here to concentrate on getting to the bottom of the blackmail situation, but I think it's important to consider the very distinct possibility that the unfortunate incident in the tiger cage may not have been an accident."

"W-wh-what are you saying, Freddie?" Waters stuttered.

"Are you suggesting that that poor girl was murdered? You too?" Hearst barked. "I've heard enough cockamamie theories to last a lifetime. I suppose that a private investigator has a vested interest in making everything seem inexplicable and dire. But the truth is, any man of reasonable intelligence can solve most crimes. Do you know why? Because the right answer is always the most obvious one! There's no conspiracy. That colored man in the garden murdered Juliette. Dolores's death was an unfortunate accident. Stop looking for a boogey-man."

"Or woman," Freddie muttered inaudibly under his breath.

"What was that? Did I hear you contradict me?"

"No, sir. I was just clearing my throat."

"You listen, and you listen good," Hearst snapped. "There is no murder investigation! We have the murderer incarcerated!" He glared at Freddie. "If you don't stop this nonsense, you will be asked to leave the premises, and no doubt your job with Mr. Waters will be terminated forthwith."

Freddie had no choice but to bite his tongue.

But he wondered why Hearst was so adamant about refusing to allow even the possibility of a real murder investigation. Was it just to keep fuss and publicity to a minimum? Or did he have a deeper, more personal motivation? Was he trying to protect someone?

Was he trying to cover for Marion?

# *Fifteen*

**L**ulu set Charlie down on the bed and furiously began throwing clothes and sundries into her bags.

Veronica knocked on the half-open door and came in before Lulu could tell her to butt out. "What in the name of Louis B. Mayer do you think you're doing? You can't leave."

"Watch me," Lulu snapped as she shoved a sparkling pair of diamanté hair combs—last night's gift to all remaining actresses—into her cosmetics case. "This whole event is a bloody nightmare. The competition is insane, and Hearst does nothing but lie, lie, lie to everyone—tricking us into thinking we're being arrested, or that someone's drowning—just so he can sit back and watch our reactions for his own amusement." Her face twisted in disgust. "And now there are *two* murders and no one seems interested in investigating any of it."

"What do you mean—two murders?" Veronica asked.

"I'm certain that Dolores was tied up when she went into the tiger's cage," Lulu said. "She had bruises and what looked like rope burns on her wrists. Someone forced her in there, but nobody will listen to me." She shook her head. "So I say fine, let them clean up their own mess and catch their own murderers, and oh! In the meantime, make young talented women demean themselves so that they can get a hypothetical part in a movie that may never materialize! I'm telling you, Veronica, I'm leaving."

"Lulu Kelly! I forbid it! I know you're frustrated, but I don't think you know what you may be walking away from. It's my job to save you from yourself, and I'm not going to let you throw away this—"

"Veronica Imrie!" interrupted Lulu, mocking her relentless publicist. "Does Mr. Hearst really think any of us are showing our 'true character' here? We're *all* acting, as always, and scrambling for the part and trying to impress. Never mind that there has been at least one bona fide murder in the last forty-eight hours on the property—a fact that everyone is blithely happy to ignore because if we actually dealt with the horror of it, it would ruin everyone's ferociously desperate and egomaniacal plans! Now, if you'll excuse me, I'm leaving. Kindly send the rest of my things to the station." With Charlie in one hand and a bag in the other, she tried to shove her way past her friend.

"Lulu, listen to me. It's been a nutty day. You're exhausted and . . ."

Lulu looked at Veronica levelly.

"Nutty? I just found a girl I had dinner with last night in a wild animal's cage, strewn about like she'd been separated into the four food groups!"

"I know. I know," Veronica said soothingly. "You've been through so much. First Ruby, and now all this?" She spread her hands. "No wonder you're a mess. But you know what our slogan is out here. The show must go on, come hell or high water."

"Veronica, you're not listening to me. Some things are more important than getting a part." *Or catching a murderer?* Lulu's better nature asked accusingly. *What if another girl gets killed and you could have stopped it, but you ran away with your tail between your legs, whining like a little kid just because men don't listen to you and your boyfriend dismissed you?* "High water is here, and I'm catching the next boat out."

Veronica threw her hands up in the air. "Then think about me," she implored. "You're Lux Studios' one and only hope for this. Isn't this why you came to Hollywood? This is the golden ticket! If you win this competition, you will be the biggest star Lux has, and just so you know, the publicity will be beyond our realm of understanding. That's why every studio wants their girl to get this part. Lulu, I'll get down on my hands and knobby knees, but I'm begging you to not run away from this."

"I'm not running away," Lulu started uncertainly.

"They'll fire me if you leave!" Veronica insisted.

"Veronica! That's low," Lulu said dangerously. "You know I don't want to do anything that would hurt you. Just . . . oh, please just get out of my way." She shouldered past, leaving Veronica watching helplessly. Lulu was frankly surprised her publicist let her go. She fully expected to be physically tackled and held down for yet another imploring lecture.

Lulu made her way through the main house, certain that Veronica was exaggerating and more convinced than ever that she needed to get away from the Ranch immediately. No footman or butler seemed to be on duty, so she let herself out, shifting Charlie against her chest to give him a more comfortable ride. She suspected he was more bruised than broken, but he seemed to be enjoying the free transportation. Hugging him gave her comfort that she desperately needed. She could always rely on her Charlie. Lulu headed to the garage. She found the drivers lolling at ease, smoking and playing dice.

"Excuse me," she said politely. "I need a car to the station, please."

"Sorry, ma'am," one of them said. "All the cars are out of commission today."

"I don't believe it!" she said. "They can't all be broken."

"Lady, I just do what I'm told."

A little prickling worry began around the edge of her consciousness. Was she actually trapped here? Was everyone being held prisoner, albeit in the fanciest prison on earth, without knowing it? She went back to the mansion and called a taxi, giving him directions to meet her half a mile down the road from the Ranch. Then she went up to her room to change into something sensible enough to make it through an off-road journey.

"Oh, thank heavens! You came to your senses," Veronica said when she saw Lulu had returned. "Take a nap—take a pill, whatever—and relax. Lulu, believe me, I'm well aware that bad things happen in the world, but you don't have to let them ruin your chance at happiness and success."

Lulu nodded very carefully and lay down on top of her covers until Veronica was distracted on a phone call with the studio. Then she slipped out the side door with Charlie and made her way through the gardens, past the Neptune Pool, and into the picturesque woods beyond. Though the noon sun shone strongly, it didn't fully penetrate the tree canopy. With every step, her speed and sense of urgency increased. Her heart was pounding, and she could feel a growing sense of panic beginning to overwhelm her. Any minute now she'd reach the winding road that snaked up the hillside. Then she'd just follow it down until she met her cab.

When the man rose up out of the greenery, she was sure she was having a hallucination. No vision that bizarre could ever emerge in real life. He was painted in black and green greasepaint, and he had vines tied around his forehead, twined around his arms and waist until he looked like part of the landscape itself. This wild man rose up and loomed over her. She froze in her tracks.

He pointed a gun at her chest. That part was all too real.

"Name?" he barked.

"L-Lulu Kelly."

He checked it against a piece of paper he had in his pocket. Lulu wasn't sure exactly how he managed this, because he didn't seem to take his eyes off her for a second.

"All right, miss, turn around and head back to the Ranch."

"No!" she said, surprising even herself. The man looked surprised too. "Perhaps you don't realize that this isn't the first time I've had a gun pointed at me. I have to leave. My taxi is meeting me down the road."

"Nobody leaves," he said flatly.

"What? You can't do that!"

"I'm not doing it. Mr. Hearst is. No one enters or leaves the property until he says so."

Lulu glowered at him. "You mean I'm a prisoner?"

The camouflaged guard flashed a row of uneven but shining white teeth. "Naw, not a prisoner. A guest!" He holstered his gun, apparently convinced she was no threat.

*If they made any kind of practical shoes for women, I might try to outrun him*, Lulu thought. But he'd easily outpace her in his loose clothes and boots, even with vines trailing around him. Then, too, she wasn't sure how seriously he'd take his guard duty. Hearst could cover up almost anything. Would the guard actually shoot her if she looked like she might escape the property? Somehow she managed to compose herself and commented on the one bright side to this ridiculous situation. "At least Mr. Hearst is taking the murders seriously," she said. "The perpetrator is certainly one of the guests, so I guess it's a good thing that no one is allowed to leave."

"Murders?" the man asked. "Perpetrator? The negro who killed that poor girl is still in the hospital, far as I know."

"No, he didn't . . . Oh, what's the use? No one believes me

anyway. But Dolores, the girl killed by the tiger, she was murdered, and the killer is still on the loose!"

"Look, Miss Kelly, I don't know what you're talking about, but this lockdown has nothing to do with any murder."

"I don't understand," Lulu said, reeling. "Why can't I leave, then?"

"It's all very hush-hush," the guard said in a low voice. But like so many men, he couldn't quite resist prolonging a conversation with a pretty girl. Especially one whom he fantasized about from the movies. "It seems Mr. Hearst got a threatening letter, and he's sure one of the guests or staff delivered it, and most likely wrote it. He's not letting anyone leave the property until this situation is . . . well . . . dealt with."

Lulu closed her eyes as she felt her world slip further out of kilter. Two women were dead, and Hearst was treating it all as a casual inconvenience. But someone blackmails him—for an amount he could pay without so much as a pang—and the world stops, secret guards come out of the landscape, and every guest is suddenly a prisoner.

"What is wrong with you people?" she asked of no one in particular, and walked away, leaving the guard to disappear back into the underbrush.

"Told you that you couldn't leave," Veronica said smugly when Lulu returned with leaves in her hair and mud on her shoes.

"You failed to mention we were incarcerated at gunpoint," Lulu said, plopping down heavily in a gilded chair in front of a vanity overwrought with curlicues. She reached for her hairbrush and began viciously yanking through the tangled mess.

"Easy there, girl," Veronica said, taking the brush from her hands. She began to coax the snarls out, and Lulu gradually calmed down a bit. It was hard *not* to relax when someone was brushing your hair, she thought absently. But she was still furious.

"Can't you call someone?" she asked Veronica. "The studio? The police? It can't be legal to keep us here against our will."

"Well, there's legal, and then there's . . ."

"Hearst," Lulu finished dryly. "I understand. It's just wrong."

"Maybe so. But all we can do is play along until the puppet masters get bored and we can pick up our own strings."

"I guess I don't have any choice now," Lulu said, biting her lip.

"That's the spirit!" Veronica slapped Lulu on the back. "Get back on that horse and win, win, win! Speaking of which, I heard a rumor that Hearst is asking all of you to go horseback riding this afternoon. Then there's talk of a pool party tomorrow. Did you see that skimpy little number that I packed for you? When Hearst sees you, he's gonna need a surgeon. It's a heart attack in red and white polka dots."

"No, I mean I don't have any choice but to solve the murders. Everyone thinks one of 'em is already solved, and no one believes Dolores's death is actually a murder. Veronica, I didn't want to be involved." She rubbed her eyes wearily. "That was bad of me, but I just wanted to go home where it's nice and safe. But now I guess it's all going to have to be up to me."

"You know, my shrink would probably say you've got a very warped hero complex. You want to save the world all by yourself."

"I promise you, I decidedly do not," Lulu insisted. "But Freddie has his own problems, and no one else will help. Will *you*?"

"Abso-tutely not! Listen, young lady, I need you focused and calm, with your head squarely in the game. I guarantee you the rest will sort itself out. Speaking of which, I've got to get to work. I'm going to put itching powder in all the other girls' bathing costumes. Lord knows, every little advantage helps. Plus, how fun will that be to watch!"

Veronica sailed off, and as usual Lulu had no idea whether her sarcastic friend was serious or not.

"What should I do, Charlie?" she asked, lying down on her back on her rumpled bed. The little dog was on the floor now, and looked none the worse for his encounter with the tiger. He nosed diligently around the room he'd already searched half a hundred times since their arrival, just in case a rat had managed to sneak in or someone had dropped a piece of ham since his last visit.

"Exactly!" she cried, inspired by Charlie's determined snufflings. After a few minutes of staring at the meticulously paneled and painstakingly frescoed ceiling, her mind sorting through her various alternatives and willing painful thoughts of Freddie away, she rolled over with new resolve and determination. "I have to keep looking. Now, where to start?" With a heavy heart she knew she'd have to go back to the tiger's cage. She sighed. It was the last thing she wanted to do.

"It's the leash for you this time, my boy," she told Charlie, tossing aside the pillow and jumping to her feet. "You're so cocky from beating a tiger, next thing I know you'll be tangling with the lions or the elephant." She clipped on his braided leather leash and strolled toward the menagerie under pretext of taking Charlie to do his business.

*Sixteen*

**T**hough Lulu tried to avoid meeting anyone, Marion's dachshund Gandhi sniffed out Charlie, pulling Patricia in his wake.

"What's the haps, Lulu?" she asked, her slang at odds with her starched pink eyelet dress and Mary Janes. "Tell me, was that woman in the tiger cage murdered?"

Lulu was surprised by the young girl's seeming clairvoyance. "What on earth would make you ask that?"

"Sardines," Patricia said, tapping the side of her head. "Brain food. I eat 'em like candy. That, plus there are some books in the library here that would convince you to never leave your house again. Murders galore! It's practically become a hobby of mine. Combine that with the constant exposure to scandal one hears living with a major motion picture star and a newspaperman, and voilà, you have a kid always willing to believe the worst of mankind. So, why do you think it was a murder, and who do you think did it? Spill!"

Lulu considered the pros and cons—and the appropriateness—of sharing her thoughts with the disarmingly precocious girl. She remembered not long ago being the same age and having to truly be the woman of her house in so many ways, helping her mother care for her disabled father, navigating the slums of New York. Truth and respect were more important to her than food some days, when her sense of dignity was so diminished.

She kept more than a few details from the ten-year-old. She didn't breathe a word about Dolores spending the night with Sal. Still, she found herself confiding much more than she probably should. It was just so refreshing to talk with someone who believed her. Patricia listened earnestly, nodded, and said, "Do you think the same person killed both girls? It could be unrelated, you know."

"True, but in my admittedly limited experience, coincidences like that only happen in novels and screenplays."

"It does seem like there's been a lot more misfortune here than usual. I'm sorry no one is taking you seriously," Patricia said with the air of someone who truly understood.

"At least *you* do," Lulu answered. "Not that I should be encouraging your hobby, as you call it. You shouldn't be anywhere near a murder investigation."

"Do you have any new suspects?" the girl asked.

Lulu bit her lip, but finally told Patricia about the lipstick on Emerson's collar. She figured that a girl as cheeky as Patricia had to have some idea about marriage and infidelity, given her surroundings.

"Oh, *everyone* knows about John Emerson," Patricia said in a blasé tone. "He's notorious for, well, kissing people other than his wife."

Lulu had the dismal suspicion that this ten-year-old was more worldly than she was.

"So I definitely want to talk to Emerson," Lulu said.

"Is that really such a good idea, if you think he's the killer?"

"Well, I just want to get a feel for him. I won't ask him anything directly. I won't let him know I suspect him." It occurred to Lulu that she should have been reading murder mysteries all her life, instead of Shakespeare.

"I agree he looks suspicious in Juliette's death," Patricia said. "And from what you said about the conversation the maid heard, it could have been Emerson arguing with Juliette. But what connection does he have with Dolores? I saw her flirting with that French painter on the first night and then with that gangster later on. Sal Benedetto, isn't it?"

Lulu was positively stupefied. Where did this child get her information? It was absolutely dumbfounding.

"Oh, I keep my eyes and ears open," Patricia said. "Most of the time I sit in a corner with a book and people forget I'm there. They think I'm too young to understand half the things they talk about anyway, so they say the most outrageous things in front of me." She shrugged. "I noticed that you appear to be a touch friendly with Mr. Benedetto yourself."

"We have a history," Lulu admitted. "Ancient history."

"Sure," Patricia said with a knowing nod. "But to get back to the murder. Crime is far more interesting than romance, I think. And it's all passion, however you look at it. Where were you heading?"

"Back to the tiger cage. I thought perhaps I'd try one last sweep for evidence."

"Don't you think they would have collected it already?"

"Probably, but you never know. If they declare it an accident, not a crime, they might just clean up and notify next of kin."

"Well, Gandhi and I will tag along. I'm sure they've scrubbed up by now. Why on earth didn't you run and get me right after it happened? I would have loved to see."

Lulu shuddered. Patricia really was a macabre little thing. The scene had been washed as clean as an hour or two could make it. All evidence of the corpse had been removed, and the tigers evacuated to another holding area. The plants had been propped up and sprayed, water glistening like fresh dew on the leaves, and the dirt was freshly raked. It was as if the gory horror had never happened. It might just as well have been a movie set, wheeled in for the occasion and wheeled away again when the scene was concluded.

The cage might have been vigorously scrubbed until every trace of blood was gone, but Lulu's memory had by no means been washed so clean. The staring eyes, the metallic tang of blood on the air, the gamey smell of the tiger. Though she was grateful she didn't have to see it one more time, it didn't seem right, somehow, that the crime had been washed away so quickly and easily. It typified Hearst's desire to wipe away problems as quickly as possible. The facade of perfection had to be maintained, no matter what filth was swept under the carpet.

*I saw you*, Lulu told the departed Dolores silently. *I saw what happened to you and to Juliette. I will never forget, and I won't rest until I find out who did it and bring them to justice.*

Patricia took her hand, and the girls and the dogs walked slowly around the cage, looking, without much hope, for anything that might hold a clue. The cage and the area immediately behind and around it were sterile. "*Not* the way you're supposed to treat a crime scene," Lulu said heatedly.

It was only when they got a little farther away from the cage that they found something out of place. There, obscured from view by the shrubberies that divided it from the rest of the menagerie, was a tie crumpled up in the dirt.

"I recognize that tie!" both Lulu and Patricia said at the same time. They looked at each other, wide eyed.

"Emerson was wearing it on our first night here," Lulu said, struggling to recall an incident that had seemed trivial at the time. "Anita Loos made a comment about his tiepin—a golden lion head. I noticed it then." It was very distinctive, a broad silk tie with an undulating pattern in various shades of purple. "No one else could have a tie as peculiar as that. Is that where you saw it too?"

"I hate to be a bucket of cold water, but that tie was given as a gift to all the male guests at the Ranch last Christmas. Marion probably bought about twenty or thirty of them, at least."

First the scarf, now the tie? Lulu felt herself deflate. Every time she seemed to get close to a suspect, the clue got diluted. She had been so sure it was Emerson when she saw that tie. Coupled with the lipstick stain, his obvious interest in Juliette, and the overheard argument (which could easily have been his voice, though she had to admit it could be a lot of other men, too), it seemed like Emerson was pulling ahead in the race for prime suspect.

"So it could belong to anyone who stayed here at Christmas," Lulu said with a sigh.

"Emerson, Docky, the painter, a dozen actors . . . Plus, just because it's *near* the crime scene doesn't mean it was part of the crime. It's circumstantial at best."

Lulu was growing used to being astonished by this astonishing young girl.

"Emerson—or whoever—could have come here days ago, weeks ago. One of the dogs could have dragged it out here from someone's bedroom. There are a million possibilities."

Lulu closed her eyes. She'd felt so close. If she could somehow link Emerson to both murders, it might not be absolute proof, but it might be damning enough that someone in authority would listen to her speculations.

They walked back to the front of the cage, while the dogs snuffled at the farthest limits of their tethers, straining for freedom. Charlie managed to pull Lulu so off-balance that she gave him enough slack to slip through the bars again. He yipped excitedly.

"Looks like he wants to relive the scene of his past glory," Patricia said, after Lulu told her how boldly Charlie had stood up to the tiger.

"Come *on*, Charlie," Lulu said, tugging at the leash. "There's no point in hanging around here any longer." She reached through the bars to catch him under the armpits, when her eye caught something shiny.

It was barely visible, lodged in a crevice between concrete slabs at the very edge of the tiger cage. Lulu felt her stomach tighten and her heart flutter. She knew what it was, and didn't even care when she broke a fingernail prying it out. With a grin of triumph, she held the tiny golden lion-head tiepin in the air.

"We've got you, John Emerson!"

Much to Patricia's vociferously expressed disappointment, Lulu steadfastly refused to let the child join her when she sought out John Emerson later that afternoon. It was the first time Patricia legitimately sounded her age instead of like a sophisticated, jaded teenager. She whined exactly like the ten-year-old she was.

"If he is a killer, you can't be anywhere near him," Lulu said for at least the tenth time.

Patricia didn't seem to see the logic. "I've read heaps more mysteries than you. I might be able to ferret out his secrets with my evil literary genius. Besides, like I told you, no one suspects a kid." Her eyes glowed with excitement. "Why, the best thing to do would be to let me go after him myself." She widened her eyes, looking angelic. "My tender innocence will be his downfall."

"Nothing doing. Now, skedaddle," Lulu said, and sent her away to the safety of her apparently exciting books.

Patricia did get her thinking that perhaps it wasn't the best idea to be alone with Emerson, even if she wasn't going to talk directly about the murder. She wished she could ask Freddie to accompany her, but he'd made it rather clear he was occupied with his own—or rather Hearst's—concerns. Besides, she was still angry with him. She'd forgive him, eventually, once he apologized, but it was up to him to come groveling back to her.

Who, then? Sal was, in some ways, a natural choice. Lulu had no idea what Sal had actually felt for Dolores, whether she'd been a pleasant diversion or a burgeoning true love, but it was clear that Sal was enraged that his girl had been killed.

But even though Lulu found that perhaps she didn't hate Sal quite as much now as she thought she should, she knew that consorting with him would be unwise. At the very least, Freddie would be provoked.

She had just about resigned herself to approaching Emerson without backup. One of the housemaids had told her that he was alone in the library, and she did her best to calm herself as she walked there. *This is stupid*, she thought. *I can't ask him about the murder and let him know I'm onto him. If I just make casual conversation, do I really think he's going to incriminate himself out of the blue?*

Self-doubt made her stop in the middle of the tiled corridor.

"Lost?" a gentle voice drawled behind her.

She whirled and smiled with unmitigated relief when she saw Paul Raleigh. Of course! Paul might not be physically imposing, but he was smart and understanding and, most importantly, he would certainly believe her when she told him her suspicions. It occurred to her that maybe as a writer used to parsing human motivations, he could provide some insight. With a relieved smile, she took his arm.

"I need to tell you something," she said softly. "Where can we go to talk? Alone."

A veil of intrigue crept into his dark eyes as he whispered, "My room is just upstairs." If he'd been any other man Lulu might have felt uncomfortable about that proposition. She'd have suspected his motives and been worried what Freddie— or anyone else, for that matter—might think if they found her in a man's bedroom. But instinctively she knew that for the gentlemanly Southern writer, the bedroom was simply a private place to talk—not a room with a bed.

"Okay," Lulu said, and took his arm. By the time they got to his door, Paul seemed to be breathing a little heavily. Of course, she thought, a writer has to sit at his typewriter endlessly. He must not get much chance to exercise.

Inside, she perched on a chair upholstered in ivory and gold brocade and said bluntly, "I think I know who killed Juliette and Dolores."

Paul had just settled down on the edge of his bed and was smoothing the coverlet, but when she spoke, his head snapped up. The color seemed to drain visibly from his face.

"Oh, Paul! I'm so sorry! I didn't mean to shock you!" *I*

*should have introduced the subject more gently,* Lulu thought with chagrin. *He's a sensitive artist. Of course he'll be more affected than normal people.*

Paul crossed to the door purposefully, swaying slightly as he walked, and threw the bolt.

"But I'm not completely sure," Lulu demurred, grateful that he'd thoughtfully locked the world out for their meeting. "I believe there's some evidence that John Emerson might have killed both of the girls."

Paul stood there staring at her breathlessly, then very slowly, his eyes softening, shook his head and muttered, "Emerson? But . . . I can't believe it."

"I might be wrong, and I don't want anyone else to know until I'm completely sure. Promise you won't tell?"

Paul nodded earnestly.

"I can see you're upset. It's a serious accusation, I know. Are the two of you friends?"

He found his voice at last. "Not particularly. I don't know him very well, though we've crossed paths. This is the first I've spent any real time with him. Apparently he's here often, but this is my first visit to the Ranch." He crossed back to the bed and sat down heavily. "He just doesn't seem like a murderer."

"No," Lulu admitted, "he doesn't. But probably most murderers don't. From what I've gathered, most victims trust their killers, at least at first. If killers looked crazy and dangerous, no one would get near them. The killer must be a guest, so he can pass as a sane man."

"Or woman," Paul added.

She couldn't help but smile at him. "Of course."

"What kind of evidence do you have?" he asked.

She told him about the lipstick, the overheard argument, and the lion tiepin.

"Well, it all seems very damning," Paul said. "But I would hate to accuse a possibly innocent man based on what might also be completely circumstantial evidence. So you really do believe the man they arrested for Juliette's death is innocent?"

"Oh yes!" He looked skeptical, and Lulu wished she were free to share her reasons. Without revealing Honey's secret, she simply sounded delusional. "I'm asking you to trust me. I have my reasons, and, well . . . It isn't my secret to tell."

He turned away from her for a moment, and in the instant he did so, she saw something resembling anxiety on his face. She bit her lip and prayed that there was someone on the property other than a child who empathized with her, and believed her.

When he turned back, his face was relaxed and composed. "You were about to speak with Emerson, I take it?" She nodded. "I think you and I should talk about this a little more before we do." He brightened with a sudden inspiration. "I always think better with coffee. Let me go down to the kitchen and get some, and I'll be right back." He left her with a smile.

Lulu was glad she'd decided to confide in Paul. He had no obvious agenda, and treated her with respect. He neither overtly wanted her physically nor demanded anything of her emotionally. He was like a port in a storm, and though he might not be a man of action, she had the unshakable feeling that if she stuck with him, together they would arrive at the truth eventually.

She swiveled around to face the little writing desk dominated by a typewriter and strewn with papers. The typewriter bore a WR stamp. It was one of Hearst's new ones with his special typeface. Lulu absently scanned the pages in a jumbled heap next to the typewriter. It was written in manuscript form, not divided into character lines like a screenplay. Still, it might have something to do with the script he and Anita (and Emerson) would craft for the winning actress. Maybe it was an early treatment of the plot.

"I really shouldn't," she whispered to herself, and as if that admission of her fault somehow made it more acceptable, she immediately began to read the first page.

"Oh!" she cried. It was a description of a woman, a jumbled, rambling sketch of character and appearance.

*Hair so pale, yet colored with an inner incandescence so that it becomes light itself, putting golden blondes to shame with its silvery shine...*

Her hand reached to touch her own hair. There were not many girls with her color hair, though the bottle had given some the platinum shade she'd had from birth. Could he be writing about her?

*A smile wise and mocking, eyes that dance. But the dance is different each time I see them. At one moment they seem to dance a merry jig, intoxicated on life. At others, they seem to sway solemnly to a funeral dirge, looking backward or inward at some secret sorrow. She is deep, and the deepest waters are dangerous.*

No, Lulu decided. She must be mistaken. The idea that she may have inspired this beautiful artist to create a character was too much for her to take in. Paul couldn't possibly have been writing about her. She placed the sheet on the pile and pushed it away across the desk, a little annoyed at herself for fantasizing. As she did so, the pages pushed a crystal paperweight over the edge and into the rosewood trash can. Luckily it wasn't broken, because it had been cushioned by torn scraps of paper.

She retrieved it, and as she was shaking off a piece of paper trapped in her fingers, a word caught her eye. *Blonde.* Intrigued, she fished out the scrap.

She squinted at the type on the scrap. It was just a fragment, really, and the only words were . . . *up on the blonde who* . . . That by itself was gibberish, but—she couldn't help herself, though her cheeks pinkened in shame—she took out another, a little larger, and read: *The silk was smooth in my hands, but it would not feel so soft when it was around* . . .

For a moment the world seemed to stop, and everything, including her own heart, was still. Then it came back in a rush, her heart pounding wildly, her ears filled with sound like a harsh gale wind. She dumped the trash onto the ground and fell to her knees, pawing through the scraps. . . . *she made a sound like a kitten, a helpless sound . . . feet kicked as if she were walking on air . . . looked at her dead body and felt . . . nobody missed that trashy blonde actress . . .*

It was a confession. A written confession.

Paul Raleigh had killed Juliette.

# Seventeen

**L**ulu stumbled to her feet, her legs numb from kneeling so long—and from shock. Seconds that felt like hours crept by, frozen in time. Despite the evidence on the typed scraps of paper that were slipping through her fingers, she couldn't believe it. Not Paul. Never Paul.

He was gentle, an artist of astounding sensitivity who delved into the human psyche. He wrote works of truly astonishing depth and beauty. She admired him. She *trusted* him.

And yet these torn bits of paper, taken together, seemed to offer inarguable proof of his guilt. The pieces she'd read were certainly an admission that he'd killed Juliette. From what the studio psychologist had told her during that movie, killers like to revel in their crimes afterward. Paul must have relished writing down exactly what he'd done . . . and then thought to destroy that evidence.

Only, he hadn't really destroyed it. That was the baffling part. He could have easily burned the writing instead of just tearing it up. It made no sense: a man as brilliant as Paul, so meticulous with words, so precise and thorough in his vicious executions, but so sloppy and slapdash in covering his tracks? Perhaps, awash with guilt, he yearned to be caught. But why?

She could see it as clearly as if it were projected on a movie screen. Paul twisting the silk scarf tight around Juliette's neck while she gasped and struggled. Paul shoving a bound and gagged Dolores into the tiger cage, a look of maniacal glee on his heretofore gentle face. She could picture those hands, the smooth, soft hands of a writer, with their smudge of ink from the typewriter ribbon, reaching slowly for her own throat . . . squeezing. . . . The room seemed to tilt. And then her sense of survival set in. The only thing she had to do was get these scraps of paper with their damning confession to Freddie. He would know what to do.

No, she amended. The most important thing was to get out of the murderer's bedroom.

But somehow her legs seemed to have forgotten how to move. She remained paralyzed, clutching the desk with white-knuckled fingers.

Finally, her legs found their power and she ran to the door, shoving the scraps into her pocket as she went. She jerked the door open and hurled herself through . . . and crashed head-long into Paul Raleigh. Scalding coffee flew over her blouse, and she screamed, for the pain and because Paul instantly dropped the porcelain cups and took her by the shoulders, shoving her back inside.

The streetwise New York slum kid in her wanted to fight. But instinct told her to try talking her way out of this first. He didn't know she knew.

"Lulu, are you badly hurt?" Paul asked anxiously. He whipped a handkerchief from his pocket, totally disarming her by handing it over. Any other man, she thought dimly, would have snatched the opportunity to dab at her chest. She was baffled. This was the Paul she had gotten to know and admired so much. Polite. Concerned and well mannered. Caring. Lulu knew she had to play this scene with great care. She didn't want Paul to be a killer. But the evidence . . .

"I'm such a clumsy idiot," he said, blushing deep red. "And Mrs. Mortimer made your coffee special when I told her who it was for. Said she was adding a spice you'd particularly enjoy. Oh, can you ever forgive me? Shall I call a maid to help you, or to bring you a new shirt?" He reached for the buzzer on the wall that would summon one of the staff to his room.

Just then Paul's eyes wandered to the overturned waste-basket, where they lingered for a moment before swiveling to meet hers.

"So you've found me out," he said carefully.

She tried to steel herself. He wouldn't hurt her. She was a moderately famous actress in the most expensive mansion on the West Coast. Most likely, one of the Ranch staff had heard her scream and was already on the way to offer assistance. If not, another scream would surely bring help. Between guests and staff, there were hundreds of people on the property.

But that hadn't stopped him from killing two other girls.

"I read your confession," she said as calmly as she could. Only her acting coach's rigorous teaching allowed her to keep her voice steady. "You killed Juliette. You strangled her, and then you couldn't help yourself: You had to relive it by writing about it. And Dolores—did you drug her before you threw her in the tiger cage? Did you write about her, too?"

She gingerly stood up and pulled the incriminating scraps of paper out of her pocket. "These tell me everything I need to know about you."

She thought he would attack her, or perhaps run away. At the very least, he would deny it.

"You must be so disappointed in me," he said in his gentle voice. Then he hung his head and . . . Were those tears? This was not how Lulu imagined the scene playing out.

"Why did you kill them?" she pressed. It didn't matter, but Lulu's insatiable curiosity got the best of her. Had Juliette or Dolores done something to him?

And then the denial came. "I didn't kill them."

Strangely, her first impulse was to believe him. She *wanted* to believe him. Confusion began to wash over her, but she stood her ground and gestured with as much certainty as she could muster to the typed scraps. "These say differently."

Paul fell to his knees before her so fast she half expected a proposal. Instead he took out a briefcase and removed a large brown envelope. She could see others stacked in the case. He shut and locked it.

"I never planned to show this to anyone, but too much has happened now. It's all gotten out of control." He thrust the envelope into her hands. "Read this. I think you'll understand."

With shaky hands she unwound the coarse twine that held the flap closed and pulled out a sheaf of pages. There were two packets, each bound with a paper clip. She began to read the first one and became overwhelmed with a growing sense of nausea and horror.

It was more terrible than she'd imagined. The fragments had been bad enough, letting her fill in the gaps with her own already active imagination. But this . . .

In the space of four or five pages was every excruciating detail of Juliette's death. The actress wasn't named, but from the description, it was clearly Juliette. He described the brassy tint of her hair, the way her dark roots were just barely showing. He wrote of the way her skin was so heavily coated in pancake makeup that her complexion looked corpselike even while she was still alive. He even described her voice with its patina of culture.

It was unbearable. Maintaining a veneer of calm, Lulu continued to read and tried very hard to not scream and run. The pages went on to describe the way he crept up silently behind his victim and paused, listening to the soft susurrus of her breathing, knowing those hushed sounds represented her final moments, the very last air her body would ever have, or need. How the whisper of the silk as he uncoiled it was almost like a breath itself . . . the feel of her body jerking spasmodically against his as she struggled . . . Paul was still kneeling at her side like a penitent, looking up at her with his head slightly bowed, as if waiting for absolution.

"I just don't want you to judge me. You, of all people. You see, when I found out about the murders, I felt like I had to take the opportunity to explore them. As a writer, you understand." His voice was pained, ragged. "Maybe it sounds perverse, but no matter how painful the experience was to me personally, I needed to. Perhaps it was a mistake, but you're an artist too! You have to understand! As wrenching as it was, I put myself into the mind of a killer. I studied the scene, imagined how the murderer must have felt at every moment. I stared at poor Juliette's body, and as if in a trance, found myself describing every moment of her exquisite suffering, of the killer's twisted pleasure. I sat at that desk and typed detailed descriptions of the murders exactly as if I were the one who committed them. I typed them over and over, adding details each time until I got it perfect."

He grabbed Lulu's hand, and intuitively, she didn't pull away. *Never do anything to upset a crazy person or be prepared to pay the consequences!* her mother had told her many times over.

Paul looked into her eyes, and in one split second, he seemed to harden a bit. "Then again, perhaps you can't understand. I have to feel and penetrate everything, simply *everything* about human nature if I'm to be a great writer. My art is my life. Please. Don't think me a monster. I'm just a writer. That's all. I didn't kill anyone."

He bent his head over her hand, and she felt the dampness of his tears.

"I'm sorry," Lulu whispered soothingly. "I'm so sorry. I was wrong to suspect you." Still, she shuddered, not absolutely certain he was telling the truth but knowing how important it was to her safety that she defuse the situation. It was hard to imagine that anyone could write with such sickening detail without some direct experience. "I admire your dedication. You are truly a great artist."

He looked up at her like a hopeful puppy, his eyes shining. "Then you forgive me?" he asked.

"Of course," Lulu assured him.

"And you won't tell anyone?"

She hesitated just a second. *I have to tell Freddie,* she thought. But she found herself comforting him instead. "No, I won't tell anyone. Your secret is safe with me."

Paul stared up at her, a strange, satisfied look in his reddened eyes. He delicately kissed her hand and rose to his feet. "Well, then," he said with a smile. "That's settled." He began picking up the shards of coffee cup. "Let me clean up this unfortunate mess, and then we can focus on what's really important: proving that John Emerson is the killer."

*Eighteen*

Lulu went back to her room to shower and change her clothes. She left the coffee-soaked garments in the hamper, where the maid Ginnie would have them clean by the next morning. Once she was refreshed and in a crisp cream-colored dress, she planned to find Freddie and mend whatever fences needed repair, then explain everything that had happened and try to put all of the clues together into absolute proof. Veronica burst in with her usual bustle and said, "That dress is gorgeous to the Nth degree, but it won't cut it for the saddle—outside of a photo shoot, of course. And from what I hear of Hearst, he takes his horseback excursions very seriously." She began to dig through Lulu's wardrobe. "I'm sure we packed a riding habit in here somewhere. Aha!"

Lulu rolled her eyes, wondering why she had ever let

Veronica and Lolly come up with her utterly fabricated history as a serious equestrian for the press. Even with the countless hours of studio-paid-for lessons, she knew this lie would catch up to her one day, and it seemed that day had arrived. Veronica pulled out a very chic moleskin ensemble. (Lulu had fiercely rejected it until Veronica explained that is was just a soft fabric and not actually made from the pelts of a thousand moles.) The jacket was tailored within an inch of its life, and the jodhpurs ballooned alarmingly before tapering to skintight below her knees. Her riding boots were black leather, soft as butter.

"But I don't feel like riding," Lulu protested.

"*Nobody* here feels like riding. But Hearst wants to ride, and so we all must. Now, scoot and get into these clothes. The posse leaves in fifteen minutes."

It took Lulu nearly that long to squeeze into her outfit, and she needed Veronica's help to put on her boots. But once she examined herself in the mirror, she was decidedly pleased with the results. She looked like an action heroine, ready for any kind of adventure. It boosted her confidence immensely.

Lulu felt oddly buoyant as she left the guesthouse to rendezvous at the stables. The golden California sun warmed her skin as the light played across the fountains and ponds. The air was perfumed with blooming star jasmine and hyacinth. She was intoxicated by the beauty, and her sense of peril melted, giving way to a sense of peaceful euphoria. She could hear people chattering just ahead, heard the whinny and stamp of a virtual cavalry of horses.

She strode past Joan Crawford barking orders at a stable boy and Ginger Rogers gracefully kicking up to her seat on the spotted Appaloosa she was assigned and plunged into the melee of horses and riders, where she was introduced to her mount.

"Have you ever ridden?" the groom asked her as he led up a dark bay horse. His coat was such a deep brown it was almost the same color as the black on his mane and tail. He was as glossy as if he'd been rubbed down with Vaseline (which she knew they did to star horses on film), and he tossed his head like he was ready for his close-up.

Lulu nodded, and the groom looked relieved. "Good! You're late, and all the swaybacked old nags are taken. This one's got some mettle, and not everyone can handle him."

She looked into the horse's dark eye. "I think I'll be fine."

She patted the big bay along the jaw and breathed into his velvety nostrils in the way she'd been taught horses say hello. "How are ya, big boy?" she asked in a low, soothing voice. She let her hand trail down his neck and back to his shoulder, to that sensitive spot where mothers nibble their foals, and dug her knuckles in gently. The horse nickered, and the groom laughed.

"You're all right, lady," he said, and gave her a leg up. She needed it. This was the tallest horse she'd ever ridden.

She turned in her saddle, trying to spot if Paul had joined the group. All of the remaining actresses were there (although some plainly wished they weren't), as were most of the guests. She didn't see Paul, though. He'd said he wanted to meet with her later to review the clues, and she assumed he'd join the ride just to do so. Maybe he'd assumed she'd find a way to get out of it and was waiting for her back inside. She muttered a curse under her breath and wondered if it was too late to slip away from what felt like a truly trivial activity that would waste precious sleuthing time. But no, there was Hearst, mounted on a rangy-looking sorrel and wearing full Western kit. Marion, who was usually loyally at his side, was nowhere to be found.

Anita Loos, diminutive and smart-looking, sidled up to her, riding a dainty, spirited gray that seemed chosen to match her dove-and-pearl-colored habit. "Who are you looking for?" she asked.

"Marion. Doesn't she ride?"

"Oh, Marion does absolutely *everything*," Anita said with heavy insinuation. "It's what endeared her to Hearst in the first place. But she's *kept* him by not doing absolutely everything all of the time."

"I see," Lulu answered, though she didn't quite see. "And what about Mr. Loos—I mean Mr. Emerson!" Her hand flew to her mouth as if she could cram the faux pas back in.

"Don't worry. You're certainly not the first to make that slip. As long as he doesn't hear it, his ego will survive. Funny, that ego of his. It pretends to be such a delicate little worm of a thing, bruised by the world, but in reality it is a small and deadly serpent, quite capable of looking after itself."

Lulu peered intently into Anita's face. There was something bitter there, she decided, some dark knowledge. Did she suspect that her husband was a murderer? Worse, was it possible that she *knew*? Lulu decided to corner her on this ride—as well as you could corner anyone in an open mountain range—and probe.

"You look pretty comfortable on a horse," Lulu said conversationally. "Do you ride often?"

"Only when I'm here, these days. I rode more when I was younger."

"I just learned a year ago, and I love it."

"You might change your mind after this jaunt," Anita said, leaning sideways over her horse and talking in a low voice. "Hearst's rides are beyond tedious. He won't go past a slow trot, but he'll ride for hours, and keeps everyone lined up like a chain gang."

"No open fields? No galloping?" Lulu asked, surprised. "What's the point of riding if you and the horse can't let loose?"

Anita seemed to wholeheartedly agree, and her eyes danced with mischief. "I know these mountains pretty well. What do you say we *get lost* after a mile or so? There's a lovely open dale just off the trail where we can gallop."

Lulu smiled. "Perfect," she said, not just for the fun or riding, but because it had proved so ridiculously easy to get Anita alone. "But won't we get in trouble with Hearst?"

Anita raised one sculpted black eyebrow. "Trouble? I could use a little trouble. Why should everyone else have all the fun? Besides, Hearst is a big baby. If he kicks up a fuss about anything, just stick his pacifier in his mouth and he'll stop bawling."

"And what's his pacifier?"

Anita's other eyebrow joined the first. "Why, Marion, of course."

Lulu and Anita maneuvered to the back of the long caravan, squinting their eyes against everyone else's dust until they had an opportune moment to slip away. For a while they let the horses pick their careful and silent way, wary of pursuit. But when no one called after them, they trotted to Anita's field and with a mutual nod dug in their knees and urged their horses forward.

Lulu won the impromptu race easily, but Anita, flushed and laughing, didn't seem to care. She pulled off her little cap and ran her fingers through her dark hair, letting it cascade over her shoulders. It occurred to Lulu that the other actresses would give their eyeteeth to have just a few meaningful moments alone with one of the foremost writers in the country—not to mention one of the people who was choosing an actress for the plum role she'd be writing.

But all of Lulu's focus was on the murders, and she felt no interest in charming Anita. All she wanted was information about her prime suspect, Emerson. She brought the topic back around to him as they settled their horses into an easy walk, hoping she sounded natural.

"So you never said. Does your husband like to ride? I didn't see him in the group."

Anita turned a sharp eye on Lulu. "Do you have designs on him?" she asked point-blank.

Lulu was startled, and her confusion showed. "No . . . I . . . Gosh no!"

Anita's flashing eyes softened just a bit. "Well, then, does he have designs on you?"

"I certainly hope not!" she said with feeling. If Emerson was indeed the murderer, the last thing she wanted was to be the subject of his creepy attention.

Anita shrugged and stroked her horse's mane absently. "A girl like you would be a welcome change, actually," she said, avoiding Lulu's eye, staring across the wildflower-strewn field as a brush rabbit bounded in the distance.

*Pay dirt*, Lulu thought, and forced herself not to sound anxious as she asked softly, "May I ask why you would say such a thing?" She didn't know why Anita seemed to be opening up to her, a girl much her junior whom she hardly knew. Maybe she'd simply reached her limit with secrets and had to be honest or burst.

"Most of his affairs are with horrible ambitious, money-grubbing little tramps with a few obvious assets and nothing at all in their brains. At least *you* I can talk to." There was profound sadness and bitter surrender wrapped around each of Anita's words.

"You mean you actually have to talk to his . . . his . . ."

"Sidepieces?" She laughed ruefully. "Of course, my dear. He picks them from our social circle. Well, the bottom tier of our circle, anyway. Or would that be a pyramid? I've had half of them to dinner, and I meet the rest at my friends' parties. It would be better if he settled down with a nice girl like you. With you, at least, I'd probably know what time he'd be home. You'd likely be considerate about that. It's amazing what little thought mistresses give to wives. Not that most last long enough to count as mistresses. Marion at least shows that being a mistress can be a noble profession. John's affairs aren't grand love stories. They're really just sad little flings."

Emerson, Lulu thought, was not a good man. But just because he ran around on his wife didn't mean that he was a murderer. He had been flirting with Juliette, though, enough to have her lipstick on his collar. And there was the tiepin. . . .

"How do the flings end?" Lulu asked gingerly.

Anita waved her hand. "Oh, they just peter out. John's attention span is pitifully short."

"Anita, why are you telling me all this?"

Anita looked at her evenly. "Because you already knew. Or if you didn't, you would soon. People talk, or haven't you noticed? Better to pretend it's all aboveboard and that I don't mind one single bit. Why, the word on the street is that I actually give him a day off from his wedding vows once a week. Ain't I just a dandy wife? Never bitter. So forgiving. Faithful until the very end."

"But don't you hate those other girls?" Lulu asked. Maybe, despite her small stature, Anita *had* managed to kill Juliette. But she wouldn't have had anything against Dolores, would she?

Anita thought a moment. "I suppose I did at first. But I've matured. After all, I can't blame them. John is an exciting man. Very handsome, of course. Arrogant in the most alluring way possible, and girls eat that up, you know. I can see how they all get swept away—at first. Then his little problems emerge, and he doesn't seem half so fascinating."

Lulu was on point like a setter. "Problems?"

"He's—well, each doctor we go to has a different name for it. Stress, they say when they want to be kind. But people under stress don't hear voices, do they? Or have manic fits of rage? When that nonsense starts up, the girls go running, and it's home to wifey he flies. Come on, enough of this folderol. Our horses have rested. I want to race again!" She urged her swift little horse forward and Lulu's big stallion had to struggle to catch up with her.

Lulu had a lot to think about as she galloped. Was Anita implying her husband was a schizophrenic? How ghastly. He certainly didn't look it, though she didn't really know what a schizophrenic looked like. She always imagined they wore their illness on their faces, like Lon Chaney in *The Phantom of the Opera*. Grotesque and deranged. But from what little Anita said, his fits must come and go. Most of the time, John Emerson was a suave seducer, apparently in his right mind. Every now and again, though, he heard voices. Lulu shuddered, and her horse, feeling her odd movement, checked his headlong rush. What did the voices tell him to do? Kill young women?

Her horse pranced to a stop beside Anita on the far side of the field.

"Anita," she asked after another moment's consideration. "Did you know that your husband and Juliette were . . . flirting before she was killed?"

Anita just looked off toward the distant ocean. "Oh yes. He's been after her for quite some time. She didn't say yes as fast as most. Come to think of it, I have no idea if she *ever* said yes."

"How did you know about the two of them?"

She laughed, and to Lulu it sounded forced. "John doesn't keep many secrets from me. Not that he's free with the details, but he's far from discreet. A few days before Juliette died I found a rough draft of a letter he was apparently sending her. Ugh, really nauseating stuff! Vowed he'd leave me, pledged his undying love—that kind of hooey."

"He must have been distraught when she was murdered," Lulu said.

"No, not particularly," Anita said, turning and looking Lulu dead in the eye. "If anything, he seemed relieved."

*Nineteen*

**Mr. Hearst** kept Freddie and Waters laboring fruitlessly in his office until midafternoon. With no new clues and no organic opening to broach the subject of Marion as suspect, the men found themselves poring over the employment records of the current staff, but nothing of note seemed to be pointing in any particular direction. Hearst himself was in and out of the office, disappearing for a while, then quizzing them manically whenever he checked in, never satisfied with any of their theories.

"That's enough for now," he finally said, stacking paperwork and photos of the blackmail letters in a haphazard pile on his already chaotic desk. He waved a dismissal at Freddie's boss. "Mr. Waters, I'd like you to type out a briefing of your progress so far and forward it to the police both here and in Los Angeles."

Freddie assumed he would be joining his boss, but Hearst met his eye and gave him a subtle hand gesture ordering him to stay behind, a gesture that did not go unnoticed by the increasingly paranoid Mr. Waters. Puzzled, Freddie complied.

Hearst settled back into his chair with an audible *oof*. He shrugged his hefty shoulders. "I've reached the grunting age," he confessed. "Can't stand or sit without a groan."

"Remember thou art mortal," Freddie said softly.

Hearst regarded him with his sharp little eyes. "A quote?" He seemed annoyed to not immediately recognize the source.

"Shakespeare, via Rome. When the ancient Romans gave someone a triumph—that's a sort of huge religious parade to honor a military commander who just won a great victory . . ."

"I know what a triumph is, boy." The eagle eyes narrowed and turned peevish. "I've staged three of 'em in movies."

Freddie inclined his head respectfully and went on. "The general became like a god for one day. All of Rome worshipped him, and he was driven through the streets on a chariot, with a man standing behind him holding a crown of laurel leaves above his head. The general wore a purple toga—he was divine. But all through the parade that man standing behind him murmured over and over into his ear, '*memento mori*'—remember that you must die."

Hearst regarded Freddie for a long moment. "You're more educated, and far more depressing, than I'd given you credit for. You do know that I know all about you, young Frederick van der Waals."

Freddie stood stock-still, eye contact never wavering, maintaining a totally false air of ease. He couldn't predict how this conversation would go. Hearst and Freddie's father, Jacob van der Waals, were not competitors, but he knew that they circled each other in the shark-infested social waters of the obscenely rich. His father was nothing but a common criminal, as far as Freddie was concerned, though he had put presidents in place, funded faraway wars that he profited from, and taken down more than his fair share of high-ranking judges and politicians who crossed him in the process. Who knew how much Hearst knew and what he planned to do with the information.

"I have no interest in playing games. My business is information. Spreading it to the world via my newspapers and movies, most would think. But also collecting it for my own personal use." He raised an eyebrow at Freddie. "I collect more than art. I've found the most important thing to remember when gathering information is to use a variety of sources. Do you think you and Mr. Waters are the only private investigators I have in my employ? The only ones at the Ranch at this moment? No. You're just the visible ones. And I've been made aware that for some very personal reason, you have disavowed your father and intend to make your own way. Why, is none of my business, but between you and me, I never could stand the fellow. I always found him a bit oily for my tastes, and I just want to tell you that I deeply respect your actions."

Freddie, not wanting to give any of his cards away in case Hearst was playing him, simply nodded politely and said, "Thank you, sir."

"I'm not finished," Hearst went on. "You have a theory

about the blackmailer that you've been keeping to yourself. I can tell by the way you avoid looking at me when we're talking about the various scenarios. I have no time or interest in withholding. Especially when it's someone I already suspect."

Freddie thought long and hard. He did not want to make an enemy of Hearst. However, blatantly lying to the great newspaperman wasn't an option.

"Sir, if you already know . . ."

"I want to hear it from your lips."

"Well, there is a suspect I've been considering," Freddie began.

"For the murder that's been solved, and the accidental death?" Hearst asked wryly. "Yes, I'm aware that you think the issues are connected."

"You've been crystal clear that *you* don't believe that they are, sir. But what you are really saying is that you don't want a thorough investigation. And I want to know why. At the very least, you don't want Waters and me to be the ones doing it. Maybe your *sub rosa* team . . ."

"Enough Latin," Hearst snapped. "Go on."

"I just began to wonder, why wouldn't you want us to find out the truth? I know you don't want scandal, but this would be a mere three-day wonder, soon forgotten. It's not as if *you* killed the girls. But if you know—or suspect—who did, and you want to protect them . . ."

"Say it," Hearst insisted, his voice tight, though strangely he didn't seem either angry or upset. More resigned, Freddie sensed. "Say the name."

Knowing it could mean the end of his budding career—or worse, given the scope of Hearst's influence and power—Freddie gulped, looked straight at his employer, and spoke. "Miss Davies. She has the access, and, forgive me, sir, but I've observed that she seems to have a drinking problem. She's impulsive, unpredictable, and we both know that all bets are off when an alcoholic is off to the races. I was speaking with her recently, and I don't know if you're aware, but she hated Juliette with a passion. In fact, she seemed to harbor an ugly grudge against all of the young actresses here. She could easily be the blackmailer. She's definitely the most likely candidate by miles, just because of her ability to move about any part of the Ranch without anyone giving it a thought. But more than that, I believe it would be ill advised not to consider her as one of the murder suspects."

Freddie felt beads of nervous sweat on his upper lip and was astonished that Hearst had let him go on so long without interruption, but Hearst responded without dropping a beat.

"It isn't her," he said briefly, calmly.

"But, sir, do you know for a fact? I can't account for all her movements at the crucial time, but you could. Can you just tell me . . . ?"

Hearst shook his head. "No. You simply have to take my word for it. Whether I have proof or not doesn't matter. She is not blackmailing me, and she would never, ever commit such a ghastly crime as murder. She has her moral failings, but they are not so drastic as that." He spoke with the firm, faithful voice of the true believer. "I *know* Marion is innocent."

"But if you have proof . . ."

"Proof is not necessary. I know." There was an almost religious fervor in Hearst's eyes, and all at once Freddie felt deeply ashamed. Not just because he had accused Marion of a crime. No, his shame was much deeper and more personal.

*With so many indisputable reasons not to trust her, Hearst trusts Marion implicitly. Evidence be damned. He loves her, and knows her heart, and believes with every fiber of his being that she is not capable of that enormity. He's not just covering for her. He's sure.*

Freddie's mind drifted back to his own situation and the uncomfortable feeling that his problems with Lulu were of his own making. *Why can't I be just as sure about Lulu?* he asked himself.

Hearst interrupted his musings. "There, that's settled now, isn't it?"

It had to be, Freddie realized.

"Yes, sir," Freddie said.

To his surprise, Hearst then said, "That accounts for the something on your mind, son. Now, what about the thing that's lying so heavily on your heart?"

It was astounding how Hearst could transform from an overwhelming authority figure into a man who was almost avuncular. Remarkably, Hearst seemed to be taking a friendly interest in his underling. The cynic in Freddie thought this was a masterwork of manipulation, designed to get as much information about—and thus power over—every person in his sphere. On the other hand, it might be genuine, and the reason a woman like Marion loved him.

Still, Freddie was reluctant to share.

"It's that platinum-blonde peach, isn't it? It's obvious that you and Miss Kelly are . . . well . . . close. She's a lovely girl, but trouble seems to follow her like a stray cat once you've given it cream. I'd be very careful with her. Believe me, no one can tell me anything about falling in love with an actress. Fraught with peril, but in good times the rewards are sweeter than any material success I have ever known. So what is it? One of you playing around?"

Freddie stiffened. "Just a misunderstanding, sir."

"Let me tell you, son, you have to decide early on whether there will be—'misunderstandings,' as you call them—or whether you are simply willing to love her and all the nonsense that trails behind her. Will you walk away entirely? Or are you prepared to accept the woman you love, not the starlet but the woman, and put her ahead of all of your silly selfishness?"

"I don't quite follow you," Freddie admitted.

"Look at me, and then look at Marion. Particularly look at her a few years ago. I'm sure you've heard the gossip. Charlie Chaplin was just the beginning. The truth is, a girl like her is going to be constantly surrounded by temptation. Maybe she'll stray, maybe not. That Miss Kelly seems to have a strong will, and a decidedly independent point of view. But she's an actress by trade, a projection of the public's fantasy: sometimes luminous and sublime, sometimes sordid and messy. If she's doing her job well, half of the world is going to believe she's stepping out on you, because no one wants to believe that a mere mortal could actually ensnare a goddess. Movie stars are gods and goddesses to their fans. Earthly rules don't apply. So you have to decide early on whether you can live with that."

Hearst looked him in the eye. "Decide now whether you do or do not trust her, and once you decide, stand firm, no matter what evidence appears to the contrary. Love her, and trust her . . . or walk away today."

Hearst broke away abruptly and shuffled through his papers. "I'm heading out on the horseback riding expedition. Why don't you take a break from the investigation and find her? Maybe she'd rather not ride today. Give you a chance to talk a spell." His voice was suddenly folksy, the kind that would appeal to middle-American masses. Freddie wondered which part of the great man was an act. Or was it all an act? Or all real?

With a lot on his mind, he took Hearst's advice and went in search of Lulu. Most people seemed to be reporting as ordered to the stables for their trek across Hearst's mountains, but finally he opened the door to an isolated sitting room and saw a slender figure with platinum-blonde hair facing away from him, gazing out the window.

"Hello, darling, what are you looking at?" Freddie asked as he moved up behind her. He was shocked when she turned and he found himself inches away from the mischievous grin of newly minted It Girl Jean Harlow.

"Darling? Well, hello to you too, handsome! I didn't know you cared!" she said with a flirty chuckle.

He'd first met Jean at a party Lulu had taken him to, and

since they'd been seated next to each other at dinner, they'd developed a fast friendship. She was a funny girl, smarter than most people probably gave her credit for. And she was certainly easy on the eyes.

"Sorry, Jean. I was just looking for Lulu."

"Well, you got close. I do love the color of her hair." She pointed out the window. Freddie peered out. Beyond the manicured part of the property, he could see the stables. The figures were distant and small, but some of the more distinctive ones stood out. There was the recognizable bulk of Hearst, astride a hefty horse. There was Louella in an outlandish purple outfit, a magenta marabou capelet around her shoulders. He noted a starlet with dyed red hair. And there, her pale silver-gold head glowing like a halo, was none other than Lulu.

So much for his plan for talking things over. In a way, he was relieved. Hearst's words were still playing on an endless loop in his mind. He loved Lulu. That was beyond a doubt. But was that love strong enough to weather the gossip that would undoubtedly dog their relationship? He knew some of it would be orchestrated by the studio. That, he thought, he could just about live with, because it would be a creation, obviously (he hoped) fake. But he had already spent enough time in the Hollywood system to know that she would be endlessly surrounded by actors, producers, moguls, and fans, and that was in itself enough to make even the most stalwart and confident man gravely insecure.

"Don't you like riding?" Jean asked, managing to make that simple sentence unbelievably provocative.

"I . . . Well, I . . ." Freddie choked, but Jean dissolved into laughter, her entire demeanor changing in an instant. One moment she was a seductive starlet who could have any man she wanted; the next she was like a sister, or the kid next door. Her face relaxed, she stopped holding her stomach in and her bosom out, and she was a real person again.

"Sorry, chum. Force of habit. Lord, I get sick of keeping all of this nonsense up on these godforsaken work trips. There really is a limit to how long a girl can play the happy-go-lucky siren, laughing gaily at terrible jokes, stroking the egos of this executive and that director, and holding in her stomach before she feels like she's going to explode! Oh, come on, Freddie, join me for a good gossip huddle about all of our friends down there." The way she said the word "friends" made him sure some of them were anything but. And yet Jean Harlow was known to be among the less catty young actresses.

"I don't listen to much gossip," Freddie admitted.

She feigned shock. "And you a private eye? Or whatever you may be. Don't look at me like I'm nuts! There's more to you than meets the eye or my hair color is real! Hey, don't worry. I won't pry. But I have to admit, I haven't heard any really juicy gossip about you. Maybe I'll have to invent some. Anyway, Freddie, you won't survive in this town without listening to the rumors. Even if half of 'em are false, there's at the very least a grain of truth in the other half."

"Can't I just read Louella Parsons's column for that?" Freddie asked.

Jean scoffed. "That's entertainment, not real, valuable

dirt. Especially given that the best dirt is about her . . . and her husband."

"Louella has a husband?" This was shocking news to Freddie. She was often seen in the company of good-looking younger men serving some quasi-official role in her work: photographers, personal secretaries. Had she married one of them?

She shook her head, laughing. "Pity the poor beaten puppy who had to shack up with that jackal! Didn't you know? Docky Martin is her husband."

It took Freddie a moment to register what Jean was telling him. "You mean the medical director for Lux Studios? How did I not know this?"

Jean shrugged. "It's a well-kept, very public secret. She married him a year or two ago, but for some reason we all pretend not to know. We all figure they killed someone together, and the only way they won't have to testify against each other when they're caught is if they're married." She winked at him. "Of course, that's just gossip!"

Why would Louella and Docky keep their marriage under wraps? What possible harm could come from people knowing? Freddie felt a tingling of suspicion. If it was such a closely guarded secret, clearly, it followed, there was some reason to keep it so. But why?

"Is that the dirt you were talking about?" he asked Jean.

"That's just the tip of a very big, dirty iceberg . . . if the gossip is even partly true."

"Do tell."

And she did. She was a lively and entertaining storyteller, but the tales she told so lightly were dark indeed. If even a fraction of them were true . . .

Docky, it seems, was whispered to be the man an actress could go to when she was in trouble. If she committed an indiscretion and caught a disease or fell pregnant, Docky could take care of it quickly, quietly, and without possibility of discovery. Of course, his price was high, and lately part of the price was that Louella would inevitably know all about it. She wouldn't use the information—otherwise Docky's business would dry up pretty fast—but she'd save it up and use it as a kind of currency. She had the goods on nearly every actress who had gotten in trouble over the past few years. If they crossed her, or if she needed information or a favor from them, she only had to remind them about their abortion or their clap, and she'd get whatever she wanted from them. Docky and Louella were business partners, and their stock in trade was Hollywood scandal.

"And of course there's the pills," Jean added. "Plenty of girls here this weekend could tell you all about that. You wouldn't believe his list of customers. Not me. Tried 'em once and they made my heart go all stupid. I'd rather skip a meal than bounce off the walls like a maniac. But whenever a girl gets a little plump, he'll give her a bottle of pills that will knock the weight off. Or if she's feeling a little high, or a little low, he has a pill for that, too. You should see some of those girls after he's had at 'em. He can get 'em cocaine, opium, anything they want."

In other words, Freddie thought, Docky was a mobile pharmacy and easily had the resources to drug a tall, strong girl like Dolores to the point where she was unable to resist being fed to a tiger.

"Do you know which girls were using any of his services?"

"Oh, the girls talk about that pretty openly. Joan Crawford takes a little something from Docky that she says helps her focus. Bette Davis has trouble sleeping and says the stuff Docky gives her will put her out for an entire day."

"Anyone else?"

Jean tapped a finger to her cheek, considering. "Well, there was Dolores."

"What was she taking?"

"Diet pills, of course. At least, she was taking them for a while, until she ran out of money. She told me Docky wouldn't front her any more unless she had cash. I would have loaned her some, but I didn't like to see her take that garbage. Then later she told me she'd worked out a way to make him keep giving her the pills."

"Do you know what she meant by that?" Freddie asked. Jean shook her head. "Do you think you could find out?" She told him she'd try.

"Poor Dolores," Jean said. "She is—was—so beautiful, wasn't she? Such a strong, curvy, glamorous figure. I always wished I was built like that, instead of being a scrawny little midget. But, of course, this being Hollywood, she wasn't happy with herself and had a hundred people telling her to lose weight. Oh, she could keep the big bosom, but not the rest of it." She shook her head ruefully. "It's not a very nice place, is it? Every little girl dreams of coming here, but if they only knew what was in store for them, they'd run away screaming."

# *Twenty*

**L**ulu and Anita got back to the Ranch long before the rest of the riders. Anita went inside to, in her words, have a liquid pick-me-up. Lulu, though, lingered outside the main entrance, torn between impulses. She wanted to find Freddie and tell him everything she'd learned. But he had made very clear his position on her investigating, and frankly, she wasn't sure where she stood with him at this moment. Neither of them was making any clear move to apologize or reconcile, and though she believed in her heart they were fine, *they had to be fine*, she found herself in new and uncertain waters here. She understood that justifiably or not, he was angry and hurt. He was a proud man, which was one of the things she loved so very much about him, and it would take some time. Still, time was not something she felt she had the luxury of. Not as long as there was a murderer roaming freely.

Maybe she could tell Veronica? No, she thought. The publicist would tell Lulu that she was paranoid and overwhelmed and just needed a stiff drink and a good night's sleep. Boots? Eleanor? Toshia? They had pretty much proven their capacity for hysteria in the menagerie, and hysteria was never a good thing in a murder investigation.

While she was hesitating, a police car pulled up in the driveway. Lulu scooted to the side, assuming the officer who stepped out of the big black-and-white car would have pressing business inside. But to her surprise he walked up to her. He looked like he was in a hurry.

"Pardon me, ma'am. Can you take this?" he asked without preamble, thrusting a package into her hands. "No one else was available to deliver it, and I was just told to hand it off here on my way home. I'd be much obliged if you could get it to the appropriate person. My wife will rip me limb from limb if I miss dinner while the mother-in-law is visiting."

"Of course! We wouldn't want that, now, would we?" Lulu said, and he headed back to his cruiser and skidded down the hill.

Lulu looked down at the scrawled label on the brown paper wrapping. *Juliette Claire, personal effects. Deliver to next of kin.*

"Oh," she breathed softly. It was such a small package, and that struck Lulu as so terribly sad, as if all Juliette's life could be wrapped up in paper, tied up with string.

But why was it delivered here? Shouldn't the police have

tracked down Juliette's family? Maybe she didn't have a family or, like so many girls who came to Hollywood, had cut them out of her life. So many had run to Hollywood, pursuing something and fleeing something at the same time, and never looked back. Lulu supposed she should deliver the package to Mrs. Mortimer, who seemed to have all the household affairs in perfect running order. She'd certainly know what to do. But . . . Lulu squeezed the package gently. There was something soft, probably the clothes Juliette had been wearing.

Then something crunched inside the package. Paper? There were harder things, too. Perhaps jewelry.

*It's not mine,* Lulu thought. *I have no right.*

On the other hand . . . what if there was something import-ant inside, a clue to solving the murder? The police thought Zing did it, so they would probably discount anything they found. Lulu clutched the package tightly and raced up to her room. Once the door was shut and locked, she stood there for a long while considering her next move. *I shouldn't. But there are lives at stake. It's irresponsible to not do everything I can to find Juliette's killer and bring him or her to justice! Lulu Kelly, you're going to do it, so just get on with it.*

She carefully untied and unwrapped the package and opened it reverently on her bed. There was the chartreuse dress with the diamante spangles Juliette had worn the night she was killed. Lulu took a deep breath and looked through the rest of the things. There was a jeweled hair clip and a sparkling bracelet, both set with huge rhinestones.

And there, folded into a tiny square, was a piece of worn paper. It was creamy white with the slight variations in color and the faint embedded threads that marked the most expensive handmade stationery. She could see that it had been folded, opened, and refolded many times. The creased edges were wearing thin. Even before she read it, Lulu thought she knew what it would be.

My beloved Juliette,

I love you. There, I write it plainly. I am yours, if you will be mine. A. is nothing more to me than a burden, a necessity, but I will be tied to my millstone, my ball and chain no longer. I swear it. I will leave her . . . if you will prove to me that you will be my comfort and consolation for all that I am giving up. If only you will give yourself to me completely, I will give myself to you in kind. I swear to you, I'll divorce A. the very next morning, as long as you are mine, body and soul, as I am yours.

We will be together at the Ranch very soon. Just give me a sign that you will come to me, and I will envelop you in my arms and dedicate to you my life, never to be parted.

Until that time when you will be made flesh of my flesh, I remain your devoted,

John

Lulu narrowed her eyes and tapped her finger to her lips, considering the text carefully. Any foolish romantic would succumb happily to Emerson's heartfelt oath to end his marriage for the sake of true love. But what Lulu read between the love-soaked lines was something entirely different. He was declaring his intention to leave his wife, true, but there were conditions. The letter was an exercise in calculation and manipulation. *Sleep with me*, he was saying, *and then I'll leave my wife*.

Whispering promises in the darkness was one thing. Whispers don't hold up in divorce court. But Emerson had put it in writing, which Lulu knew from scanning the scandal sheets was the worst thing to do. He'd been an idiot to write such a letter, much less send it.

And here, thought Lulu, was a motive for murder.

Juliette had a letter from Emerson where he swore his love and offered to leave his wife. That would be powerful ammunition for blackmail. Juliette was just the type to threaten to show it to Anita. Of course, she didn't know that Anita knew all about it. Did Emerson himself know she was aware of the letter already? Would he be afraid of his wife finding out?

But Lulu knew full well that in the very public and publicized world of Hollywood, a wife's ire wasn't nearly as important as the world's opinion. If Juliette had threatened to give the letter to the press, the ensuing scandal could have meant unmitigated public humiliation for Emerson.

Once he realized what a mistake he'd made giving Juliette that letter, he'd probably do anything to get it back. Had he searched her room? Someone had, but Lulu needed proof it was him. After having her theories repeatedly shot down, she was afraid to commit herself without irrefutable evidence.

Lulu wrapped up Juliette's things and shoved them under the bed. It was getting late, so she decided to change for dinner. She took care to find just the right dress: demure, but satin, for a little added glamour tonight.

She found Paul a few minutes later in the Assembly Room. A few guests were scattered about in the vast chamber, and for just a minute they were virtually alone. She hastily approached him, eyes alight, eager to share her discovery. But just when she'd almost reached him, her hands outstretched to take his arms in her excitement, Freddie walked in the door.

He stopped abruptly when he saw them in that almost-compromising position, then regained his nonchalance.

Lulu decided right then that there was nothing that irritated her more than this put-on coolness Freddie had reverted to. It was time to burst that icy bubble he was hiding in. In fact, she suspected that a huge screaming fight would set everything straight between them. Given their surroundings, though, a good old-fashioned covert confrontation would have to do.

However, now was apparently not the time for it. Freddie sat down on the immense leather couch at the exact calculated distance that showed that Lulu was more his than Paul's, but not so close that he seemed to be marking his territory. He then proceeded to make polite, even entertaining conversation with them both, until other people joined them.

It was infuriating. Lulu wanted to grab him by the collar and shake him.

But instead, being an actress, she kept a smile on her face and met him cool for cool, chatting as if there wasn't some ludicrous chilly wall between them.

It irritated her that she had to act normal—and that everyone was acting normal. Of course, they'd been told one murder was solved and the other wasn't a murder at all. But even if they accepted all that, two girls were dead in particularly brutal ways, and surely she wasn't the only one who knew they were all being held prisoner. Were they all too grotesquely ambitious to care?

Soon she was directed to her same old seat near the head of the table. Her legs were sore from riding and she stretched them out as she sat down . . . then remembered what was discovered the last time she did that and jerked them in tightly back under her chair. Freddie was still seated across from her. She caught his eye, and he smiled at her, making her heart tremble. But the smile was brief, and he gave the same one a moment later to Jean Harlow when she sat down. Lulu pressed her lips together and cracked her delicate knuckles. She was determined to fix this.

He wasn't there yet, but she could see from the place card that John Emerson would again be sitting to one side of her, which made goose pimples rise on her arms. But what could he do to her in the middle of dinner? She eyeballed the sharp, serrated steak knife at the side of the plate. Well, actually, a madman could do plenty, she acknowledged gravely. But a calculating killer would wait for a more opportune moment. She was probably safe.

Probably.

The look on Emerson's face when he entered could only be described as controlled mania. His eyes seemed to burn. They were glassy and bloodshot, open unnaturally wide. The rest of his usually handsome face was stiff and pale, as if it had been coated in plaster and left to dry.

He made Lulu an exaggerated theatrical bow, adjusted his trousers, pulled at his suit jacket, and sat down.

"How are you?" Lulu asked, the only conversational opener she could manage at the moment.

"Terrific, thanks!" he said, trying to manage a half-cocked smile as his eyes slid around the room. "They're watching, you know." He lowered his voice. "They all think they're onto me . . . but they have no idea. Not really."

Lulu's hands clenched in her lap. Did he mean the murders? Was he about to confess? There was something odd and otherworldly about his voice, as if he wasn't really there. She remembered that Anita had mentioned her husband's "little problems." The voices, the rage. He was mentally ill.

And then it occurred to her: This was probably the safest place for an interrogation, and he might be driven to incriminate himself.

"How could they be onto you?" she asked carefully. "Have you been careless?"

"Oh, never!" he bellowed loudly with a brazen guffaw and shifted uncomfortably in his chair. The diners who were just settling themselves looked over in curiosity. Then, bringing his voice down, he said, "I made sure to cover my tracks expertly. A trick I learned from a Bushman in the Kalahari. Walk backward everywhere, don't you see?"

"And . . . no one knows what you did?" Lulu ventured carefully. She glanced over at Freddie, but he, frustratingly, wouldn't make eye contact.

"No one has a clue." Emerson patted her hand too swiftly for her to jerk it away. "Except you, my dear. I can see you are a young woman of the most profound perspicacity." He gave her a little wink. "What do you say we do it together, after dinner, eh? Just you and me? The only sensible people in this madhouse?"

"Er . . . ," Lulu began, looking frantically at Freddie, who seemed to be still lost in Jean Harlow's undeniable charms.

Emerson leaned toward her and whispered, "We'll discuss it later. It's snouts to the trough now."

At that moment Paul swooped into the seat next to her. She'd never been so happy to see anyone in her life. She tried to telegraph everything that was happening with her eyes and thought that, with his sensitivity, Paul certainly understood some of it. She felt in the midst of uncertain terrain, not sure whether Emerson's statements were those of a murderer or madman or both. Did he know she suspected him?

But then dinner was served, and Emerson seemed abruptly and unnervingly normal again. He was clear-eyed and hungry, the color returning to his cheeks, shouting political opinions down the table to Hearst, flirting boldly with any female who caught his eye. Just before dessert, Hearst announced which actresses were being eliminated. One took her dismissal with what looked to Lulu like relieved serenity. *I don't blame her*, Lulu thought, half wishing she'd been sent home herself. She should have thought of that when formulating her escape plan.

The other, a pale waiflike girl named Audrey whom Lulu hadn't spent much time with, broke down completely and had to be carried out by a member of the staff. Under normal circumstances, Lulu would have felt intense pity for her and might have even excused herself from the table to comfort her. But now her mind was on other things: John Emerson was incessantly tugging at his suit.

At first she thought it was just a sign of nerves, or a tic perhaps, caused by his rather obvious instability. It was only at the end of the meal that it occurred to her that it was the same suit he'd worn on the night of Juliette's murder. She could still see the faint smear of fuchsia lipstick on the collar.

All at once the housemaid Ginnie's words came back to her. She hadn't tried to wash the entire jacket, because that material would shrink. The other night, the suit had fit to perfection. Tonight, though, it pulled under the arms, the trousers seemed to bind him, and the sleeves were a bit short. The suit had evidently gotten a thorough soaking.

And then it struck her: the girls' prank! When Eleanor, Toshia, and Boots had set the water-bucket trap, someone had sprung it. Someone who ransacked Juliette's room, probably looking for the love letter, and had taken the scarf that was later used to kill her.

She remembered now that when Emerson appeared later

that night, Anita commented that he'd changed his suit! Later, when it had dried, he must have given it to Ginnie to clean.

Lulu felt a surge of triumph course through her and smiled down into her dish of raspberry trifle. This was the last piece of evidence she needed, she was sure. The tiepin in the tiger cage. The overheard argument in the garden. And now irrefutable proof that he had snuck into Juliette's room just before her murder.

She had to tell Freddie. Standing abruptly, she murmured, "I feel unwell. Please excuse me." Instantly three men were standing at her side: Paul, looking sweetly concerned. Emerson, manic and a bit wobbly. And . . . a footman, politely pulling back her chair.

Lulu glared hard at Freddie, who didn't break from conversation with Jean Harlow for an instant. How dare he! He was her beau. Even if they were momentarily on the outs, it was *his* job to rush to her aid. She opened her mouth to call him, then snapped it shut, thinking better of making a scene.

With a sigh of indignation, she left the dining hall, not looking back to see which man was following her.

# Twenty-One

She was so irate with Freddie that she didn't notice the footsteps behind her until Emerson grabbed her hand and pulled her into the spacious coatroom. She squealed, and he clamped a hand hard over her mouth.

"Hush. They'll hear you!" he hissed. Slowly, he uncupped his hand from her lips.

She stared into his frantic eyes, adrenaline coursing through her veins. "Well, that would be the point, now, wouldn't it?" she said evenly, ice in her voice. Lulu Kelly, born Lucille O'Malley in the slums of New York, was never going to be a girl who shrank in the face of danger.

"No! Please don't! The Communists will hear you! Either them or the Bureau of Investigation. The BOI *knows* things, you know. About the aliens, but they don't want us to know.

And the Communists are working with them. They're all watching us. All of them! Did you know that the president himself . . ."

Even through her fear, Lulu felt saddened for the delusional man as he ranted about a bizarre array of impossible conspiracies. Sometimes he talked directly to Lulu, foam gathering in the corners of his mouth, sweat beading on his brow as he shifted back and forth, shaking. Other times he seemed to address unseen companions.

She began to edge sideways, moving to the door. At any moment Emerson might switch from his verbal ranting to something more violent. Lulu was completely sure she was alone in a coatroom with the murderer, and if she didn't play her cards right, she might be his next victim.

It was with profound relief that she heard the door open, and Paul was standing there, casual as a spring breeze. "Mind if I borrow Lulu for a while, old fellow?" he asked, seeming to ignore the pale and utterly unhinged man before him, and calmly stepped in and took her arm. In an instant he had her out in the now empty Assembly Hall.

"Rather a questionable place for an interrogation, don't you think?" Paul quipped.

"Oh, Paul, be serious. He's mad as a hatter!" Lulu said, breathless. "He was going on and on in the most insane way, and I was sure at any moment . . ."

He patted her hand reassuringly, though Lulu couldn't help but feel there was a hint of condescension to the action.

"Paul, listen to me. I've found other evidence. There's a

letter, and I know for a fact now that Emerson was in Juliette's room before she was murdered. We have to tell the police."

Paul stopped her rapid flow of words with a raised hand. "Not here," he said earnestly. "I have something important to tell you, too. Let's go to the stables. They'll be deserted at this hour. We can be completely alone."

Without question, Lulu took his arm and went with him. She was shaken from her jarring encounter with Emerson and upset that Freddie hadn't picked up on her cue and followed her. Why couldn't he see how ridiculous he was acting? There was nothing between her and any other man, so why hadn't he run after her and taken her in his arms? She took a deep breath and shook off these nagging thoughts. For now she needed to focus. She'd confide everything to Paul, and together they'd convince the police who the real murderer was.

Paul was right; the building was deserted. Drowsy horses quietly nickered in the shadows of the darkened stables. A row of overhead bulbs cast dim yellowish pools of hazy light on the dusty floor. "In here," Paul said, and drew her toward the tack room, where the equestrian supplies were kept. He held the door open and stood aside gallantly to let her in. As she entered, Lulu saw the array of leather and metal equipment neatly arranged inside—burnished bridles, iron bits, riding crops, and coach whips. She felt Paul's hand against the small of her back, the most intimate he'd ever been, guiding her gently inside the deserted room.

"Lulu!" a voice called out just as Paul was closing the door. Sal shoved his foot into the doorway. He was smiling, a cocky, confident twist of a grin, but his stance made it clear that door would close only over his dead body.

"Doin' okay, Lu?" Sal asked as Paul reluctantly opened the door. "You looked a little queasy at dinner, and one of the butlers said they saw you two headed down this way."

"I'm fine, Sal," Lulu said with forced patience. "Go back to the dining hall."

"Ain't gonna happen," he said flatly. "I need to talk to you. Alone." He shifted his gaze to Paul, who took a deliberate step back.

"Are you okay with this?" Paul asked her softly.

She wasn't, really, but it occurred to her that Sal might have more information about Dolores's death, or maybe even Juliette's, so she nodded. Paul brushed her hand softly with his as he left, and the lightness of the touch made her shiver. He looked over his shoulder at Lulu, slowing as he strolled away, and she perceived deep regret in his eyes. She watched him as he went.

"You got the hots for writer-boy now?" Sal asked, sounding amused. "Good thing you're not my girl . . . yet. I'd be sore if you were messing around. Does noble young Freddie know? Or care?"

"None of your beeswax! And anyway, no," she snapped.

"Just pipe down for one minute and listen to me. I followed you down here to make sure that John wasn't gettin' funny with you and to tell you I heard from one of the worker bees here that John Emerson was seen wandering around the estate before dawn, yapping to himself about what he was going to do to all the people who were out to get him. From what the guy said, Emerson was upset about a broad who thinks she's too good for him. Talked about pulling out her *black hair* by the roots."

Lulu's hand involuntarily rose to her lips. Dolores had black hair. Had Emerson propositioned her and turned murderous after being rebuffed? On the other hand, Anita Loos also had black hair, and the world knew Emerson had reason to resent his wife's stellar success. Maybe he was talking about her.

Lulu told Sal about the other evidence she'd gathered and how it all pointed in one direction: John Emerson, unbalanced and enraged, had murdered Juliette and Dolores.

"I'm gonna gut the bastard," Sal growled. He pulled out a knife and held it low between them. Lulu stared at it, spellbound. The blade was wide at the hilt and curved outward slightly before tapering to a point. At first she thought it was dirty, and recoiled, thinking it might be covered with old blood. But a moment later she realized the blade was made with dark metal that didn't glint at all in the moonlight. That must have been an advantage in his line of work. Let the show-offs have shiny blades. Serious killers have dark weapons.

It wasn't a big knife, but its purpose was certain and grisly. Even though she was sure Sal meant her no harm, she felt afraid with that deadly weapon so close.

Impulsively, she put her hand on his and pushed the knife down. "You can't."

"Give me one good reason why not!" he shouted, jerking his hand away. "When I think what he did to that poor dame!

She was a good egg, Lulu. Wouldn't hurt a fly. She didn't deserve that ugly ending. . . ." He rubbed his temples with his free hand, covering his eyes at the same time. Was he crying?

"She was . . . She talked so tough, you know, carrying on like she was high class for Hollywood, but she was just a goof. She was a good kid . . . like you."

"Did you love her?" Lulu asked.

When he moved his hand to look at her, his eyes were dry. "Love? Does that matter? But she shouldn't have died. Nothing that beautiful should die. When I get my hands on Emerson, I'm gonna carve the flesh off his face and—"

"Sal, don't be an idiot. You have to leave it to the police."

"My kind doesn't leave revenge to the police. *They* didn't nail the man who killed my father. I did." He pounded his chest with the fist that clutched the knife.

"We have enough evidence for them to arrest Emerson and put him on trial. This has to be done the right way. If you kill him, you'll go to jail, Sal. It's a sure bet."

"There's so much you don't understand, Lu. I'm untouchable," he snarled.

"Just give me enough time to make my case to the police. Give them a chance to do their job. No matter what Emerson deserves, you don't need another death on your conscience."

"My conscience feels pretty clean, and I've killed an awful lot of people." He brandished the knife in front of her again. "I'll give you one more day. But if the cops don't arrest him by tomorrow night, I'm handling it myself."

★   ★   ★

Freddie sat at the dinner table for a full five minutes after Lulu left, considering his next move. Visions kept assaulting his brain: Lulu in Sal's arms, Lulu sitting intimately with Paul Raleigh, her hand brushing against his. Freddie knew that Lulu loved him, but somewhere inside he heard the voice of burning doubt. He wanted to build a life with this extraordinary woman, but what did he have to offer? Creatively, he didn't hold a candle to the writer Paul, who must understand the passions and motivations of an actor so much better than Freddie ever could. He vividly recalled the glow of interest in Lulu's eyes when she'd sat pressed close to Paul's side.

And when Lulu was in mortal peril it had been Sal who saved her, not him. Sal the gangster, with his broad shoulders and arrogant swagger, that curling lip, half smile, half sneer.

Suddenly he balled up his napkin and threw it down on the table. With his eyes burning and his jaw set, he stormed after Lulu and her followers.

"About time," Veronica said audibly, chewing a mouthful of string beans amandine as she watched him leave.

With the help of some observant servants Freddie discovered what door she'd exited through, and after a moment he heard a rough male voice. The words were for the most part indistinct, but one carried unmistakably through the landscaped grounds: "kill."

Freddie broke into a run. The path was cobblestone, but it was covered in soft decorative moss, and his footsteps were silent. For a second he stopped at the edge of the clearing near the stables.

Sal. Lulu. And between them, the dark but unmistakable wedge of a knife.

He didn't hesitate. Back in New York, Freddie's valet-cum-bodyguard Mugsy had made sure his charge was prepared for any manly confrontation. From an early age, Freddie was schooled in boxing and hand-to-hand combat. Ostensibly, this was so he could thwart any kidnapping attempt. Really, though, Freddie suspected it was because the former fighter Mugsy wanted a sparring partner.

Adrenaline propelled Freddie forward with lightning speed as he dashed to save Lulu. He grabbed Sal's knife hand at the wrist and twisted it up behind him. Then with a savage jerk he all but dislocated Sal's shoulder, sending the knife flying. He stomped hard with his foot against the back of Sal's knee, bringing the gangster down. Then, foolishly, he began to let up, thinking he'd won.

But Sal—whose idea of a fight was usually that only one fighter left it alive—spun on his knee and caught Freddie with a punch to the gut that doubled him over. Rising smoothly to his feet, he swung for Freddie's jaw. Freddie managed to get his hands up just in time to block it, and tucked into a boxing stance, sidestepping away.

"Stop it!" Lulu shrieked, but Freddie didn't know if she was talking to him or to Sal, so he darted in with a neat left jab that made Sal's head rock back.

Sal shook his head, looking surprised, then with a roar charged like a bull and knocked Freddie down to the ground. For a moment it was all dust and confusion as they rolled, first one on top, then the other, punches flying as Lulu shouted. Both of their faces were bloody. Then Sal was on top, straddling Freddie's chest, his fist raised to smash Freddie's face.

He stopped, his arm shaking with controlled power. Freddie, pinned helplessly, waited for the blow he knew would knock him unconscious at the very least. It would definitely break his nose and probably knock out a few teeth too.

And then Sal looked over at Lulu, a bloody trail running from the corner of his contorted mouth, down his jawline and neck, and blooming on the starched white collar of his shirt.

"You wouldn't forgive me if I messed up that pretty face of his, would you?" Sal gave Lulu a little smirk. "I won't have any chance with you then." He looked to Freddie and whispered, "This is your lucky day, pretty boy." And with that, he jumped to his feet, caught up the knife and sheathed it under his jacket, and stalked away, saying over his shoulder, "Tomorrow night, unless you give me a damn good reason not to."

Freddie dragged himself up, straightening slowly as his bruised midsection protested. He found Lulu regarding him with eyes that were filled with terror, fury, and tears. "What. Were. You. Thinking?" Each word seemed to cost her a tremendous effort.

"I saw the knife. I thought . . ."

"So you jumped in and risked your life to save me?" She moved closer until she was standing right before him. She sounded so angry, but there was something else there too.

"Of course," he said, stifling a groan. He was pretty sure a rib was cracked.

Suddenly she shoved him hard, two hands on his chest. He staggered and winced. "Then why didn't you do it before?" she shouted at him.

He was confused. Save her from Sal? Or did she mean save her from the tiger? "Did he accost you before?" he asked.

"Sal wasn't threatening me, Freddie. More important, he wasn't threatening *you*. No man is, not as far as *we're* concerned. I don't love Sal. I don't love Paul. I love *you*." She gave a quick sniff, and he saw the sorrow beneath the anger. "I thought you loved me."

He felt his eyes get hot. "How could you doubt—" he began.

"How could *you*?" she countered before he could get any further.

"I was . . . well, I was jealous," Freddie admitted with supreme effort. "Lulu, I swear I have never been jealous before in my life. But when I saw you with one man, then the other, I couldn't help thinking maybe there was a better man out there for you. Someone who could understand and excite you more than I can. Or who could keep you safe as I never could. Maybe if I was still rich . . ."

She raised a hand swiftly, and for an instant he was sure she was going to slap him. But instead, she covered his lips with her fingertips.

"*You* are the man I want," she said with absolute certainty. "And you always will be." He felt a smile start to creep up on his mouth, straining the fat lip one of Sal's punches had given him. "Unless," Lulu added, stopping the smile in its tracks, "you ever treat me like that again. Start thinking you're not good enough for me, and maybe I'll start agreeing with you."

"I'm sorry I was such a fool," he said, taking her hand and softly, painfully kissing her palm.

Lulu wiped away a tear and sighed. "Just don't let it happen again. I've had to resort to writers and children to help me with this case, for goodness' sake! I need a real private eye in my corner."

Freddie chuckled. "Oh, is that all I'm good for?"

"Not all," she said teasingly. "Now, let's get you back to your room and cleaned up. I can get Ginnie to bring in some iodine and bandages for those cuts. Frederick van der Waals, you are a certified mess." And with that, she leaned forward and kissed him with a passion and abandon that seemed to make time stand still.

When they finally separated, they just stood looking into each other's eyes, basking in the feelings that overwhelmed them both. Finally, Lulu, not able to help herself, blurted out, "I think I've thoroughly cracked the case," prompting a great belly laugh from the love-struck young detective. "Wait till you hear all the evidence I have. We have to convince the police to make the arrest before tomorrow night. Otherwise, Sal will take matters into his own hands. That's why he was waving a knife around. Just making a *point*."

"I see. Well, you could warn me next time. Avoid all this bothersome medical attention," Freddie said, grinning. Life suddenly seemed joyous again now that he and Lulu had cleared the air. "Though I trust your judgment, I came up with a couple more suspects myself—for both the murders and the blackmail. You might want to hear about them before you tell the police—or let Sal and his knife loose. I'll tell you after you tell me about what you've got on Emerson. Maybe together we can get to the bottom of both cases."

She looked at him with earnest, loving eyes. "Just make sure whatever we do, we do it together."

## Twenty-Two

**L**ulu went to sleep feeling intoxicated with love and relieved by the knowledge that she and Freddie were no longer on the outs. After she'd told Freddie everything she knew about the murders, he reciprocated by sharing all he had. And there they were, synchronized again.

"Marion is an appealing suspect on a certain level," Lulu admitted. "I can see how her addiction and insecurities could make her crack. And it certainly would tickle Lolly and the other gossip columnists. But I have to say, though she might be capable of it, not enough evidence points directly to her."

"And what about Docky?"

"How on earth did Lolly keep him a secret all this time? Can you imagine anyone so . . . ?" She had been about to say "vile," but she stopped herself. Hollywood—particularly the men inhabiting it—had a tendency to destroy innocent young girls. How many of them had made one mistake or been pressured into doing something they regretted only to find themselves punished with a potentially lifelong consequence? Some of what he did might not be legal, but Docky gave these girls a second chance. As for the pills, well, most of them were legal. As much as it disturbed Lulu to think of girls drugging themselves to become perkier or thinner, they bore some responsibility too. She had to admit Docky might have his place in this already disturbing world she lived in. *She* just planned to stay well away from him.

Still, she didn't think he was the murderer. He and Lolly had almost certainly been together when Juliette was killed.

"No," Lulu said with assurance. "It's John Emerson. I'm certain."

Freddie agreed he would go over all of the evidence she'd gathered and present it first to Hearst, then to the police tomorrow morning. If all went well and they believed him, Emerson would be arrested and the whole nightmare would be over.

She'd been a little worried about him waiting until the next morning to come forward, but Freddie wanted to make sure the argument for Emerson's guilt was airtight, so the authorities would act quickly and decisively, and that, he said, required some preparation. Lulu was concerned that another day's delay could mean another victim, but after a few discreet inquiries with the staff, Freddie found out that Emerson and Docky had gone on a private bender in the billiard room and were both currently unconscious and drooling on the green felt. Emerson would neither be alone nor capable of crime that night. If there was any movement, Freddie would be notified immediately.

So Lulu's night was uncharacteristically peaceful. The morning, though, began far too early, with Veronica's face inches from her own cooing, "Rise and shine, sleepyhead. It's time to wax Shakespearean! Good Lord, your fingernails look like you've been on a chain gang! And how long have you let your eyebrows go? They're like rogue caterpillars on a spree. There's *character* and then there's *character actors*. It's a little soon for you to be playing the hillbilly aunt. We've got work to do."

She clapped her hands, making Lulu wince and burrow deeper under the crisp linens. "Is the show really today?" she asked blearily.

"Of course it's today! All those other girls have been tapping, high-kicking, and warbling their heads off for the last two days! Personally, I'm still against you doing Shakespeare. This is Hollywood, not Stratford-upon-Avon. Hopefully your talent is not making everyone fall asleep with those speeches. Do you have your sonnets memorized? Can I convince you to jump through flaming hoops while you're doing them? It's just a thought."

"I have them memorized, and no flaming hoops, thank you."

Lulu washed her face, tied her hair back with a scarlet kerchief, and looked for something sensible to put on.

Comfortable in trousers and a red silk blouse, Lulu headed out to the gardens so she could rehearse in peace. The Ranch, however, was not designed for peace, at least not when a house party was in full swing.

Finally, she found an undisturbed spot by a yew tree that had been shipped across the Atlantic from a Welsh church-yard. She took out a slim copy of Shakespeare's sonnets she'd found in Hearst's library and started reading over her chosen set. But the words were so familiar that her mind seemed to blur, then go restless, and before long she turned her attention to the other reading material she'd brought with her.

Though Hearst being blackmailed seemed rather sleepy in comparison to dual homicide, it was nonetheless an interesting mystery. Lulu pulled the reports from the envelope and began to study them.

Freddie and his boss had made very little progress. None of the staff had seen anything suspicious; none of the guests had been seen in the family's personal wing, where Hearst's office was located. Other than Marion, no real suspects had emerged, and Freddie still didn't know what secret Hearst was afraid might be revealed.

Freddie had included photographic prints of the blackmail letters too. Lulu looked with interest at the disparate words cut from newspapers and magazines and glued to paper to form the blackmailer's demands. The first letter contained a vague threat. The second asked for a specific sum—$30,468—and threatened to expose some shameful truth if the money wasn't paid. The third had very specific instructions: Place non-sequential, small bills in a leather satchel and leave the money in the freezer of the St. Vincent de Paul soup kitchen. If the money wasn't delivered by that very night, the blackmailer would "reveal Hearst's darkest secret to the world." Lulu stared at the photos, though she didn't think she would discover anything new. After all, Hearst, Mr. Waters, and Freddie had been poring over them for days now. What could a person tell from cut-out words, anyway? Maybe one could trace which periodical they'd come from, but most of the words were so commonplace they could be found in any newspaper, published on any given day.

But wait, perhaps there was something a little bit odd. She squinted and looked closer. It wasn't so obvious on the shorter words, but the edges of the longer ones had small but distinct curves. The longest had a crescent moon, and part of another. How strange.

Before she could give the matter any more thought, she heard the joy-filled yipping of dogs and was nearly knocked off her perch by Charlie and Gandhi, who were tugging Patricia in their wake.

"So! How goes the investigation?" Patricia asked, plopping down beside Lulu and turning the dogs loose to play in the gardens. The child looked nervous and, unlike every other time, didn't seem graphically curious about the crimes. While Lulu started to fill her in, Patricia absently opened a little ostrich-skin purse and pulled out a manicure set. As Lulu spoke, Patricia stared into the distance, filing her nails.

"It's a big night," Patricia said disinterestedly. "Lots will happen, I suppose."

"Patricia, is something wrong?" Lulu asked.

The girl seemed to force herself to look cheerful and set her file down on the bench between them. "It's a rotten old world," she said lightly. "Of course there's something wrong. Terrible things happen all the time to good, innocent people. Luckily, not to me, though!" She smiled, tears pooling in her eyes, and spread her arms, encompassing the dogs, the gardens, the Ranch, the riches. "I'm very lucky. I have the perfect life. I'm Marion Davies's niece and William Randolph Hearst's very special friend. Who could ask for anything more? Now, will you please excuse me?"

She got up, hugged Lulu, and ran away, leaving the dogs and her manicure set behind. Lulu called after her, but Patricia didn't turn. *Well,* Lulu thought, *even very privileged children can have problems.* She felt sad for the lonely girl, but helpless at the same time. She would check in on Patricia tomorrow morning before everyone left the Ranch, but for now she had work to do.

She slid the blackmail documents back into their envelopes and managed to focus on the other task at hand, running through each of the sonnets one time before searching out Freddie. He should be making his case for Emerson's arrest soon. He'd talk to Waters and Hearst first, then summon the police. They were probably on their way already. Emerson would be in custody within a few hours. Then she could truly rest easy. She might even enjoy the night's performance.

She was almost looking forward to it. It would be delightful to see what kind of acts her friends had dreamed up. She didn't have particularly high hopes for her own show—reciting poetry was fairly low-key in her world, though Veronica assured her it would have an old-fashioned charm. Still, she began to feel a little gnaw of competition stirring in her. Other girls had certainly done much more than she to ingratiate themselves with Marion and Mr. Hearst while she was off investigating. Oh well, she didn't really care. She might not win, but she would shine. Lulu was going to make sure she came off well. In the movie business, every moment in front of people was an audition for something.

She ran through the sonnets once again, losing herself in the emotion of the words, rehearsing her gestures and stance, modulating her voice to add music to the poetry. When she was satisfied, she remembered Veronica's testy comments about her eyebrows and fingernails. She'd have to go back to her room to deal with the brows, but she might as well use Patricia's manicure set before she went back.

As the dogs played happily around her and the sun warmed her skin, she began to relax and file her nails smooth. One was a little too long, and she fished for the manicure scissors to trim it before filing.

As she opened the tiny pair of scissors and prepared to cut, she froze. A little scrap of something that had been wedged where the blades joined fell into her lap. She stared.

That slight curve in the cut-out words of the blackmail letters.

The curve of the manicure scissors.

No, it wasn't possible. Most of the women at the Ranch

probably had a pair of curving manicure scissors exactly like Patricia's. That said, almost none of the women had unfettered access to Hearst's private office. The door might be unlocked half of the time, as Hearst himself admitted, but guests weren't allowed in that wing of the house unless specifically invited, and only the most trusted servants ever entered it.

Holding her breath, Lulu picked up the scrap that had fallen when she'd opened the scissors. It was a shred of newspaper.

She closed her eyes. It couldn't be Patricia. Why, she was just a kid. A precocious kid, to be sure, but what could her motivation possibly be? What secret could she know? Why would she want money when she had everything her heart could desire? Lulu's mind raced to find a reason.

Lulu took out the photos of the letters. They had been enlarged, which made it impossible to tell if the scissors fit. The angle of the curve looked the same, but she'd have to see the originals to tell if the size was a match.

With the dogs at her heels, she ran inside to find Mr. Hearst. But he was meeting behind closed doors with Freddie and Mr. Waters in the library, and the butler standing sentry outside the door wouldn't let her in. She waited, pacing one moment, then tapping her foot impatiently for minutes on end. The wait gave her time to second-guess herself. What would Mr. Hearst say if she charged up and accused Marion's niece of blackmail? He wouldn't believe Lulu for a second, especially on such flimsy evidence. He already thought she was a troublemaker, seeing crimes where there were none, pointing fingers at the innocent. She had to get something more conclusive.

Turning on her heel, she made her way to Hearst's private wing. She told the attending housemaid that Marion had summoned her to her boudoir, and she was granted admittance to the area. But as soon as the maid's back was turned, Lulu dashed back down the hall, then slowed as she approached Mr. Hearst's private office. She turned the knob slowly, expecting it to be locked. But it wasn't, and she let herself in. Freddie had told her that Hearst kept the original letters in his desk drawer.

The office was a mess, with tip-tilting piles of newspapers— Hearst's own, and his competitors'—piled on almost every available surface. There was a shiny new typewriter on the main desk and another one on a smaller desk, apparently for Hearst's secretary. A picture of Marion looking chic and ethereal was propped on one side of the desk; one of Marion with her arms around Patricia was on the other.

Lulu sat in Hearst's chair, sinking deeply into the well-worn leather, and carefully, breathlessly, opened the drawers. In the top left hand, she found what she was looking for. She delicately removed the letters, and then after gently unfolding them, held them up next to the curve of the scissors. It certainly looked like a match, but she needed to be sure. She took the topmost newspaper from the nearest pile and cut out a word at random. Then she placed it over the blackmail letter.

The curve of the cut was exactly the same. It wasn't absolute proof, but it made Patricia a much more likely suspect.

Lulu sighed. She did not want to have this kind of responsibility. Solving a murder was a moral obligation to her, with no shred of guilty feelings involved. However, implicating a child in a crime was something else entirely. Maybe she was wrong. Maybe this was just some sort of joke that Patricia was playing, and she should stay out of it.

Or maybe someone was forcing her to do it? For the life of her, Lulu couldn't see through her suspicions to any reasonable explanation.

She held up the word she'd just cut out, reading it for the first time. *Guilty*, it read ominously enough. She'd randomly snipped it from an article about a mob trial in Chicago.

When the police came into the office, Lulu was still sitting transfixed, the scissors in one hand, the paper in the other.

"Miss Kelly, you're under arrest for blackmail and extortion."

# Twenty-Three

**W**hat are you doing? Let me go!" Lulu cried as the officer caught her under the arm and roughly pulled her to her feet.

"Caught red-handed," the officer said. "How convenient."

"You're making a mistake—it wasn't me!"

"Is that so? Everyone I've ever arrested was innocent—until proven guilty."

Lulu closed her eyes, searching for the wisdom to know what to do. Where was Freddie? She tried to explain to the officer. "It *couldn't* have been me. The first blackmail letter was delivered before I even arrived at the Ranch."

"Now, isn't that strange," the officer snarled. "Only the guilty party would be privy to that kind of inside information."

"You have to listen to me," she said evenly. "I think I know who the blackmailer might be. That's why I came here, to confirm my suspicions."

"Darling, do tell!" came a cool, louche voice from the doorway. Marion lounged against the frame, glassy eyed, her tone dark. "Is it really you, you crafty little thing? What gumption to blackmail my old man!" She didn't seem to be very upset by the idea.

"Of course I didn't do it, Marion," Lulu said quietly. "But I think I know who did."

"Really? And who might that be?" Marion asked acidly, arching her elegant eyebrows.

Lulu opened her mouth . . . and closed it again.

"You heard the lady. Spit it out," the officer said harshly.

How could she tell Marion that her beloved niece was a blackmailer? Marion would never believe her, not without more convincing evidence. What she had now made Patricia a suspect, nothing more.

"I . . . I'd rather not say," Lulu muttered at last.

"I figured. Now, let's go down to the station and you can work on your story a little more. I'm sure it will be a good one—once you get your facts straight." The officer started to pull her toward the door.

"Marion, please!" Lulu begged, truly afraid now. "You know I didn't do this. Please get Mr. Hearst! Get Freddie! I can explain everything!"

"Oh, you poor dear girl," Marion said, sliding unsteadily to the side to let them pass. "You were my favorite, too. Why did you have to do it? The contract for Anita's new movie alone would have been far more than the blackmail amount, and you're one of the top contenders."

Lulu struggled against the officer's grip. This couldn't be happening again!

But she was hustled through the Ranch, where she seemed to pass every single guest. They looked at her in amazement, curiosity, and in the case of a few of the actresses, gloating satisfaction. They couldn't know what she was in custody for (though no doubt the gossip machine would spread versions both true and false within minutes), but those unpleasant competitive few were heartlessly glad to see a rival removed from the game. The humiliation was brutal.

"Take your hands off her this instant!" Toshia said, suddenly jumping in front of them. "How dare you!"

"And that goes double for me!" Boots said, running to Toshia's side.

The officer stopped, uncertain. He could barely handle one headstrong actress. A wall of them was another story, especially when Eleanor joined them. She was wearing a sleeveless sundress, and her strong swimmer's muscles made her look particularly imposing.

Eleanor crossed her arms and said, "Nothin' doin', mister. You let her go. Whatever you think she did, she didn't do it!"

They stalled him, but it was Honey who ran in search of Freddie. Thankfully, he was close by in the upper garden talking to Waters. Seeing Honey waving her arms maniacally, he excused himself, and together they arrived at the standoff moments later.

"Lulu!" Freddie called, and she had never been so happy to hear his voice in her life. "What's happening?"

"They think I'm the blackmailer!"

Freddie stopped . . . and laughed. He laughed until he was doubled over, panting for breath.

"Only you, Lulu," he gasped out at last. "Only you."

"When you've finished amusing yourself at my expense, could you ask this upstanding officer of the law to let me go so I can tell you who the blackmailer actually is?"

After a lengthy negotiation—to the interested delight of the spectators—the officer begrudgingly agreed to bring Lulu to Mr. Hearst before she was formally arrested and charged.

To her surprise and deep embarrassment, the meeting took place in Mr. Hearst's bedroom. He shuffled around in his slippers, a robe wrapped around his generous midsection, looking like a benevolent uncle. Lulu sat in an armchair with the officer standing on one side of her, Freddie on the other.

"Now, Miss Kelly," Hearst said, regarding her sharply with his keen little eyes. "Just who do you believe is blackmailing me?"

After taking a deep breath, Lulu looked up and said plainly, "I believe Patricia is the blackmailer." Then she carefully presented her scant evidence and explained her hunch.

She was certain Hearst would rage and roar, that spittle would fly from his mouth as he shouted that such a thing was impossible, that his darling Marion's sweet little niece could never, ever . . .

But to her amazement he simply blinked and pressed his thin lips together. "Thirty thousand dollars," he said. "Of course. It just never occurred to me that . . . This is terrible. But the letter specified another amount. How much was it, Freddie?"

"It was $30,468."

"Yes. If what you say is true, Lulu, the thirty thousand dollars makes sense. But what about the four hundred and sixty-eight? I don't know. I don't know. I feel like it couldn't be true. And yet . . . Oh, the poor child. I have to find her. Don't tell Marion yet. If I'm wrong . . ." He called for his valet and set the servants to finding out where Patricia was. Someone had seen her in riding clothes, so Hearst began marching for the stables, leaving the others to scramble after his long steps. As he walked he said, "If it's true, she'll never admit it, even if she's cornered. She's a tough little one. But, Lulu, if you'll play along, we might be able to get her to confess. She'll be strong for herself, but I don't think she'd let someone she likes take the fall. Just follow my lead."

They found Patricia on a sprightly pinto, just about to ride off with Paul Raleigh. Funny, Lulu thought, she distinctly remembered Paul telling her he didn't know how to ride when she'd asked him afterward why he hadn't been on Hearst's group trail excursion.

"My, this is a nice sendoff," Patricia said.

Hearst addressed Paul Raleigh. "I beg your pardon, Paul, but I'm going to have to steal Patricia away for a while. Family business."

"No!" Paul exclaimed loudly enough to make his horse shy and lay back his ears. "I mean, what a shame," he amended more softly. "We had such a lovely route planned."

"Aw, shucks," Patricia said. "Paul was going to show me this lovely wildflower field he found just miles from anywhere. And I was going to pitch him story ideas until he got positively sick of me. What's up, WR?"

"We'll speak of it inside. It is, as I said, family business."

"But they're not family," Patricia said, eyeballing Lulu, Freddie, and the plainclothes officer. She looked suspicious, but Lulu couldn't tell if she had a glimmer of the real situation yet.

"True, but it seems they are intimately connected to this affair. Come. I'll explain inside."

Patricia swung her leg over her pinto and hopped down. She shot Lulu a questioning look, but Lulu only shrugged. Now Patricia looked positively worried, and that added to Lulu's belief that she'd read the facts right.

They gathered in Hearst's messy office. Hearst disappeared for a moment, then came back in with Marion on his arm. Then he shut the door solidly behind him, turning the lock.

"Now, then," he said, clearing his throat. "As all of you know, someone has been blackmailing me under my very roof. While taking advantage of my hospitality, they have crept into my personal domain and left threatening correspondence. Well, I'm happy to say that thanks to some excellent detective work, and a bit of luck, we've identified the criminal."

After a brief flutter, Patricia gathered herself together

and looked as cool as the other side of the pillow. Lulu had to admire her. She didn't think most ten-year-olds would be so self-possessed.

"Officer Milligan, our investigation is complete. If you would be so good as to take Miss Lulu Kelly into custody and escort her to the station, and thence, I'm sure, to prison for a very long time." Hearst seemed to gain inches and pounds as he feigned rage, towering over Lulu. He frowned darkly at her, and even though she knew it was an act for Patricia's benefit, she trembled. "You'll rot in prison for the rest of your life! You've made yourself my enemy, young lady. And my enemies always get crushed. Take her away!"

The officer jerked her toward the door and Lulu couldn't help but cry out. She pulled against his tight grip. "I didn't do it, I swear! You're making a mistake!"

She glanced sidelong at Patricia, but the girl didn't move, didn't speak. *Is she really going to let me take the blame?* Lulu wondered. The officer dragged her across the room as she continued to struggle.

"Freddie, help me!"

"Your career is over, Miss Kelly," Hearst growled. "Your life as you know it is over. No one can help you now. *No one.*" Lulu had to steel herself to keep from looking at Patricia again. Was the girl made of stone? Was she really going to let Lulu take the fall?

The officer had hauled Lulu out the door when Patricia finally jumped to her feet and cried, "Stop! It wasn't Lulu!"

"Nonsense," Hearst said. "We have all the evidence. We

actually caught her using the same manicure scissors used in the blackmail letter—sitting at my desk, no less, cutting out words for another malicious threat." He addressed the officer. "Get her out of my sight!"

Patricia clenched her fingers together. "It wasn't her!" she said again, but this time her voice trembled.

Hearst rounded on her sharply and asked, "Who was it, then?"

"It was . . . I don't know. But it wasn't Lulu. I know that for a fact."

"Come, now, a girl's entire life and future are at stake. If you know something, you have to tell us."

Still, Patricia hesitated. Lulu hated seeing her so torn up.

Marion jumped in with, "Didn't your parents raise you to be an honest girl, Patricia?"

With those words, something seemed to snap in Patricia. She rounded on Marion and shouted, "My parents? You have the nerve to talk about my *parents*? And honesty? Don't make me laugh. As if the two of you ever told the truth when you could conveniently buy a lie. You're both despicable, and I hate you!"

Marion and Hearst looked at each other, and Lulu read volumes of unfathomable emotion in that glance. She felt her pulse quicken, as if she almost knew what was coming next.

"What are you talking about, dear girl?" Hearst asked, his voice heavy and unnatural-sounding.

There were tears in Patricia's eyes, but she didn't let them fall. She stood tall and glared defiantly first at Hearst and then at Marion. The little girl fell away, and she suddenly looked years older.

"You're right, WR. It is time for me to tell you, and the world, exactly what I'm talking about." She practically bristled with ferocity. "Do you want to bring Louella Parsons in too, or will these people be enough to spread the truth at last?"

Hearst looked alarmed, an expression Lulu never expected to see on his usually supremely confident face. "Officer Milligan, will you kindly leave the room and clear every staff member from this wing?"

He looked disappointed, but he complied.

"Now, then," Hearst said. "Have a seat, my dear, and tell us what's on your mind." His voice was gentle and conciliatory, which was apparently entirely the wrong tone to take with Patricia at the moment.

"Stop treating me like a child!" she roared, so loud that any staff that hadn't yet been evacuated would surely hear. "I will not sit down. I will not be made small! I will stand and I'll be heard, damn it!" Every jaw in the room dropped at this mature oath.

"Yes, it was me," she admitted proudly, Lulu thought, as she started to pace the small room. "You would never admit the truth, even to me. But I knew! I found the records! Good old Aunt Marion and sort of, kind of Uncle WR have been *so kind* to give me such a good home, haven't they?" Her lip curled in a snarl. "But what would the world say if it knew the truth?" She fixed her eyes on Hearst. "What would your wife say . . . Dad?"

The entire room fell silent.

Patricia turned to Marion. "How about you, Mom?"

Marion burst into tears.

"Thirty thousand," Hearst muttered to himself.

"Yes, the price you paid in hush money for Marion's sister Rose to take me in and pretend I was her own."

"And the four hundred and sixty-eight dollars?" Hearst asked.

Patricia gave a mirthless laugh. "Oh, that's the best part. Mama Rose wasn't content with the thirty thousand dollars. She wanted a new mink cape, too. She even kept the receipt, with a note scribbled on it: 'partial payment for P.' Isn't that rich? Oh, believe me, I know it all now. I found everything, eventually, in Rose's attic. I had to dig and dig, but I even found the original birth certificate."

"No," Marion breathed. "You couldn't. It was destroyed."

"Rose might have told you that, but her husband—my supposed father—must have thought the documents would come in handy one day. If I hadn't blackmailed you, he would have, eventually. Fine family we have, eh? I found the original birth certificate for Rose's baby, the one who lived only a few days. Then I found the altered one with my name on it. How convenient, that your bastard could just take that other baby's place."

"We never . . . ," Marion began, but Patricia held up her hand.

"The only problem was, I was already three years old when Rose's baby was born." She turned to Lulu and Freddie.

"How do you think they took care of that? They had my fake father kidnap me for five years. Anyone can tell a three-year-old from a newborn. But by the time I was nine or ten, you all could just pass me off as a seven-year-old who was big for my age and fiendishly clever."

The tears began to fall now. Hearst, who usually dominated every conversation, was completely silent.

"Do you know what it was like for me?" Patricia asked, anguished. "I never felt love from them, not once. They were supposed to be my parents, but I always knew they didn't feel for me anything like a parent's love. Can you imagine what that's like for a little girl? And then, when I found out the truth after you took me in, I waited . . . and waited . . . and waited for you to tell me. Hell, I wouldn't have even cared if you hadn't told me, if you'd only *shown* me. Here I was at last with my true parents, and you still treated me like no more than some relative you're fostering out of the goodness of your heart."

"We love you, Patricia," Marion said, choking back her sobs.

"If you loved me you would have owned me!" Patricia countered.

"WR is married. And my career would have been over," Marion said. "What do you think would have happened to me if the world knew I had a baby? An unwed mother?"

"You had WR! You didn't need a career. You had a choice, and you picked acting over your own child."

"But if I wasn't an actress, WR would never—" Marion broke off abruptly and looked down at her fingernails. Lulu knew exactly what she was going to say. Hearst wasn't just in love with Marion the woman. He was in in love with Marion the actress. He was fascinated by her power to charm the world. If Marion had given up her career for the sake of her daughter, then Hearst would have given up her. She and her daughter would have been cast adrift. Oh, maybe Hearst would have supported them. But neither of them would be rich beyond measure, the center of glamour and style.

"And hiding my age," Patricia went on bitterly. "Do you know, I was hardly taught to count until I was seven, just so I wouldn't accidentally give anything away. I didn't even understand the concept of years for the longest time! I was shipped around the world, and every time someone said 'what a charming little girl; how old is she,' we moved on again. I didn't have a birthday until I came here. You dressed me in short frocks and ribbons and did your best to convince me I'm ten years old. I always felt like a freak and didn't know why. But I'm not ten! I'm almost thirteen, almost a woman with a woman's feelings and dreams and brain!"

Remembering herself at thirteen, Lulu thought Patricia's claims a bit dramatic. But then, drama is what being thirteen is all about.

"Oh, my poor darling girl," Marion said, rushing to embrace her. Patricia stood stiff as Marion's arms went around her. "You don't know how hard it has been for me. For us." She gave Hearst a look, begging for his support. He stood still and stony while Marion showered her daughter with kisses. Lulu could suddenly see a strong resemblance between Hearst and his daughter: the pride, the stubbornness, the hard set of the cheeks. Patricia didn't soften under Marion's affection.

"Hard for *you*?" Patricia said. "That's rich."

"Don't you realize it broke my heart to give you up? But I have you back now, as my very own darling girl. I'll never let you go again."

"Why did you go to all this fuss?" Hearst asked suddenly. "Why didn't you just tell us you knew? You disappoint me, demanding money. Don't I give you everything you need?"

Patricia held her own against his steely gaze. "I wasn't going to keep your money for myself," she said with contempt. "I was going to leave it at the St. Vincent de Paul soup kitchen when it was delivered. All I want—all I've ever wanted—was to know who I am and who I belong to. I thought if I made up the blackmail, then the truth would all come out in the investigation. Once you brought in Mr. Waters and Mr. Van, I was sure they'd find the evidence themselves, and it would all be exposed."

"You *wanted* to expose our family secrets to the world?" Hearst asked.

"If that's what it took." She sighed, and finally put her arms weakly around the caressing Marion. "I just wanted you to admit what you did. I just want to be your daughter. For real."

Hearst shifted his great weight from foot to foot, pondering. Lulu half thought that even now he was considering that if he threw a great deal of money at this problem, he could make it go away again. How far would he go? Would he get rid of Patricia somehow to protect himself? And Lulu and Freddie, too? Lulu held her breath as she watched the family drama. At last Hearst's shoulders sagged, and he held out his arms to Patricia.

"You *are* my daughter. Our daughter," he said, as if it cost him great effort to admit it. All the same, Lulu was almost sure she saw relief in his face. "But you must be content with that. I won't have it known. In this house, though, when we're alone, you are our child."

Patricia paused, looked up at her father, and nodded as she was enfolded in his arms. Finally.

"Thank you, Lulu, for bringing this to a crisis," Hearst said over Patricia's bent head.

Inspired, Lulu said, "Oh, it wasn't me at all. Freddie had the idea. I was the one silly enough to try to sneak into your office, but Freddie was the one who figured the whole thing out."

Freddie opened his mouth to protest, but Lulu shushed him with a significant look. "In fact," she went on, "Freddie has some compelling new evidence about the two deaths at the Ranch." She controlled herself and didn't say "murders." "I hate to interrupt this happy time, but if you could give him your attention for a while, I think you'll be surprised by what he's come up with."

It was the way of the world, she knew. Hearst would be far more likely to listen to a man than he would to hear the evidence from her. It wasn't right. It wasn't fair . . . but it was a sacrifice she was willing to make if it meant the man who'd murdered two innocent girls would get what he deserved.

"Very well," Hearst said. "If you'll come back in an hour or so, we can discuss anything you like. For now, though, we have some family matters to work through. May I trust in your discretion?"

Lulu and Freddie both nodded. Hand in hand, they left the family alone to sort things out.

# Twenty-Four

**A**s much as I appreciated that absolute lie you just told in there, you *do* know that that was totally unnecessary," Freddie protested as they walked slowly down the dimly lit hallway. "Why wouldn't you graciously take the credit you deserve? All of it! *You* cracked the blackmail case. And without you, that man lying unconscious in the hospital would take the fall for a crime he didn't commit."

"Frederick Van, what good could it possibly do for me to get a reputation as a private eye? Maybe another week of gossip, a spread in *Photoplay*? Honestly, Freddie, I only want the public to know me as the characters I play. I have nothing to gain, but you stand to profit tremendously by taking the credit."

"Is that so?" he asked coyly.

"You know full well that's so! Waters is a lush, yet Hearst has been supporting his investigation business for years. Waters must have done something, sometime to gain Hearst's endless gratitude. What do you think he could do for you, the one who actually solved the crime?" Lulu stopped and gave him a quick kiss on the cheek. "But now you have to get ready to present the evidence about Emerson's guilt to Mr. Hearst. And I have to get ready for that unfortunate competition tonight."

"After all, the show must go on." Freddie sighed, giving her a peck on the nose.

As Lulu walked dreamily through the grounds of the Ranch she thought that while she might not stand any real chance of winning the competition, she had accomplished everything that really mattered. She and Freddie were reconciled and stronger than ever. She'd not only found the blackmailer but also brought about a family reconciliation. And most important, she had solved two murders. Within a few hours the murderer would be under arrest and the girls of the world would be much safer.

She felt free and light for the first time in days. All of her burdens and worries had been lifted, and life was sweet again. *Maybe I do have a chance after all,* she thought. The other girls were pulling out all of the stops and doing lavish numbers in glittery outfits that would showcase all of their assets. Her poetry reading was distinctly tame by comparison. But at least it was different. Quiet, substantive, and authentic. That might count for something.

For almost the first time since coming to the Ranch,

Lulu considered taking her performance that night seriously. Tonight she could stand before the highest glitterati of the entertainment business and present herself as the serious actress she longed to be and had worked so hard to become.

So far her practice had been mostly simple, purist recitation. She needed to add true emotion to her performance. She needed guidance, but she had no access to her acting coach, Vasily. This was a terribly inconvenient moment for her to be coachless. Then it occurred to her. She might not have Vasily, but she did have access to another artist who was uniquely skilled in unearthing deep emotional resonance. Paul Raleigh might be able to offer her some insight.

She couldn't find him in any of the obvious places, and when she asked the grooms at the stable, they said he'd abandoned his ride once Patricia was called away. *Maybe he's in his room,* she thought, and with hardly a qualm about propriety, she made her way there and knocked.

There was no answer. She hesitated only a moment, then went inside, flipping on a tall marble lamp on a table just inside the door. She knew Paul wouldn't mind if she waited there for him. Then, after pacing around for a few minutes, she sat at his desk, fiddling with his paperweight and looking idly over the pages scattered on the surface.

Naturally enough, she mused about finding the lurid, disturbing writing that had seemed to incriminate Paul. How frightened she'd been . . . until he'd explained. Of course a writer had to take what chance they could to explore even the most terrible facets of human nature. She didn't envy him.

She supposed some people must have sick fantasies exactly like that, but of course Paul was just a kind man who was willing to suffer for his art. He had no bad thoughts or intentions toward anyone. He probably wrote scenarios about bridge parties, golf games, lovers' quarrels—everything, just to hone his skills.

So it was with an easy mind that she started to read the typed pages scattered on Paul's desk.

A moment later, Lulu's mouth went dry and her heart began to race. Her mind recoiled with disgust as she read page after page of sick fantasies. These weren't explorations of the human psyche that tormented Paul's delicate artist's soul. They were his personal fantasies of gruesome murders.

What kind of twisted mind could write these things?

Her heart was thudding wildly in her chest. How had she been so easily deluded by the innocent, gentle-seeming Paul? As she read the pages, she realized that these must be his blueprints, which he'd later acted out in real life.

Lulu tore through the pages. The words filled her with revulsion.

```
I drugged her so she wouldn't cry out, although it
dulled the keen edge of my pleasure that I could
not hear her scream as the tiger tore into her. She
was conscious, though, which was almost enough.
Her sluggish body fought as well as it could, but
she was alive as the great ravening beast ripped
her viscera from that tender belly and ate it
before her dying eyes. . . .
```

And there was more, and more. . . . Lulu skimmed through, sickened and terrified.

Then she saw her own name.

```
When I saw her pawing through my trash like a spy,
I wanted to wrap my hands around her throat and
squeeze the life out of her, killing her the same
way that other blond tart died, her face turning
slowly blue . . .
```

*He wanted to kill me, the way he'd killed Juliette*, she thought as she fumbled through more pages of grotesque confessions.

```
She was a child still, but almost with a woman's
body, a young Diana, racing her steed across the
flower-strewn field. How alive she was . . . until
I looped the rope around her neck and pulled her
from her horse.
```

Patricia had been about to go riding with Paul. If they hadn't called her away, would this have been her grisly fate?

The door creaked behind her.

"Hello, Lulu," Paul said in his soft, slow voice. "I imagine you remember Bluebeard's wife. Don't you know what happens to girls who snoop?"

## Twenty-Five

**can't** believe it! Emerson!" Hearst ran his hands over the wave of gray-blond hair that fell over his forehead. "Are you sure? Tell me everything again."

Hearst had now fully embraced Freddie as his principal confidant following his unraveling of the blackmail case, so much so that he had sent a rather intoxicated Waters back to Los Angeles, confused and none too pleased with his subordinate. But it was taking much longer than Freddie had anticipated to convince Hearst of Emerson's guilt. It had been midday when he started, and now it was late afternoon, not more than an hour before the actresses' competition was slated to begin.

Freddie was getting frustrated, and he imagined that Lulu, as she waited for news, was as well. His primary fear, of course, was that Emerson could very well kill again if action weren't taken soon. But convincing his employer that the husband of one of his closest friends was potentially a serial killer was deeply problematic. Freddie would have liked to go straight to the police, but he desperately needed Hearst's support. If Hearst didn't believe him, he'd quash even the soundest investigation.

For at least the fourth time, Freddie, attempting to quell his aggravation, presented the evidence that Lulu had gathered. He once again named and quickly eliminated all of the other suspects he had considered, from Docky to Sal to Marion herself.

"Now, Marion I would almost believe," Hearst said with what sounded to Freddie like grudging respect. "I joke, of course, though hell hath no fury like a woman scorned for getting older. But if she wanted that part, or any blasted movie she desired, she could have had it. I'd buy that woman the sun if it would make her happy. She did ask, once, about this role, but truthfully I didn't think she'd be quite right, and I suppose I hinted that. She never mentioned it again. But if she'd pressed me, I would have made sure she got it, whatever her age. But Emerson! I know he has his . . . issues. In my experience, all geniuses do. But murder? It's . . . it's too much. I can't believe it."

"The facts all fit," Freddie insisted. "He had a clear motive to kill Juliette, who was blackmailing him over their love affair and that letter. He went into her room and searched it. He was heard fighting with her. And as for Dolores, he all but admitted it, and his possessions were found at the crime scene."

"But what about that colored man . . . ?"

"No, it wasn't him. He was here to propose to his girl. Suffice it to say I have ample evidence of his innocence."

"If you're wrong, and I direct the police to arrest an innocent man . . ."

"I'm sure of this, Mr. Hearst. As sure as can be. We've gone over every possibility, and Emerson is the only one who fits."

"You are aware what this will do to Anita Loos? Between the scandal, shame, and humiliation, she will be utterly devastated. I love my friend, and I would do anything to shield her from the pain she will experience once she finds out," Hearst said darkly.

"Mr. Hearst, you're not responsible for the actions of a deranged murderer. I'm certain you will do everything you can to spare Anita, but right now the most important thing is to stop it from happening again."

At last Hearst agreed to bring in the police. Soon Emerson would be judging the competition in plain sight. When it was over Hearst would summon him and he could be quietly arrested.

"What is it with writers?" Hearst asked as Freddie left to find Lulu. "They're all just a bunch of arrogant drunks and nut jobs."

"Well, I don't like to generalize, but I'd bet it's a curse living with so many people in your head," Freddie said, and went in search of Lulu.

But he couldn't find her, and no one he asked had seen her. Veronica was practically frantic. "She goes on in an hour, and it's going to take nearly that long to lace her into her corset!"

Paul stepped swiftly into his bedroom and locked the door. "You shouldn't have done it, Lulu," he admonished, clicking his tongue. "You've been a bad girl, poking through my things. I let you in on some of my secrets, but now you're snooping without my permission. You'll have to make it up to me in some way." He stroked his chin. "Let's see. What shall we do?"

Lulu felt on the verge of panic. Her head swam, and the edges of her vision grew blurry. *I can't faint*, she told herself. *I can't be one of those dumb girls who passes out at the first sign of danger! No. I just need to get out of this room. Now.*

"Why did you do it?" Lulu asked, feigning composure. How could she have been so wrong about Emerson, swayed by circumstantial evidence? Everything that had looked like proof before suddenly seemed flimsy and insubstantial. John Emerson might be a bit deranged, but it was Paul who had the truly sick mind of a killer.

Paul took a step nearer. The desk was still between them, giving Lulu a small measure of comfort.

"Why?" He cocked his head. "As my mother used to say, because 'Y' is a crooked letter." He chuckled. "You beautiful, ignorant child. You think you can reach into the depths of your soul and drag out art, but your passions are infantile compared to mine! You don't have the capacity to understand what I do. How I feel."

His voice was rising in a manic tone, and Lulu thought her best bet might be to appeal to his artistic vanity. If she could just slip past him and out the door . . .

"I've always thought writers were something almost magical," she began, but he surged toward her, slamming his palms on the desk between them.

"Shut up, you lying tramp! You're just a mimic, a pantomiming floozy. How can you possibly understand what I do—what I am!"

To her horror, Paul picked up a letter opener that was lying on the desk. Her breath began to come faster as he pointed it at her.

"Paul," she said in a conciliatory voice, "I'm sure you didn't mean to . . ."

"You presume to judge me? You . . . you *actress*!" He spat the word as if it were the ultimate insult.

He shook the letter opener toward her face, and she cringed back out of reach, but was afraid to run and leave the relative safety of the desk's barrier. "Writers mean *nothing* to people like you. All you actresses are the same. I create beauty, power, passion, and you think your ridiculous little nattering can express the glory that I manifest from thin air? I make a world that is a thousand times more real than the one you know. You are nothing but shadows pantomiming the truth."

"Please, Paul," Lulu said desperately as she stared into

his crazed eyes. How had he kept it hidden before, all that demented rage? She grasped the heavy paperweight on the desk. It felt solid and substantial in her hands . . . but would it possibly keep him from stabbing her? If she was only brave enough, fast enough, to run for the door.

Then, just as he started to move, there was a loud staccato knock, and someone pushed the door open.

Mrs. Mortimer stepped inside and said, "Mr. Raleigh, the other judges are waiting for you."

"Look out. He has a knife!" Lulu shrieked.

Paul whirled toward the housekeeper, the long, sharp letter opener in his hand. For some reason Lulu thought he looked almost confused. He looked down at the weapon as if he couldn't believe he was holding it. "I'm not . . . ," he stammered. "I wouldn't . . ." But he was still pointing the knifelike letter opener at the housekeeper.

Then Mrs. Mortimer snatched up the marble lamp and wielded it like a club, smashing Paul in the side of the head. He crumpled to the ground, his hair matted with blood.

"Oh, thank goodness!" Lulu cried as she ran around the desk and threw her arms around the housekeeper. She babbled in her relief. "I found his papers, the most horrible things . . . he's the murderer . . . he was going to kill me . . . he's crazy . . . you saved me!"

Mrs. Mortimer stood stiffly in her embrace for a moment, then patted her on the back exactly twice.

"Are you implying he killed those two girls?" the housekeeper asked with a tremor in her voice.

"I thought it was John Emerson. I thought I had so much evidence against him. But when I found those horrible things Paul wrote, I realized it must be him."

"This is monstrous! He actually tried to kill you?" Mrs. Mortimer asked, looking down at Paul sprawled on the ground, bleeding onto the Persian carpet.

"Well . . . ," Lulu began. She certainly thought he had at first. "He yelled and came at me with that sharp letter opener." Now that she thought about it, Paul had seemed to be gesticulating with it rather than threatening her.

Mrs. Mortimer nodded coldly.

"Shouldn't I go and tell someone?"

"He's not going anywhere, and you need something to fortify you, poor girl." It sounded a little strange to hear sympathy coming from the housekeeper. She was usually so brusque. "Drag him over to the chair and I'll find something to tie him with."

Lulu was so flustered that she let herself be guided. It was much easier to let the competent housekeeper take charge than to try to think for herself in this dizzying moment. Gingerly, she grabbed Paul under the armpits, but when she tried to haul him toward the chair, she only managed to shift him a few inches. She didn't like to think of herself as weak, but it was almost impossible to shift the dead weight. Not, she thought with some relief, that he was literally dead weight.

Lulu tugged again and gave a grunt of frustration. Mrs. Mortimer looked up from rifling through the drawers for a bondage-suitable tie. "Oh, shove over, girl. Let me do that." She caught Paul around the waist and manhandled him up into the chair. Lulu was amazed at her strength, and said so. "Those who work for a living are strong," Mrs. Mortimer said in that way that people who frequently use the same life mottos do. Scripted and self-convinced.

Lulu thought—but did not say—that her mother had worked for a living and was never that strong.

Mrs. Mortimer didn't give her time to think. "I'll tie him so you don't get blood on your clean clothes." After she did so, she took Lulu's arm and led her down to her private office off the kitchen. Everyone was ready for the talent show, and they didn't even meet any of the staff en route. "Let's make you a nice cup of tea. After you've calmed down, we can call the police."

Lulu sat down gratefully. It was over at last! The murderer was not only discovered, but captured, unconscious, and bound, and no more girls would be gruesomely murdered. She sighed with relief, and didn't even notice when Mrs. Mortimer locked the door before she started boiling the water for tea.

Freddie's frantic first thought was that Lulu had decided to confront Emerson, or that the suspect had gotten wind of her investigation of him. With sickening dread Freddie sought Emerson out, only to find him already under unobtrusive guard by one of Hearst's undercover men. Hearst was discreetly keeping an eye on him until the police could get the arrest warrant ready. He breathed a deep sigh of relief. So Lulu was safe. But where could she be?

He decided to check one more time in case Lulu had gone back to her room. On the way through the grounds he found a quieter, rather pensive Patricia taking Charlie and Gandhi for a sunset walk. "Patricia, have you seen Lulu?" he asked.

"Not since the big family reunion," she replied in something of a daze.

"You doing okay?"

She shrugged. "Not much is going to change, I suppose. But any psychoanalyst will tell you that it's best to get secrets out into the open." Now that he knew her real age, he wondered how anyone had ever believed that the precocious girl was only ten. Well, he thought, people believe what they're told. When a credible source tells you something is true, you accept it.

"If you see her, let her know I'm looking for her."

Then, as if recharged by the notion that a mystery was afoot, she seemed to perk up. "Golly, the show's just about to start, isn't it? Does she have stage fright? We can help you look for her, can't we, fellas?" She reached down to pat the dogs. "Charlie has been longing for her, as always, and wanders about whining like a disheveled sad sack whenever she's not around. Charlie! Where's Lulu? Find Lulu! Seek!"

Freddie knew that Charlie couldn't have any idea what Patricia was talking about, but the little dog became immediately excited at the mention of Lulu's name, dancing on his hind paws as Patricia encouraged him. Freddie smiled indulgently at the endearing little terrier.

"Go on! Where's Lulu? Go find her! Good boy!" And Charlie was off and running, dragging the portly Gandhi along reluctantly in his wake. Freddie and Patricia ran after him. He headed back to the main house, yipping madly. Once inside he circled, sniffing the air and snuffling at the floor. Then, with a little growl, he ran for the stairs that led down toward the kitchen and the housekeeper's and butler's offices.

# Twenty-Six

**T**he heavy ring of keys rattled and clinked about Mrs. Mortimer's waist as she made tea at the little stove and counter in one corner of her spacious office. Well, of course, Lulu thought absently. The housekeeper would have to get into every room in the house. She bet that big one was the key to the elaborate front door, which had been pulled from a Spanish church. Others were small and pedestrian, no doubt room keys. One brass key had a lion's head on it. She tried to remember where she'd seen that before.

Mrs. Mortimer bustled with things Lulu couldn't see while the tea steeped. Lulu was anxious. Why were they wasting so much time here when they should be telling someone about Paul Raleigh? What if he regained consciousness and escaped?

As she tapped her fingertips impatiently against her leg,

288

Lulu began to replay the scene with Paul. He'd been emotional, verbally aggressive . . . but had he actually threatened her with that letter opener? "You know," she said to Mrs. Mortimer, "the more I think about it, the more I think maybe Paul didn't actually mean to harm anyone. Is that crazy? I was so scared at the time, but now that I'm calm I wonder if . . ."

Mrs. Mortimer turned and looked at Lulu sharply. "Wondering will get you into trouble, girl."

"Yes, but what if he's not the murderer? Maybe it really is John Emerson. Or someone else entirely. I always thought maybe a woman . . ."

The housekeeper fixed Lulu with a long, strange look. Then she gave a little sigh. "You're better than the others," she said. "What a shame. Still . . ."

To Lulu's frustration, Mrs. Mortimer returned to her tea preparations. She scooped a heaping spoonful of pale crystals from a pink-flowered porcelain bowl and sprinkled it in one of the cups. Lulu opened her mouth to tell Mrs. Mortimer she didn't care for any sugar but then reconsidered. The mandates of her nutrition coach shouldn't matter at a time like this. So she didn't say anything as the stoic housekeeper set down two matching teacups, the sugared one in front of Lulu, the other across the intimate round table.

As she set the teacups down, Lulu noticed that the housekeeper's large, square hands were shaking slightly.

There was a soft knock, and a look of annoyance crossed the housekeeper's face, but she unlocked the door and opened it a crack. Lulu heard her talking to one of the maids about whether she'd found the missing judge, Paul Raleigh.

For whatever reason, most likely the nagging voice of Lulu's nutrition coach relentlessly ringing in her ears, she used this opportunity to switch the identical flowered teacups. The vain, actress obsession with keeping her figure didn't even dissipate in the face of mortal danger, she noted wryly. This seemed less fuss than asking the gravely shaken Mrs. Mortimer for a fresh cup. Lulu took a sip of the plain oolong, sighing as the soothing brew warmed and calmed her. *The English have it right,* she thought. *A nice cup of tea can help almost any trouble.*

Mrs. Mortimer closed the door and sat down across from Lulu. "Drink up, my dear," she said, and Lulu obliged. Mrs. Mortimer didn't touch her own tea, but watched Lulu intensely. *Probably expecting me to break into delayed hysterics at any moment,* Lulu thought. But all the young actress felt was relief, and a strong desire to leave Hearst and his Ranch behind.

"You really are an interesting girl, Lulu Kelly," Mrs. Mortimer said. "I happen to know that Anita was quite gung ho in your favor. She thought you'd be ideal for the role." Her breath made ripples on the surface of her tea as she lifted it to her thin lips. "You'd think, being a more mature woman, Anita would have the sense to see that pretty little chits like you will never have the experience, the passion to be great actresses."

Lulu frowned slightly and started to rise. "Shouldn't we . . . ?"

"Sit down!" Mrs. Mortimer snapped, and half rose herself. The ring of keys jingled, and suddenly Lulu remembered where she'd seen that lion-head key before. It was the key that opened all of the carnivore cages in Hearst's menagerie. But the keeper said he had the only one.

And then Lulu froze. No, it couldn't be. She couldn't have been wrong *twice*.

The maid bringing in the shoes she'd just cleaned, saying she got off all the mud.

The rip in the shoulder of the black dress, torn after great exertion.

Ginnie looking for her supervisor after hearing the argument, but she was nowhere to be found . . . right at the time of the murder.

Mrs. Mortimer had the keys to the tiger cage, keys to every locked door in the Ranch.

She was big, powerful. Look how she'd hit Paul with that heavy marble lamp, how easily she'd dragged his limp body to the chair.

It fit. But why would Mrs. Mortimer kill Juliette and Dolores? It couldn't be possible. Unless . . .

She remembered the snippet Freddie had told her about the housekeeper's long connection with Marion. Lulu had been thinking the murders were crimes of passion, or insanity. What if the motivating factor was not just a combination of those two things, but above all, an act of loyalty?

Lulu realized she'd been staring at the lion-head key, and tore her eyes away, but not, she thought, before Mrs. Mortimer noticed what she was looking at.

*I have to be calm,* Lulu told herself. *She can't suspect I know. Right now she thinks I'm convinced Paul is the killer. And maybe he is.* Probably *he is. It can't be Mrs. Mortimer. Can it?*

"I see you admiring my menagerie key. It's quite beautiful, don't you think?" She smiled and took a long sip of her tea.

"Too clever for your own good," the housekeeper murmured. "Smart enough to get into a fix but not quite smart enough to get out of it again. I was so pleased when you put together all the clues that led to Emerson as your chief suspect. The police and Mr. Hearst's own investigators should have done it long before you." She gave a little chuckle that made shivers creep down Lulu's spine. "After all, I set up the evidence so neatly for them."

That nonchalant confession made Lulu more frightened than Emerson's paranoid ravings, more terrified even than the moment Paul brandished the deadly sharp letter opener. This woman killed two young actresses! And here she was, sitting calmly across from Lulu, brazenly admitting what she'd done.

Lulu glanced desperately toward the door. Confessing in a locked room—a room with a row of knives, from fillet blades to heavy cleavers, hanging on the wall.

But Mrs. Mortimer made no move.

"Of course," she went on calmly, "Emerson incriminated himself with his own foolish ties to Juliette. I just helped it along. Do you have the love letter I stole from Juliette's room and hid on her body? When it wasn't with the personal effects you gave me, I had high hopes that the police would close in on him fast. But those incompetent fools didn't even find

Emerson's tiepin I left at the scene of Dolores's death. That was you again. You were meddling so helpfully . . . for a while."

She held her teacup in both hands, warming them.

"But I don't understand," Lulu said gently, once again relying on her acting experience. "Why did you kill them?"

The housekeeper jumped to her feet, setting her teacup down so violently that half the contents sloshed out. Even in her fury, she scooped up a cloth from the counter and blotted up the spill. "Those little tramps were taking my lady's place!"

"You mean . . . Marion?"

"Marion Davies is a great star. You little snot-nose pretenders can't rightfully even breathe the same air as her. She is more than a legend, though. She is the noblest, kindest, most beautiful woman in the world. That role should have been hers! A custom creation from the great Anita Loos and some cute little nobody of an ingenue gets it? Over my dead body!" She chuckled. "Or theirs, I should say."

"You killed them so that Marion could have the role?" Lulu asked.

"Juliette was blackmailing Emerson with that letter he wrote to her, promising to divorce Anita. Juliette was a clever girl, too. She didn't want marriage from Emerson. She wanted the role of a lifetime. In that argument the maid overheard, he had all but agreed to force Anita to join him in naming Juliette the winner."

"Would she have agreed?" Lulu didn't think the strong-minded Anita could be so easily convinced.

"Oh, my dear, you still don't understand what a precarious

life we women lead. Even with all of Anita's fame, do you think the studios take her seriously without a man's name attached to her? Emerson gets her into the meetings. Even at the peak of her success, no one would read her scripts unless they were a Loos-Emerson affair." Despite her terrified state, Lulu was indignant on Anita's behalf.

"During the fight, Emerson accused Juliette of infidelity. He'd seen the wrapped present on her bed and snatched it up. He thought that scarf—the one all the actresses were supposed to get—was a present from a lover. He threw it at her. They screamed and fought, they made up, and amid tender whispers that the maid couldn't hear, he promised her the part. I had followed that little tramp, and I heard everything. When he left, it was a simple matter to strangle that insignificant nothing right out of the running."

The housekeeper made a twisting motion with her meaty hands.

"And you dragged her into the dining room? But there were no muddy footprints."

Mrs. Mortimer raised her eyebrows and regarded Lulu archly. "When you've cleaned floors for a living, you leave your muddy shoes outside. Even if you have others to clean up after you."

The motivations beginning to click, Lulu said, "And you must have found out that Sal Benedetto had made a deal with Hearst to give Dolores the role after that."

"Those powerful men are always scheming. You'd think Hearst would have insisted Marion have the part. But no. I think he was afraid. He's kept her in roles that are beneath her all these years. What if she won an Academy Award? Maybe she wouldn't need him anymore. He's supremely selfish, but he loves her. That's the only reason he's still alive."

*She'd kill Hearst?* Lulu shivered.

"So you drugged Dolores and . . . and . . ."

"It was easy pinning the first on Emerson, but he had no real connection to Dolores. I set up the evidence implicating him, but I made sure that at first glance it would look like an accident, a foolish whim of a silly, drunk actress that went horribly wrong. The police would have left it at that, if it weren't for you."

Lulu glanced at the door. "I admire your loyalty, Mrs. Mortimer. I won't tell. I promise."

Mrs. Mortimer chuckled. "Of course you won't, my dear. Do you think I would have spilled the beans otherwise? You won't reveal my secrets, and you won't be Anita's pick for the role of a lifetime. No, you won't tell anything to anyone ever again."

"You're . . . you're going to kill me?" Lulu asked, wondering if she could get to the knives before Mrs. Mortimer, and if she'd have the fortitude to use one.

The laugh grew wilder. "You poor child, I already *have* killed you!"

Lulu felt a sick dread in the pit of her stomach. "What do you mean?"

"I tried it before, but you spilled the coffee. Oh, that time I only wanted to make you ill. I figured if you were vomiting and fainting, you'd be in no state to continue your investigations."

"You poisoned my coffee?"

"Just a bit," she said coyly. "This time, though . . ."

The spoonful of crystals in one cup, but not the other.

And then Mrs. Mortimer smiled calmly, picked up her cup, and swallowed the rest of her tea. "This time I gave you enough poison to finish things off. Can't taste it, can you? These deadly crystals are sweet, and dissolve quickly. Though even if it tasted off, you're such a polite little thing you probably would have drunk it all down just to spare my feelings."

With a surge of relief so strong it made her woozy, Lulu thought, *I just have to wait.* When the poison Mrs. Mortimer accidentally swallowed herself took effect, Lulu would take the keys and . . .

Then she saw the housekeeper's face twist in disbelief . . . then rage . . . then pain. She doubled over, clutching her stomach. "You . . . What did you do? How did you know?" She staggered to her feet, shoving the table hard against Lulu, who tumbled backward and hit her head on the floor. Momentarily stunned, she blinked heavily, seeing stars. Dimly, she was aware of Mrs. Mortimer staggering across her office, not toward Lulu, but toward the little kitchen section. The part of the room where the knives were hanging.

Lulu managed to get to her knees, but her head was ringing, and she felt unsteady and sick. She saw Mrs. Mortimer pull the biggest knife off the hook and then reject it for the long, thin, deadly sharp filleting knife.

All at once there was a commotion outside the door. Snuffling and barks. A girl's voice. And then the dearest sound in the world.

"Lulu!" Freddie called. "Where are you?"

"No!" the housekeeper shrieked. "They can't save you. I won't let you be the hero, the darling who solved the murders." She lunged unsteadily toward Lulu, who started to crawl under the table. "If you live, your picture will be in all the papers. You'll be bigger than ever, and my Marion will fade into obscurity. Come out from under there, you insignificant wretch!" She slashed at Lulu, but the poison must have been taking hold, and she fell to her knees too.

Lulu heard pounding on the door. "Freddie, I'm in here!" she called at the top of her lungs as she desperately tried to scuttle out of the way of the flailing knife.

She and Mrs. Mortimer were both kneeling now, facing each other. But Lulu, recovering from the blow to her head, was getting stronger. The housekeeper, succumbing to her own poison, was weakening. The door juddered as Freddie threw himself against it again and again.

"Freddie, help me!" she shrieked as Mrs. Mortimer lunged for her, slashing at her face. She threw herself backward and felt a strange sensation across her chest, as if she'd been struck by an icicle. Then there was a huge crash and the room was a blurry, roaring confusion of snapping dogs and shouting as Freddie hurled himself on top of Mrs. Mortimer so that they both went down with a mighty *thud*. Lulu crawled backward until the table was between them, so she couldn't see what happened next. But Freddie was here! He'd saved her!

The housekeeper shoved Freddie off and somehow managed to stand, breathing hard, clutching her gut with one hand. In the other she still held the knife. It was slick with blood, which dripped down her hand.

Freddie was on the ground, pale and unmoving, a blood-stain slowly expanding on his chest.

"Not in the script," Mrs. Mortimer said, "but I can certainly work with improvisation. I used to be a great actress, you know." She staggered toward Lulu again, but the frantically yipping dogs wove around her feet, bringing her down to the floor.

She didn't get up again. Lulu saw bloody foam bubble from Mrs. Mortimer's lips as the housekeeper glared malevolently at her. Then, slowly, the hateful glare faded and her eyes were blank and staring.

Lulu all but threw herself on Freddie. "My darling, my own love," she said, kissing him. "You saved me!" She pressed at the stab wound. "You need a doctor. Patricia, stay with him!"

Freddie tried to call her back, but she was desperate to get help. She ran through the Ranch, but it was strangely deserted. Then she remembered—everyone was gathered for the competition, even the staff. She raced toward the theater where the show was taking place. The structure was a massive maze of corridors and doorways, but she was certain the entrance was close. Was that the sound of applause somewhere to her left? She threw open the unfamiliar door in front of her.

Bursting through, she found herself in a glaring spotlight. She was on the stage, looking out over an audience of all of her friends and Hearst's guests.

"The . . . the murderer! I caught her!"

But the entire packed theater just sat there, mouths agape.

"Help! Someone! Anyone . . . Why are you all just sitting there?" she shouted into the darkness, blinded by the searing light, hot tears running down her face.

"You've got to help me! He's dying!" she pleaded through her sobs to the mute, unmoving mass of bodies. "What's wrong with you? Have you no compassion or humanity?" She fell to her knees, whimpering. "Why are you just staring at me? Please do something! I'm begging you!"

And then she stood again, disheveled, frightened, determined, and lovely, blood dripping from a slash across her chest. She looked like every great heroine of stage and screen come dramatically to life.

The audience, until then silent, suddenly leaped to their feet and erupted in thunderous applause.

# Twenty-Seven

**T**here are knives to the chest . . . and then there are knives to the chest. When Lulu saw Freddie with blood pouring from his wound, she immediately assumed he'd been stabbed in the heart or lungs and was at death's door. By the time she'd staggered back to his side, though, the Ranch medics had already tended to what was a rather unpleasant but ultimately minor puncture of Freddie's surprisingly substantial right pectoral muscle.

"Good Lord, that woman was determined. That left hook of hers was a killer. Oh, and sorry if I'm, well . . . a little exposed. Sort of comes with the whole being stabbed thing, I guess," Freddie said with a wince, smiling bravely through the pain. His shirt had been cut away, and his tanned upper body, though bruised and bloody, was on impressive display.

Lulu had never seen quite so much of him before, and found herself distracted.

"I'm not sorry . . . well, I mean except for the stabbing part," Lulu said, barely pretending to not admire her spectacularly handsome beau as the medic wrapped the bandage. Veronica threw a cashmere blanket over Lulu's tattered dress.

"I guess it's no more off-the-shoulder gowns for you," Veronica said as the butler dabbed stinging antiseptic on Lulu's knife slash. It was long, stretching across her chest and shoulder, but shallow, and hurt far more now that it was being treated than it had when she got it.

"Scars give character," Freddie said, gently kissing her neck, sending a shiver of longing and comfort through her.

"And I've never seen an actress with more character than you, Lulu Kelly." William Randolph Hearst had come into the room, his bulk making it decidedly cramped. "You might have had the wrong man for a while, but you and Freddie certainly came through in the end. Truly magnificent work. I never would have imagined old Mrs. Mortimer had it in her."

To her surprise, Lulu almost bristled at this. What gave Mr. Hearst the right to call the housekeeper old, or to doubt her strength and resolve? That was the attitude that could drive women in Hollywood to tears, or madness, or pills, or suicide. Mrs. Mortimer's reaction to her treatment, and to Marion's, had taken a decidedly psychotic turn, but Lulu still rebelled at the forces of life that drove her to it.

"I think we should step outside," Freddie said delicately,

and everyone but the medics moved into the hallway.

Marion came traipsing down the corridor. "Lulu darling! Here you all are! Oh, it was absolutely divine! Your performance silenced the worst chatterboxes on the face of the earth. The other numbers were so deadly dull, just the same old song and dance routines. But then you! Blood! Murder! At first I thought you were doing a bit from *Titus Andronicus*. Oh, jeepers creepers! I just realized what a field day the press will have with this." She pouted. "I'd better change into something more conservative before the cameras come. My new Chanel! It will be perfect. Oh, and no one seems to know—who was the murderer after all?"

Lulu gasped. No one had told her! Oh, poor Marion. Lulu tried to get between her and the doorway, but Hearst whispered in Marion's ear just as she maneuvered to where she had a clear view of her friend's corpse.

Lulu expected hysterics, but Marion only breathed the word "no" very softly and sank to the floor. She pulled Mrs. Mortimer's head onto her lap and rocked gently, forward and back. "How could I not have known?" she asked no one in particular as her eyes began to pool. "Oh, of course she could hide it from me. She was a better actress than me, always."

Lulu crept over beside Marion and put an arm over her shoulder. "She was very, very loyal."

Marion's eyes lit up. "And I am—was—loyal to her. Everything I am, I owe to her. She got me my first part on the stage, gave me guidance. And then . . ." Marion's face fell, and she looked suddenly older. "Then she got too old, and they pushed her out. I was sixteen and perfect and the world opened up for me. She was forty and the best actress of her generation, and the world crushed her down. We lost track of each other for years, you know, and then just before I came to California I found her. She was scrubbing the front stairs of a dinner club. I couldn't believe it! An actress like that, falling on such hard times! So I took her with me, and she's been my most loyal companion ever since. I wanted her to act. I could have gotten her parts, though not the ones she deserved. But she said she was only fit for cleaning now. So I made her head of the whole Ranch."

Marion sniffed loudly and smoothed Mrs. Mortimer's disheveled hair. "She was the only person I ever fully trusted." Realizing what she had said, she glanced at Hearst. He looked away uncomfortably. "I would have done any-thing for her!" Marion added staunchly.

*Would you have murdered someone for her?* Lulu wondered. *Would you have hidden her crimes if you'd found out first?*

But none of that mattered now. She tactfully left Marion alone to grieve.

The others moved into the Assembly Room, some for a stiff drink, though after her brush with poison Lulu didn't want to drink *anything* for a while. Anita came in and made a beeline to Lulu. She reported that Paul was conscious and seemed to be recovering. He claimed he had never intended any threat, and in her calmer state, Lulu admitted to the authorities that this was probably true. Writers, she was starting to notice, were all deranged in their own unique ways. The first thing Paul did when his hands were untied was demand his typewriter. He began furiously documenting his recent experience even while the medics were bandaging his head.

"I know everyone is saying Freddie is the real investigator and that he caught the killer," Anita said, "but, Lulu, you seem to be everywhere the action is. Why do I get the feeling you're at the heart of everything good that's happened over the last few days?"

"Yes, isn't that something," chirped Veronica archly. "Truly curious."

Lulu demurred with a smile.

"Modest, too," Anita said. "Hmm . . . You know, I think I'm getting a peach of an idea for the main character of this next screenplay. A girl who is a secret hero. Fingers in every pie, smarter than anyone gives her credit for, and determined to fix the wrongs of the world. But she stays in the shadow of her brilliant, far-too-attractive fella. And because it's a man's world, he gets the credit, but it's the girl who really makes everything happen. Without her, the story would have an unhappy ending. It's bittersweet, though, because her hero-ism is unsung."

"That sounds good for a story," Lulu said quietly. "In real life, though, I don't think the girl would mind very much. A few people would know what she did. The people who mattered."

"I can't speak for the other judges, but as for me, I know

which actress has displayed the most inspiring character over the last few days." Anita lowered her voice and added in a confidential whisper, "Even if you thought my husband was the killer. I can't say I blame you."

Lulu started to laugh, then stopped with a gasp.

"Where is your husband?" she asked Anita in alarm. She looked at Freddie. "Where's Sal?"

"Sal wasn't in the audience at the performance," Anita said. "That's odd. Come to think of it, WR noted it and asked after him. And my husband was called away just before you came onstage. One of the servants handed him a note summoning him outside to the Neptune Pool. I don't know what it was about, but I tried to stop him. I suppose I assumed it was one of his girls—though now that I think about it, all the eligible females were in the performance. Lulu, what's happening?"

But Lulu was already snaking her way through the crowded room. "Sal still thinks Emerson did it!" she shouted over her shoulder as she ran. "Freddie! He's going to kill him!"

Even though his wound wasn't too serious, pain and blood loss were slowing Freddie down, and by the time he'd cleared the confused crowd, Lulu was far ahead of him and out of sight.

It was sunset, and the classical statues cast long shadows over the Neptune Pool. "Lulu!" Freddie called.

And then he saw her, the small, slender girl using her body as a shield. Behind her, Emerson cowered on the tile, begging for mercy. In front of her, Sal stood with his gun held out, pointed straight at the groveling Emerson.

"I want to hear it from your own mouth before I kill you," Sal snarled, his rage so raw that he hardly seemed to notice Lulu was there. "Tell me what you did to that poor, sweet, innocent girl, you scum. Confess what you did to Dolores before you die."

"Sal, listen to me. It wasn't Emerson. I made a terrible mistake. It was Mrs. Mortimer."

"Who?" Sal asked, clearly puzzled.

"The housekeeper."

"Are you crazy? That stout old lady in black? Come on. You can lie better than that. Now, get out of the way. I have something to finish. For Dolores."

Lulu stepped closer to Sal. Freddie edged nearer too, though he didn't want to make any sudden moves with Lulu in the line of fire.

"You don't want to do this, Sal," Lulu said, holding up her hands.

"Drop the gun, Sal," Freddie shouted as he made his way toward the melee.

"Stay outta this, *Frederick*," Sal thundered, glancing over his shoulder.

"Freddie, please!" Lulu begged, not wanting to make a tense situation worse. "I can handle this. Just please stay back."

"I know you're on the side of the angels, Lu, but I ain't. This bastard isn't going to go to jail and live another fifty years when Dolores was . . . She was ripped apart." Sal sniffed and rubbed his nose with the back of his hand. "He dies now. Stand aside, Lu."

"I won't. You're not thinking, Sal. He's innocent. I swear to you. And I can't let you kill an innocent man."

But Sal looked like he was in a trance, his eyes glazed and hard. Nothing she said could break him of his determination to punish the man he was certain was guilty. The man Lulu had told him was guilty.

She had to do something to snap him out of his spell, get him to listen to her long enough to get Emerson to safety and the gun away. But what could she do to distract Sal from his murderous intent?

And then, as Freddie inched closer, Lulu walked up to Sal . . . and kissed him passionately on the mouth.

In his astonishment, Sal's gun arm fell to his side, and Freddie, reeling, dashed in and twisted it out of his grasp. The two men stood face-to-face, sweating and full of unchecked fury, eyes locked, each daring the other to make the next move. But then the other guests stumbled in, laughing and shouting, not seeming to know whether this was all real or just another bunch of hijinks choreographed for their amusement. The tension was broken. Emerson, shaking with sobs, huddled against the granite wall. Sal turned abruptly and stalked away.

"Oh, Freddie!" Lulu gasped. "I . . . I didn't mean that. . . . I only . . ."

But Freddie, unflappably confident that Lulu loved him

completely, knew exactly what she was going to say. He stopped her words with a kiss so pure, so passionate, that all questions of forgiveness were eradicated. She'd been acting. It had done the trick, and no matter what, Sal was gone and Lulu was his.

He decided then and there to put the matter beyond any further discussion.

With every guest of the Ranch assembled around the Neptune Pool, thrilled by the unexpected excitement, Freddie dropped down to one knee. With his torn, bloody shirt exposing a sliver of his chest, he looked like the prototype of every dreamy romantic hero. He took Lulu's hand and gazed into her shining eyes . . .

And before he could even ask the question, Lulu simply whispered, "Yes."

Freddie stood and pulled Lulu into his arms, and neither of them noticed the standing ovation of the crowd.

**ADAM SHANKMAN** is the director and producer of the exuberant musical remake of *Hairspray,* the producer of the top-grossing *Step Up* films, and the director of the adaptation of the Nicholas Sparks bestseller *A Walk to Remember,* starring Mandy Moore, and *Bringing Down the House,* starring Steve Martin and Queen Latifah. Adam has also directed episodes of *Modern Family,* and *Glee,* and he's a popular personality as a judge on *So You Think You Can Dance.* He also produced and choreographed the 82nd Annual Academy Awards (which was itself nominated for a record twelve Emmys).

**LAURA L. SULLIVAN** is a former newspaper editor, biologist, social worker, and deputy sheriff who writes because storytelling is the easiest way to do everything in the world. Her books include *Love By the Morning Star, Delusion,* and *Ladies in Waiting.* Laura lives on the Florida coast.